Titles in The Sto

The Martyr's Stone

Published in 2021 (*v.1.1*)
by
HawkesFlight Media

ISBN 978-0-6487041-8-8

www.author-nick.com

Cover Design by Karri Klawiter

The Martyr's Stone

by

Nick Hawkes

Chapter 1

The wind sighed through the sedges like the mournful spirit of a long dead soul. But he could feel no breeze. The sedges that sang to him also shielded him from the wind, as he lay on his back in the icy bog beside the creek. The young man was vaguely aware of a chilly wetness seeping through his clothes, scalding his back. It didn't matter. He would be dead soon. But dying was taking longer than he expected.

He'd set out in the moonlight on his mission – his final mission, and now the first hint of morning, the false dawn, was becoming evident.

This was a better way to die. Gentler. Earlier that night he'd hiked up to the top of the hill that overlooked the small island just offshore. The tiny hamlet of Second Valley below him was fast asleep. A few streetlights shone bravely, including one on the jetty that thrust out into the bay. He'd thought that being night, he would be able to jump from the dreadful cliff edge into the blackness. But it wasn't black. Moonlight kissed the jagged rocks below and high-lighted the foaming crests of the waves as they crashed against the rocks. He'd stepped back in fright… and made his way back up the valley to put in motion his back-up plan.

And now it was nearly done.

His head lolled sideways. He could see strands of his long hair amongst the frosted moss, grass, and sedge. It did not feel as if it belonged to him at all. All sense of feeling had gone. But he could still smell the earth. It had the pungent odor of mud, dung, and cattle urine.

His mind was wandering in and out of reality. Disturbing images loomed out of his memory to confront him, to accuse and mock. He had failed in everything... and would be missed by no one.

Suddenly, he was aware through his drunken state of a warm breath across his cheeks, a snort, and a drooling dark nose looming down at him from above.

The young man blinked, but couldn't lift his arm to protect himself.

It was a young calf. The animal skittered backward, deciding that caution was a better option than curiosity. Its action was enough to cause the calf's mother to come trotting over. The cow saw the young man spread-eagled on his back beside the creek, put its head down and lunged, but stopped short of butting him.

The cow cared for its calf. A cow!

He would have laughed, if he could, at the irony.

Both cow and calf trotted off.

Then he died... or he thought he had, because what happened next was surreal.

St. Peter stood above him. He was carrying a staff and had hair so long that it almost reached to the belt strapped round a coarse woolen tunic. The bottom of the tunic splayed out like a skirt.

A skirt. That was funny. But he had jeans underneath. It was confusing. He didn't know St. Peter wore jeans.

Then everything went black.

The boy's pulse was weak and thready. He was barely alive. It was not surprising. The lad was dressed only in a thin windcheater and

2

jeans... and his neck was cold to the touch. If the young man was to live, there was little time to lose.

Julian Alston heaved the boy over his shoulders in a fireman's lift. He trapped the boy's leg and forearm to his chest with one arm, picked up his staff with the other, and made his way along the track beside the creek. The track, such as it was, had been made by himself as a result of his routine walks.

The boy was disturbingly light, and he stank. His clothes had a sour smell that bore eloquent testimony to a lack of hygiene.

The track led him up the bank to his own cottage. Its white-washed stone walls were beginning to show up in the dawn light. Julian made his way through the vegetable garden, skirted around the house, and walked on over the closely cropped grass to a rusted gate. It opened with a shove from his hip. The next bit was treacherous. He had to cross the bridge across the creek, the Parananakooka. The creeks of the Fleurieu Peninsula all had wonderful-sounding aboriginal names.

Crossing the bridge was fraught with danger at any time, because it had been badly made from old railway sleepers and sections of Stobie poles – the ugly steel and concrete poles that held up power lines along the streets of South Australia. There were gaps between the posts, and you had to watch your footing – even more so in the half-light of the early morning.

The bridge kept him isolated from the world – even though there were enough cottages and houses around him to make up the small hamlet of Randalsea. The settlement was one-and-a-half miles from Second Valley – the village on the coast where the creek ran into the sea. In recent years, however, both settlements had become collectively known as 'Second Valley'.

Julian loved the bridge and the isolation it gave him. He also loved the countryside round about. The English had colonized the area early in South Australia's history and left a legacy of stone cottages and houses that resulted in Randalsea looking as if it had been transplanted from Cornwall. Although the settlement was only eighty miles south of the city of Adelaide, it was a different world. The Fleurieu Peninsula was a land of steep-sided hills, bisected by creeks lined with magnificent red-gum trees. Its coastline was spectacular – rocky and rugged. Steep cliffs occasionally gave way to sandy coves. Seals loved to sunbathe on the beaches. Julian crossed the road and headed past Ellie's little shop to the grand old house that stood on the corner by the main road. After mounting the steps to the bull-nosed veranda, he rapped on the door with his staff. As he did, he reflected ruefully that it was an ungodly hour to call on anyone. But Ellie's husband, Stan, was a retired doctor.

———

After an interminable few minutes, Stan answered the door. He'd thrown an overcoat over his pajamas and was wearing slippers. Ellie stood behind him tying up her fluffy blue dressing gown.

Stan took in the scene immediately. He frowned and said without fuss, "Julian; what have we got?"

"Hypothermia. Barely alive."

"Right. Let me help you lay him on the kitchen table." Stan turned to his wife. "Ellie, run the bath. Tepid water. Not too hot. Then call the ambulance."

Ellie hurried out of the room as Stan began to check the boy's vital signs.

Julian looked on feeling helpless, until he had the presence of mind to begin going through the pockets of the boy's jeans, seeking anything that might tell them who he was. He found a plastic wallet and an empty pill-bottle. He read the label: Amytal.

Julian handed it to Stan. The doctor looked at it briefly, unscrewed the cap, and lifted it to his nose. "Dammit, it's barbiturates sure enough. He's probably taken an overdose. Breathing and blood pressure are going to be the problem – if the cold doesn't kill him first."

Julian nodded. "What can we do?"

"There's no antidote, just activated charcoal. Fortunately, I've got some, but I'll have to administer it through a naso-gastric tube." He paused. "Inserting it is a tricky business, and I'll need your help. Are you up for it?"

"Of course."

"Right. Let's get him into the bath first. I can insert the tube there. You take his shoulders. I'll take his feet. Don't bother taking the clothes off him. Speed is everything."

As the young man lay in the tub that was still filling up around him, Julian couldn't help but reflect that this was the first bath the boy had seen for some time. It was a pity he was not conscious enough to enjoy it.

Stan was kneeling beside the bath with the doctor's bag open next to him. "Right Julian; lean him forward, but let his head fall back a little."

Three minutes later, the tube was in place, and a dreadful-looking slurry of charcoal was being been poured into the end through a funnel.

When all was done, Julian stood up and stretched his cramped muscles.

Ellie was standing in the doorway of the bathroom.

He smiled apologetically at her. "Sorry to cause you drama, particularly so early in the morning."

Ellie gave a grunt that might have been a laugh. "Thirty-five years as a doctor's wife has taught me not to be surprised at anything." She paused. "Where did you find him?"

"About two-hundred yards down the creek from my cottage."

She shook her head. "He was lucky you found him."

Julian was far from sure he'd found him in time, but he kept the thought to himself. Instead, he said, "Have you looked in the boy's wallet for some identification?"

"No. I'll do it now."

Julian turned as Stan rocked back onto his heels and got up onto his feet. The doctor grunted. "We've done all we can. We can only keep him warm and monitor progress from this point on. The important thing is to keep him breathing."

Julian nodded. "What's the deal with this barbiturate?"

"Amytal, or amobarbital... Jimi Hendrix and Marilyn Monroe both committed suicide using it."

Julian couldn't think of anything to say.

5

Five minutes later, Ellie came back from the kitchen holding a small card. "I've found a government concession card which has a name on it. The boy's name is Dillon Shiffer." She paused. "I put a call through to the policeman on duty in Normanville." She noticed Julian's incomprehension. "It's what we normally do in these situations," she explained.

Stan appeared not to be listening. "Where's that blasted ambulance?"

"It will be here soon, dear," said Ellie soothingly.

Julian picked up the earlier thread of conversation. "You rang..." He left the question hanging in the air.

Ellie nodded. "Yes." She paused. "Evidently, he's wanted by the police."

Chapter 2

J ade pulled out a red ribbon and tied it over her elastic hair tie.
It was her *gulu fulgiyan gūsa* – her 'red banner'. She wore it
whenever she went into battle. Jade had done so ever since
she'd read the stories of Nurhaci, the brilliant general who ruled
much of China at the start of the 17th century. He'd first come to
power in Manchuria and had organized his army into four divisions
– each identified by a different colored banner: yellow, white, red
and blue. Jade had chosen 'red' as her banner.

She looked into the eyes of *Shifu*, the Master. They were passive,
completely inscrutable, giving nothing away. They never did. But
she also knew that she was being comprehensively assessed for
emotion, balance, and points of vulnerability. This was a fight
between a mongoose and a cobra… and she wasn't sure which
she was.

She feinted a move. The *Shifu* didn't even respond, making it
clear that he knew it was simply a testing move – one he wouldn't
even deign to acknowledge. She was in combat with a master.

Her mind was racing. *Let him come to me*, she reasoned. Human
reflexes are generally faster when acting in defense, but the deadly
cost was loss of initiative – unless, of course, you could turn the

defense instantly into attack. And that's exactly what years of training in *Kung Fu* had taught her to do. No, she decided. She would attack... and so she did, viciously and with all the speed she could muster.

The *Shifu* rocked back, parried with his arms – and spun low on his feet. He kicked her on the inside of her knee, sending her sprawling on the mat. The old Master stood upright with his hands together and bowed to signal the end of the fight.

Jade sprang to her feet. She felt nowhere ready to end the fight – but instantly acquiesced.

The *Shifu* spoke. "You are fast; you are good; and you are determined... but you must be better." He lifted his chin. "But enough of this hand-to-hand combat. Our craft's real skill is found in *Yin Shou Gun* – staff fighting. Prepare yourself, while I attend to another matter."

Jade bowed and made her way to the storeroom where she picked out a helmet and a padded jacket. It smelled of sweat... or was it fear. She donned her protective gear and selected her *gun* from the rack. The staff was six feet long and made of wax wood. This made it slightly flexible, something that belied the fact that it was a formidable weapon. The *gun* was the favored weapon of the Shaolin monks of Henan province... and no student was instructed in its use until they were first proficient in the basics of hand-to-hand combat. It was a point of honor that Jade had been allowed to train with the *gun* for the last six months.

The martial arts discipline she had schooled herself in over the years was *washu*, or *kung fu* as it was more popularly known. It was a discipline that combined *Ch'an* philosophy with the martial art skills developed by the Shaolin. The discipline had been part of China's heritage for 1,500 years.

Strictly speaking, the Shaolin were forbidden to kill. Occasionally in history, however, this rule was relaxed. In 1553, Wan Biao, Vice Commissioner in Chief of the Nanjing Chief Military Commission, conscripted the monks of Shaolin in his war against the pirates. The monks acquitted themselves spectacularly well, by all accounts.

Jade returned to the hall, sat on a bench, and waited. One thing she was sure of; she would soon be feeling pain. She asked herself for the thousandth time why she did it. Was it because the *Kuomintang* (the Chinese Nationalist Party) had declared *washu* to be *guoshu*, a 'national art' — something to be embraced that fostered national pride? Possibly. Certainly, now was a good time to be Chinese. The nation had become technologically advanced and was, for the most part, at peace — even if China's expansionist ambitions were being frustrated by the repressive and unjust reactions of the rest of the world. No. The real reason she applied herself to *washu* was that it empowered her… and it was her secret. None of her friends or relatives knew she was a student of the craft and had achieved a very high level of proficiency in it. When her Adelaide friends saw her leave Adelaide University to drive down Brighton Road to the *guan* (the school), they thought she was going to a gym. The fact that she'd been able to keep this secret was a tiny triumph, for her community was one in which everyone knew everyone else's business.

Jade glanced up at the posters that had been affixed to the wall. One was headed "Deeds" and listed the noble deeds required of the Shaolin: "humility," "virtue," "respect," "morality," and "trust." Another poster was headed "Character". Underneath, were the words: "courage," "patience," "endurance," "perseverance," and "will." Jade approved. They were good words.

The distinguished culture of *washu* heritage was, however, somewhat marred by a picture of Bruce Lee acting in one of his famous kung fu films. Jade could only think the *Shifu* allowed the poster to stay because it helped market the classes he taught.

The *Shifu* came into the hall — similarly dressed for combat. He'd seen her look at the posters for he said: "Let what we do this afternoon rescue our noble tradition from Bruce Lee and hip hop."

Jade said nothing and followed him obediently to the center of the hall.

The two of them stood sideways to each other, each holding their staff upright in their right hand. Both nested the base of their staff against the instep of the right foot. They bowed, then kicked

9

up the base of their staff into the left hand – and the battle commenced.

Jade knew that the *Shifu* was holding back his strength, but the buffeting he gave her was painful enough to teach her not to allow him through her defenses again in the same way. More pleasing was the fact that she knew the *Shifu* had to work hard to parry her own attacks.

At the end of their sparring, they turned sideways, returned the gun to one hand, and bowed once again.

The *Shifu* nodded to Jade. "You have progressed well since your *bai shi* – your discipleship ceremony."

Jade bowed her head demurely in acknowledgment and waited for him to say more.

However, the *Shifu* remained silent. She lifted her head. And there, in a brief moment of time, Jade saw something deeply disturbing. It was only an instant. She saw in the eyes of her master – the weariness of disappointment.

The Ambulance turned left at the T-junction with the main road. After giving one warning 'woop' of its siren, it revved its way up the steep hill and headed towards Adelaide. Julian watched the red and blue flashing lights for a moment before he turned to Ellie. She was standing with her arms folded, hugging herself as the adrenaline seeped away. Stan had already gone inside – to "tidy up," he'd said.

"Are you okay?" Julian asked.

"Yes. But come and have breakfast with us. Goodness knows, you deserve it."

Julian recognized a cry for help when he heard it. "Thank you."

Conversation in the kitchen proceeded in a desultory fashion. Ellie protected herself from facing her feelings by asking questions of Julian. It was as good a therapy as any, so Julian did not discourage it.

"Why do you dress in such a strange way? I've never seen a priest dress like you before."

"I'm not a priest."

"But why do you dress like you do?" she insisted. "You look like a Medieval villein – a peasant who's stepped out of the Dark Ages." She tugged at his sleeve. "It looks as if you're wearing an old army blanket – except for the leather-laced collar."

Julian shrugged. "It's warm, practical, simple, and affordable."

Ellie passed him a piece of hot toast. "I saw something like it years ago on sale at the Onkaparinga Woollen Mill when it was still running. Where did you get this one from?"

"From Leah."

"Aah. She's a strange one, sure enough. Very much the hippy." Ellie pointed at the long mane of graying hair hanging down Julian's back. "Are you a hippy?"

"No. I just choose to live simply." He could have added, *and as quietly as possible*, but chose not to elaborate.

Ellie shook her head. "For a priest, you sure don't say much. Most of the memories you've given me in the last two years have been of silences."

"I'm not a priest," Julian reminded her. "I'm just a very grateful neighbor." He decided to change the subject. "Can I pick some flowers from your garden for the church? I'll swap you for some broccoli and a cabbage."

"Of course. The vegetables would be handy. But what I really want from you is another of those bush chairs you make out of sticks. The last one sold in my shop for 180 dollars. I could sell one a week easily."

"Consider it payment for helping me look after my place."

Ellie rolled her eyes. "You're like my Stan – no head for figures at all."

Further conversation was forestalled by the arrival of a small child. He was still in his pajamas. The boy glanced at Julian briefly, yawned, and climbed up into Ellie's lap with the confidence and innocence that only a grandchild can have.

Ellie fussed over him briefly then introduced him. "Julian Alston, this is James. He's four. He is spending five days with us while his parents have a few days on Kangaroo Island."

Julian nodded. "Your daughter's son?"

"Yes."

He looked at the boy, still befuddled by sleep. He was not sleepy enough, however, to lose his grip on the small jam jar he was holding. Julian pointed to it. "What have you got in there?"

The boy drew it back protectively, paused, and then thrust it out to Julian. "It's a caterpillar. See, it's eaten a lot of the leaves.

Julian took the proffered jar. "Hmm. Indeed it is. It's a 'woolly bear' caterpillar. They turn into tiger moths when they grow up." He turned the glass around. "See; these spiky brown legs near its head are its real legs. But it's grown these pairs of prolegs along its length which it can also use for walking."

"So they're legs too."

"Yes, I suppose they are."

James frowned briefly at the foolishness of adults, and took charge of the jar again. "Granddad hates them. He swears at them when they eat his pansies."

Ellie rolled her eyes.

After a leisurely meal of poached eggs, followed by toast and marmalade, Julian took his leave.

The day, however, had not finished serving up surprises. Parked on the other side of the road on the grass clearing, not far from his bridge, was an unremarkable green saloon. When Julian drew level with it, a gangly figure unfolded itself from the front seat, opened the door, and stood awkwardly beside the car.

Although Julian had not seen the man for six years, he recognized him immediately. Indeed, he was a hard man to forget. He had the unique skill of making any situation he was in look untidy.

Caleb Kuznetsov was bumbling, gawky, and never failed to flounder in company. No matter how desperately he tried to 'fit in,' he missed the mark – often gloriously. Today was no exception. Julian glanced at his conservative gray suit, the 1950s hairstyle, and the brilliant lime-green training shoes. Someone had obviously suggested that training shoes were the 'in' thing – so Caleb had tried his best.

Julian smiled, hoping to put the man at his ease. "Hello Caleb, you're a long way from home. What brings you here?"

The man darted a nervous smile and shifted awkwardly from foot to foot. "Er... um... you actually. Can we t...t... talk?" In moments of stress, Caleb was prone to stutter.

"Yes of course." Julian looked down at the bunch of flowers he was holding. "I need to put these flowers in the church. It's just a few minutes down the road in Delamere. Would you like to come?" Julian experienced a flash of disquiet, imagining what Caleb's driving would be like, so he added: "We'll take my truck, if you like."

Caleb nodded.

Julian led him across the road to his thirty-year-old, Toyota Land Cruiser pick-up. It was parked in front of the Institute, just beyond Ellie's shop. The vehicle suited his purposes perfectly. It was uncompromisingly tough, although it gave little priority to comfort.

Caleb got in, seemingly indifferent to the dust on the seat, and sat with his palms on his knees – waiting.

Julian couldn't hold back a smile. "Seat belt," he reminded him.

"Oh. Oh, oh... yes. S... s.. sorry."

Once Caleb had strapped himself in, Julian passed him the flowers to hold. Caleb grasped them to his chest like a drowning man would clutch a lifebuoy.

Julian motored to the T-junction with the main road. Standing on the other side of the road, on a neatly clipped lawn, was the mill. It was three stories high, made of old stone, and still had much of the massive original chimney in place. The mill had first ground grain, then wattle bark... and then, incongruously, had been turned into a shearing shed. In recent years, the building had become a top-grade restaurant, which, after several years of false starts, had confounded the local pessimists with its success.

They headed south – sometimes through the steep-sided valleys dotted with fantastically shaped, gnarled gum trees – and at other times, along roads cut into the hillside. The views were spectacular. Julian loved the Fleurieu in the winter. The land looked green and productive. Lucerne and hay were being cut, and cattle grazed on the abundant pasture growth. In five month's time, the paddocks would be burned golden and brown by the harsh Australian summer.

It took just a few minutes before the tiny bell tower and the red corrugated iron roof of St. James could be seen. Julian parked the pick-up under the yew trees by the gate and led Caleb to the old stone church. He paused by its wall to lift up a slab of stone and retrieve a key that was hidden underneath.

After unlocking the door in the porch, he took the flowers from Caleb and set about replacing the old flowers in a vase by the altar. Caleb busied himself looking at the stained-glass windows.

It didn't take long for Julian to complete his task, so he sat himself in a pew near to where Caleb was examining a side window… and waited for what would transpire. Julian remembered enough about Caleb for him not to be surprised at his interest in the windows. Caleb lived in a unit in downtown Adelaide… and the only interests Julian remembered him having were leadlighting, and taking walks in Adelaide's botanic gardens. Caleb was a frequent visitor to the Museum of Economic Botany that was housed there. On some occasions, Julian had gone with him, as it was very close to Adelaide University where they had both once worked.

"How long has this window been broken?" said Caleb, poking his finger through a hole in the glass.

"For as long as I can remember. Sparrows get through the bigger hole next to where your finger is, and they poop everywhere."

"It should be fixed – particularly this bit which is part of the picture."

Julian looked at the window. It portrayed St. James at prayer, looking serenely at a bloody sword – a grim reminder of how the saint had been executed in the first century. It was not a picture Julian particularly liked. In fact, there was a great deal about the inside of the church that jarred with his spirit. It was full of memorial plaques, ornate furnishing, and gilt. He felt that a church should not be a mausoleum enshrining the past, but a place where people could be empowered to change the future. His convictions were ironic given that he was notionally in charge of the place.

He returned his attention to Caleb. "I think that used to have a piece of red glass in it… to signify a drop of blood." He paused, and patted the seat beside him. "Come and sit down. Tell me what's on your mind."

Caleb pushed his hands deep into his trouser pockets and plumped himself beside Julian.

His visitor looked at him sideways. "You were the only person I didn't mind sharing a lab with."

For a long while, Caleb remained silent, as if shocked at voicing this disclosure.

Julian waited.

The morning light was now shining through the windows, leaving splashes of color on the flagstones and pews. The effect was magical.

"I like working on my own. I think better… and can do things."

Julian nodded. Caleb might be socially awkward, but he had the most brilliant mind of any scientist he had met. The Americans had tried to lure him over to join them, but apart from the occasional visit there, Caleb always returned to Adelaide – to his lab, his lead-lighting, and his walks in the Botanic Gardens. It was where he felt safe.

Julian risked a comment. "You are a great scientist. I, on the other hand, was not great. It was one of the reasons I left."

"You left to become a monk."

It was a statement of fact, so Julian merely nodded.

Caleb continued. "I've been doing a lot of research – with some help from the Americans – and odd things are happening. I… I'm not very comfortable… in the lab."

Julian raised an eyebrow.

Caleb was now leaning forward, massaging his scalp as if trying to exorcise the demons in his head.

After a long period of silence, Julian asked. "Do you want to tell me anything more?"

Caleb shook his head.

Julian nodded, waited a while, then got to his feet. "Then come back to my house and have a cup of tea, and perhaps lunch, before you drive back to Adelaide."

Chapter 3

The young man stood in the middle of the room clutching a plastic shopping bag. It contained all he owned. He was the picture of resentment.

"This place is a dump. You can't seriously tell me that you live here?"

Julian filled the flat-bottomed kettle with water and set it on top of the wood-burning stove. "Would you like some tea?"

"Do you have any Coke?"

"No. Just tea."

The fact that Dillon Shiffer was standing in the middle of Julian's tiny cottage was a miracle. The previous week had been testing, to say the least. For the first two days, Julian had sat by Dillon's bedside at Flinders Hospital. Dillon had ignored him and spent most of the time sleeping, or affecting to be asleep.

That hadn't bothered Julian at all. He'd simply loaded up the Bible app on his cell phone and read to him the adventures of Jesus' life from one of the gospels. He read it quietly, letting the words do their own work.

After hospital, Dillon had spent a day in the Adelaide Remand Center – largely, Julian suspected, because he had nowhere else to go. Julian had also visited him there. This time, Dillon began to talk.

From the little Julian managed to learn from him, and from a helpful social worker, Dillon's story emerged. It wasn't a good one. For the first few years of his life, he'd been raised by his single mother. By the time he was six, his mother couldn't cope anymore and had handed him over to State care. Since then, Dillon had been in and out of foster homes... and had familiarized himself with the rewards of petty crime. The boy had failed to attend a court hearing for procuring and selling drugs, mostly marijuana... and that was why the police wanted him. However, the constabulary had higher priorities and had not pursued Dillon with any great vigor. It being his first offense, he would have got off with a warning, had he not earned such a reputation for vandalism and antisocial behavior whilst in foster care.

The authorities had been bemused by Julian's presence. "Mr. Alston, are you a relative?"

"No."

"A friend?"

"No."

"Who are you?"

"I'm a member of the Society of the Sacred Mission."

"What's that?"

"It's an Anglican order of monks. We operate out of St. John's church on Halifax Street here in the city."

"But you live in Second Valley."

"Yes. I'm on secondment there. The locals couldn't find a priest for their church, so I'm paid one day a week by the diocese to fill their need."

"Why should we release Dillon into your care?"

"Because I can be with him most hours of the day; because he would be away from the temptations of the city; because I have been trained in pastoral care... and because I was the one who found him after his attempt at suicide." Julian wanted to add: *and because it's what anyone should do*, but kept quiet.

"A psychiatrist will need to see him."

"Has it ever helped in the past?"

"No, but it is protocol."

"If you really want him to change, then I submit something different needs to be tried. Institutionalizing him would be the worst thing."

With great reluctance, the officials had released Dillon into his care, but only after making provision for a local social worker to visit him every two days. "You're on two weeks probation."

Julian felt that it was him who was being treated as the criminal. It was a feeling that was in no way helped by Dillon's aggressive questioning as they drove south from Adelaide in Julian's pick-up. "You're not a queer, are you?"

"No. I had a girlfriend once." He paused. "She died of cancer eight years ago."

"You look old. How old are you?"

"I'm thirty-eight."

"And you are a monk?"

"A rather bad one. Yes."

"Why are you bad?"

Julian had been hard pressed to give an answer Dillon might understand. He pondered the question, and then said, "The monks in my community are very fond of rituals, set readings... and..." he searched for the right words... "bells and smells," he added lamely. He was fairly sure that Dillon was not following him, so he added, "I love the daily disciplines of being a monk, but I'm more at home with things that are simpler."

Julian's explanation was met by an expletive and a look of disbelief.

Finally, Dillon was standing inside his tiny cottage. "Have a look around," Julian invited... "and see where things are."

It didn't take long for Dillon to do so. He returned to the front parlor with a puzzled frown. "There's a bathroom, and an office with a desk and... and this room." He shrugged. "Where do you sleep?"

Julian poured hot water into a mug of mint tea and handed it to Dillon. "I was coming to that. You need to make a hammock."

"What!"

"A hammock. I sleep in a hammock… and so will you. It's just that I haven't finished making it yet. I've left it for you to complete."

"You're kidding me!"

"Actually, no."

"What! Like they do in the navy?" Dillon frowned. "Were you in the navy or something?"

"I used to sail a bit… and still do when I can."

Julian didn't want to say too much on Dillon's first day. It was important that the boy feel his way in his own time. However, there were some things that had to be established right from the start.

"I'm a monk, so I'll be doing what we call the 'Daily Hours' of prayer. These are times when I will be quiet. The first one is 5am, so it shouldn't bother you too much. I'll sometimes leave the house to go to a rock – one that's actually very near to where I found you the other day."

"What for?"

"I go there to make sure I'm sticking close to God." He shrugged. "In other words, I pray."

"At five am!" Dillon shook his head.

"I start breakfast at six. You'll need to get up for that."

"What happens the rest of the day?"

"If I'm not praying, I'll be reading. And if I'm not reading, I'll be working. You can join me when I'm reading if you wish – like you did in hospital."

Dillon rolled his eyes. "Spare me."

Julian pressed on. "I would, however, respectfully ask you to join me in my work."

"Respectfully?"

"Yes."

"Go to hell!"

Silence hung between them. Julian waited.

"What sort of work?" asked Dillon aggressively.

"Mainly in the garden. If not there, then helping me make things for Ellie to sell in her shop. And once a week, we'll drive over to a holiday house which I'm responsible for maintaining cleaning and restocking for the next visitors."

"Who's Ellie?"

"Ellie is the one who will do your washing twice a week. She's lovely. Her husband is a retired doctor. He was the one who saved your life." Julian pointed. "It all happened in that old house across the road." He paused, then added: "Oh, and one more thing."

The young man looked at him sullenly. "What?"

"Can I ask you not to commit suicide?"

"Why?"

"It would make me sad."

"Yeah?"

Julian looked at him levelly. "Yes, it would, for you are more sacred than you can possibly believe."

Dillon interrogated Julian's expression for a while, then rubbed his neck and turned away.

Dillon didn't understand his feelings. Something heaved in his guts. For a moment, it tasted something like hope – the worst of betrayers… so he silenced it with a cynical laugh.

The monk spoke from behind him. "Have a proper look round. Explore the place. Find out where things are."

Dillon frowned. "What? Everywhere? Cupboards and everything."

"You won't find any cupboards except in the parlor, but 'yes,' everywhere."

He poked his head into the bathroom again. It was surprisingly well fitted out with a shower, basin, and toilet. Dillon then returned to the room he'd first assumed must be a bedroom, except it contained nothing other than an antique desk that had a lap-top computer sitting on it.

Julian followed him into the room. "You can use my computer or cell phone whenever you want, but you'll need me to open up both devices."

Dillon jutted out his chin. "Why?" he demanded.

"Because they're protected by facial recognition."

"Wow!" Dillon had to quickly do some rethinking. He'd thought Julian didn't trust him to use the computer, but it was just that it had facial recognition technology. That was pretty amazing. He looked at Julian with a frown. "You don't strike me as a techno-geek."

"I used to be a scientist."

"Really! Where?"

"At Adelaide University."

Dillon looked around the room. Other than the computer, there was nothing that indicated a liking for things technical. Quite the opposite. The cottage was Spartan, to say the least.

"So, you really are a geek?"

"I have a doctorate, if that's what you mean."

Dillon expressed his surprise with a profanity. "Who'd have thought: I'm staying with a geeky monk." He used the comment to mask the feeling that he was increasingly getting out of his depth. What he was experiencing was like nothing else he'd ever encountered. The monk was unsettling, both to his thinking... and to his plans.

His plan had been pretty simple: steal what he could, and run. Dillon coughed a bitter laugh. There was nothing to steal – absolutely nothing. The computer and phone were protected by facial recognition... and there was nothing else. And even escaping from the place wouldn't be easy. Buses to their rural location were not that common.

Everything about the monk was crazy. His hairstyle and his lifestyle were weird. He was like no one else he'd ever met.

One of the strangest things about him was his voice. It was soft. Listening to him was like warm honey being poured onto toast. He'd listened to the mad monk read whilst pretending to be asleep in the hospital, and he'd found his words strangely comforting. The man had read for hours – as a father might read to a child.

He wondered again if the man really was queer... but he didn't think so.

What really troubled Dillon, however, was the monk's claim that he would be saddened if he committed suicide. Could that really be true… even after knowing him for just a short time? Did someone really care?

Dillon rubbed the back of his neck. It felt cold, and he didn't like the feeling. The monk had paid for him to have a haircut in Adelaide – so the legal people "wouldn't see him as such a hooligan." He'd complied, only because the thought of going back to the Remand Center was frightening.

Dillon pulled aside the curtains that hid an alcove beside the chimney. It revealed Julian's clothing. He didn't own much. One thing of interest was a robe, and something else he didn't recognize.

He pulled at the robe. "What's this?"

"It's a cassock. And the other thing is a scapular. It hangs from the shoulders front and back. It's meant to signify an apron."

"Why?"

"To remind me to be a servant to others." Julian smiled. "It's a bit showy, so I only wear it on Sunday mornings when I take the service."

Dillon took the cassock off its hook. "Cool. Can I wear it?"

Julian nodded. "Of course you can – once you fall in love with God and commit your life to serving him."

Dillon couldn't think of anything to say, so he put the cassock back.

Leaning inside the alcove was a staff. Dillon picked it out. "Is this part of 'the look' as well?"

"No. I don't use it often: only when I'm walking when there isn't much light – such as when I found you… and when I'm walking the cliff path in the summer."

"Why?"

"Because of snakes. It's not uncommon to see them on the path."

Dillon shivered, then swore. He hated snakes.

"Where do I sleep?"

"You'll sleep in here." The monk pointed to two iron hooks that had been inserted two feet up the sides of opposite stone walls. "That's where your hammock will hang. I'll sleep in the front parlor." The monk smiled. "But if you're going to sleep at all, you'd better set about finishing off your hammock.

Dillon was soon sitting at the kitchen table (the only table) with yards of heavy canvas spilling away from him over its surface.

The monk showed him the end of the hammock that he'd already stitched. "What you're making is an American Navy Hammock."

"Why American?"

"Because you can remove the cords holding the hammock by pulling out this trapping rope… and allow the hammock to be washed."

The monk slipped what looked like a leather knuckle-duster over his hand. It had a pitted metal plate stitched into it near the base of his thumb. "This is a sail-maker's palm. It's what you use to push the needle through the canvas. You'll be pushing through three layers of twenty-four ounce canvas, so you'll need it."

The monk picked a metal ring out of a box. "This is a one-inch steel cringle. They make the islets at each end of the hammock where the cords tie on. There are twelve at each end. I've sown in all but six. The rest are yours to do."

Dillon picked up the unfinished end of the hammock and looked at a cringle Julian had sewn into place. "You've not sewn very straight," he said derisively.

"No, I haven't," said the monk. "If you put the needle holes all on the same circumference, the canvas will become like perforated paper and your cringle will pull out. So stagger your stitching to three different positions, like I have."

The monk threaded a thick triangular needle, took the sail-maker's palm from Dillon, and made the first stitch, trapping cringle in place. Then he handed the palm back to Dillon. "I'll make you a cup of tea in an hour."

"You haven't got any coffee?"

"No."

"Normal tea?"

"No."

"What have you got beside the mint stuff?"

23

"Dandelion."

Dillon rolled his eyes.

In the end, the monk had to finish the last two cringles. Dillon's forefinger and thumb had begun to blister.

Dillon was thinking he was a bit of a failure, but the monk patted him on the shoulder. "Well done. Not many could have done what you've done on their first try. Now let's put it all together with the cord lacing.

When the hammock was complete, the monk bundled it up and handed it to Dillon. "Yours is the privilege of hanging it up. You might have to adjust some of the cords, but it looks pretty good to me."

Dillon took it into the study and slipped the ring at the end of each set of cords over the steel hooks. Then he tentatively sat down in the middle of the hammock.

It instantly spun over and deposited him on the floor.

Dillon swore viciously.

The monk called to him from the parlor. "Sit dead in the middle, then twist round and pull your legs in."

Dillon did so… and to his surprise found himself hugged and secure in the hammock… and surprisingly comfortable.

The monk came to the doorway. "You get out in the same way – carefully." He was holding a duvet-comforter in his arms. This is what you'll wrap yourself in… and it will be washed each week."

Chapter 4

Dillon knew exactly what to do to free himself of Julian's oversight. It was laughable that the monk would even think Dillon would be content to say in a drafty, stone-age hut – infinitely worse than any other place he'd stayed in – except for the bathroom. That was nice. And as for sleeping in a hammock: that was plain stupid, although he had to admit, he had slept well. He had contemplated sleeping on the floor as an act of protest, but a five-minute experiment of rolling himself up in the duvet and lying on the hard flagstones had quickly ended that idea.

The list of grievances he had at having to live at Second Valley with the mad monk grew day-by-day, almost hour-by-hour.

His first grievance, if you didn't count the hammock, was being awake at 6am… for that was when he was forced to come to consciousness from his slumbers. It wasn't the monk that woke him. He was as quiet as a mouse. No, it was every feathered fiend that lived in Second Valley. They squawked and screeched and carried on as they circled and wheeled their way through the trees outside, seemingly taking cruel delight in waking him at an ungodly hour. It was a conspiracy, he thought darkly. No one could invent a sound that was so calculated to put your nerves on edge. The racket they kicked up left him wide-eyed in disbelief. Scratching fingernails across a blackboard didn't even come close.

And all this happened before he'd even got up!

Then there was the diet. There was plenty of food… but no sugar, just honey. Not only was there no sugar; there was no coffee; no chocolate; no commercially made biscuits; and nothing that looked remotely like a pizza. Almost every meal he ate tasted weird and unlike anything he'd eaten before. The only plus side to this crazy eating regime was that the gnawing ache he'd carried for months in his gut, started to ease after three days, and he was going to the toilet more regularly.

No, he decided. Staying with the monk was something he'd have to put a stop to, and he knew just how to do it.

Whilst drying up the breakfast things, he dropped Julian's mug on the stone floor, shattering it to pieces. There were only two mugs in the cottage.

"Sorry," he said with delicious insincerity.

"No problem said the monk. "I'll share yours." And the crazy man did! He seemed completely unfazed. Dillon didn't like it at all.

So he came up with a better plan. At lunchtime, he dropped a plate.

The monk looked briefly at the hundreds of pieces of broken pottery, and then handed Dillon a brush.

Dillon resented sweeping up the pieces and did so with ill grace. That night at teatime, Julian gave Dillon the one remaining plate, and ate his meal from a saucepan lid that was missing its knob. Again, the man seemed completely unfazed.

Dillon was slightly put out when the monk casually said. "It will be your turn to have the saucepan lid tomorrow."

So that plan didn't work too well either.

But Dillon was not defeated. He thought he'd give the crockery a rest, and try the furniture. The trouble was, there was almost none. But there was the kitchen table.

Whilst the monk was outside doing his meditating thing, Dillon took a small knife, and carved his initials in the top of the table. The real pity was, the tabletop was bare wood. Its surface, if it ever had one, had long since disappeared. As such, there was no varnish to disfigure. When Dillon had finished the carving, he was quite proud of the result.

The mad monk had seen the disfigurement when he came in, stared at it briefly, and gone back outside to the workshop. He'd returned with a scraping blade and some sandpaper. "Here," he said. "Let me know when it's all gone, then I'll take you to the beach at Rapid Bay to explore a cave."

It had taken him all afternoon to sand his graffiti away, and he never got to explore the cave.

And throughout all this time, the mad monk never lost his cool. He just looked at Dillon with eyes that seemed to lay bare his soul, and exude a weird peace, even affection. Whatever it was, it was deeply disturbing. It didn't matter how much Dillon sulked, was uncooperative, or just downright rude, nothing seemed to upset him.

Dillon had once blurted out in a fit of frustration, "Why aren't you pissed off at me?"

The monk looked up from the book he was always reading and said, "Why should I give your behavior the power to determine how I feel?" He smiled. "Would you like some tea?"

Bloody man.

Dillon's final desperate act of vandalism was to break a kitchen chair. When Julian came back into the house, Dillon had said in a masterful parody of contrition, "Sorry. It broke when I sat on it."

The monk nodded slowly. "Then we'll just have to share the other one until you make a new chair." He smiled. "I'll show you how to make a stick chair this week."

"A stick chair!" Dillon uttered a profanity. "I'm not going to sit on any pile of sticks."

The monk waved a finger. "Ah, but these are very specially made. I've got one out in the workshop half made. Come and see."

Dillon trailed after him reluctantly as they made their way outside to the stone outbuilding beside the house.

"This used to be a blacksmith's shed," the monk said. "But now I use it as a workshop."

Dillon viewed the walls of the shed with suspicion. Two opposite walls had a distinct lean to them.

"The walls don't look very safe."

"Don't worry about them. They've stayed in place for over a hundred-and-fifty years and are not going to fall down any time soon."

The monk lifted the chair he was making from behind the work-bench and placed it on the top.

Dillon looked at it with amazement. It was an ingenious tangle of sticks that had somehow come together to make a fabulous chair. How on earth did he do it? He caught himself wishing that someone might teach him how.

"Would you like to break this one too?" asked the monk.

Every fiber of Dillon's being cried out in protest at such a thought. It was a beautiful chair. But the only thing he said was, "I'm not going to make no stick chair."

The next day, the monk had driven him into Normanville so they could stock up on supplies. Their shopping basket at the super-market didn't contain very much, certainly nothing that excited him.

Once they'd put the shopping in Julian's pick-up, the monk walked up the street to the charity shop.

Dillon walked behind him like a reluctant puppy.

The monk turned him and smiled. "You can buy yourself a plate and a mug in here if you want to? Both should only cost you about a dollar."

With a sense of resignation, he did.

As they drove back to Second Valley, Dillon was deeply out of sorts. Longings and fears swirled around his head in a way that was bewildering. For a brief moment, the longings screamed the loudest, and before he could stop himself, he found himself saying to the monk, "Can you teach me how to make a stick chair?"

Julian had sought solitude by sitting outside on the bench seat in the garden. Whilst it was a garden, there were no flowers to be seen, just vegetables. But they were beautiful in their own way. Beyond the garden, the side of the valley rose steeply to its rounded summit. The cattle that roamed freely along the valley sides had grazed the grass that covered it. Julian was grateful for them for they kept the grass around the cottage short. Seeing them on the hillside seemed to add to the peace of the valley.

It always took a while for Julian to surface from that deep place where his spirit communed with God in prayer. Julian had learned not to rush it. So his sensibilities were brought into the reality of the present with a shock when his cell phone rang.

Chiding himself for not switching it off, he pressed it to his ear.

"Julian speaking."

"Is that Julian Alston?"

"Yes."

There was a pause. "My name is Detective Inspector, Miles Jenkins. I'm afraid I have some bad news for you."

Julian frowned. "Oh yes?"

"I believe you were once a colleague of a Dr. Kuznetsov."

"Yes."

"I'm sorry to tell you, he has died."

Julian jerked himself upright and pressed the phone to his ear. "Are you sure, Inspector? We're talking Caleb Kuznetsov?"

"Yes sir." There was a pause. "I'm sorry to be the bearer of bad news. I understand he was a friend of yours."

The policeman's comment caused Julian to rub his forehead. Was Caleb a friend? *Yes*, he decided.

"Er… He was, although we haven't seen much of each other in the last six years. We shared a lab in the Braggs Building at Adelaide Uni for a few years.

"Yes sir, so I understand."

Julian was still in disbelief. "How did Caleb die? I only saw him a few days ago… the first time in years."

"I'm sorry to tell you that he was murdered."

"Murdered!" exclaimed Julian incredulously. "But why? Caleb would have to be one of the sweetest natured, and most harmless people on the planet."

"He was very definitely murdered, sir – not at all pleasant."

Mental images of their last meeting played through his mind – and grief stabbed at his heart. Such a terrible, brutal waste... and the loss of a brilliant mind.

The policeman interrupted his thoughts. "The thing is, sir: as far as we can ascertain, you were the last person to have talked with him before he died... so we'd like to talk with you."

"Of course. Although I doubt I can help much. When?"

"Tomorrow. Mid morning."

Tomorrow was Saturday. The Detective Inspector was obviously not troubled by weekends.

"Tomorrow's fine. Park in front of the Institute here at Second Valley, then give me a ring. I'll come and get you."

"Thank you sir. And again: I'm sorry for your loss."

The phone went dead.

Chapter 5

He was late.

He was always late. It was one of the irritating things he did to remind Jade that he was the one calling the shots – and to perpetuate the illusion that he was busy.

Still, if you had to wait anywhere, waiting on a park bench beside the River Torrens adjacent to Adelaide University was as good as it gets. The Manchurian pear trees were in blossom, and people strolled in front of her, some heading for a coffee at the café next to Jolly's Boathouse. A crew of girls was rowing an impossibly thin rowing scull, and a pair of lovers were enfolded in each other's arms on the University Footbridge.

The sight of them tugged at her heart. She had never found love of any lasting kind. Jade sighed. Perhaps she expected too much. Some men were intimidated by the fact she was finishing a doctoral thesis on electrical engineering. One girlfriend had even suggested her beauty intimidated them.

Jade had responded with an angry retort. "Rubbish!" But the fact that she even remembered the exchange told her that the idea bothered her. Life had taught her that beautiful women were often the loneliest, and were the ones who felt least secure. Jade shook her head. Life was a bewildering thing.

She forced herself to take in the scene in front of her – the manicured lawns, garden beds, and the old Victorian boat-sheds. Yes, she decided. It was a good day to be alive. Gardens had always gladdened people's hearts, no matter what nationality they were. They were certainly revered in her country of China – although the fierce struggle for industrial wealth meant there were too few of them. But things were improving. Fear that the Beijing Olympics might have been compromised because of pollution had helped put a priority on beautifying public spaces. But all too often, a greater priority was put on grandiose civil engineering projects and infrastructure. What China had achieved in the last few decades was truly astonishing. By any measurement, China was now a splendid modern nation. The fact that it still insisted on being classed as a 'developing nation' in order to allow its level of pollution was an absurdity insisted on by the Chinese government – now powerful enough to insist on anything it liked. Nothing must stop progress – certainly not impositions that came from the West. Even so, she couldn't help but grieve the fact that the crisp, clear sunny day she was currently experiencing was not something often enjoyed in Chinese cities. Perhaps that might change. She hoped so.

Jade had grown to love the sleepy, easy pace of Adelaide, its gardens and old blue-stone buildings.

"*Too Bee-eh* (ground beetle), how are you?"

The shadow of Wang Lei fell across her, darkening both the vista before her and her mood.

"You are late," she retorted.

"I am a busy and an important man."

Jade scoffed.

Wang Lei sat himself beside her. As usual, he looked young and 'hip'. He was impeccably dressed in a casual Western way. Wang Lei was wearing an expensive jacket over a designer tee shirt, narrow jeans, and pointed leather shoes. Jade thought uncharitably that he looked like a tightly bound piece of roast chicken. The jacket was

too small – as was the current fashion, but in this case it was exacer-
bated by the fact that Wang Lei was putting on weight.

Jade decided to go on the offensive, but it was always a delicate
balance when sparring with someone from the CCP (the Chinese
Communist Party). Wang Lei was ostensibly part of the Chinese
diplomatic corps in Adelaide established to serve the burgeoning
Chinese community in the city. In reality, he was part of a team
whose job it was to 'milk' technical and political information from
Australia for China.

"I suppose you are continuing in your parasitic activities." She
pursed her lips. "Yours is a world I want no part of."

Wang Lei's countenance darkened. "Tread carefully, my little
'ground beetle.' You come from a dirt-poor family… and I can
return you there like that." He snapped his fingers.

He then lifted his chin and looked at Jade with disdain. "I am
not a parasite, I am a patriot. It is the duty of all Chinese to do
whatever it takes to further the interests of our motherland." He
jabbed a finger at Jade. "And that means staying ahead in the area
of computer security – your area of research. I've not had a report
from you for a long time."

"But what you are asking is immoral."

Wang Lei slapped his knee. "There is no such thing as morality.
There is only loyalty or disloyalty. You will send us reports, or you
and your dirt-poor family back home will suffer.

Jade thought briefly of her father, a schoolteacher, in the poor
province of Shanxi, and her ailing mother – and a frisson of fear
ran through her.

"You wouldn't…"

"I would… in a heartbeat. So don't you forget it." He leaned
back in the seat, now apparently at ease with the world. Jade knew
she was beaten. He had cowed her… yet again.

He continued to lecture her. "The People's Republic of China is
actively pursuing the goal of 'cyber sovereignty.' Information technology is the new thing – the new 'oil' that leads to power. We have
therefore become leaders in information warfare." He smiled. "And
it is a war that we are winning. Appropriating Western intellectual

property has to be a priority, and must remain a priority if we are to become the main world power." He paused. "Did you know that the Chinese J-31 fighter jet is a direct copy of the American F-35?"

Jade couldn't think of anything to say. Wang Lei continued. "We are now strong… and it is a national obligation to do all we can to make China even stronger."

"At what cost to our soul?" protested Jade.

Wang Lei banged a hand on his knee again. "The CCP is China's soul."

A tense silence hung between them.

Wang Lei then became conciliatory. "The father of Chinese information warfare, Major General Wang Pufeng, has said… and I quote: 'Information war is a crucial stage of high-tech war.'"

"Are we at war, then?" she asked.

"Yes. But the West doesn't realize it." He jabbed a finger at her. "So, just make sure you play your part. Remember: we shoot deserters."

Julian's normal morning routine was thrown into chaos. No sooner had Dillon's social worker left, than the police arrived.

There were two of them: a cadaverous-looking Detective Inspector, Miles Jenkins, and a Detective Sergeant, Jenny Polanski.

Julian wheeled the office chair into the front parlor to augment the remaining chair and the metal dustbin he and Dillon had been using as the other kitchen seat. The boy had not yet started on the stick chair. Through the window, he could see Dillon working at pulling up weeds in the garden – although 'working' was probably a generous term.

Julian had protected his garden with cages made from building mesh and chicken wire. He'd long since discovered that if he didn't protect his vegetables, the cattle would eat them, and what they didn't eat, kangaroos would eat… and what they didn't eat, the possums and rabbits would eat… and then, of course, there were the birds.

After the introductions were made, the Inspector got down to business. He asked Julian to recount all that he could remember of Caleb's visit.

Julian did so, and concluded by saying, "The only sense of disquiet Caleb voiced was when he said he was not feeling very comfortable in his laboratory. I'm afraid he wasn't any more specific than that." Julian shrugged. "I didn't give it a great deal of thought to be honest. I've learned that it takes very little to disturb Caleb's sense of equanimity."

The Inspector nodded. "You used to work together, I understand."

"Yes. We shared a lab for a few years when I worked as a post-doctoral researcher at Adelaide Uni."

"And you were on good terms with each other?"

"Yes. We got on well. Although, I have to say, we've hardly seen each other in the last six years. His visit was actually a bit of a surprise. I left the scientific world to study theology. I'm now the acting locum here."

The female Sergeant broke in. "How did Mr. Kuznetsov appear to you when he visited?

"He seemed to be on edge, but was unable to articulate the cause of it." Julian paused. "Perhaps he didn't know." He lifted up his hands in resignation. "I have no idea."

The Inspector took over again. "Take me through it again, sir. What did he do, and what did he say?" His lips were pressed into a straight line – only just on the right side of politeness.

It didn't take long for Julian to again recount all that had happened.

The inspector grunted. "And he went straight back to the car and drove back up the hill, presumably heading back to Adelaide?"

"That's right. I watched him turn onto the main road."

The Inspector looked at his notes and sighed. "Well, if you think of anything else – however insignificant, let me know." He slid a card across the kitchen table.

Julian nodded. "You haven't told me how Caleb died."

The Inspector looked at him levelly. "Are you sure you want to know?"

"Yes."

"He was tortured to death in his unit."

Julian was unable to process what he heard – or make sense of the obscenity of what he was hearing.

"What?"

"I'm afraid it's true sir. It was most unpleasant. I will spare you the details."

Julian rubbed his temples – appalled. But even as he fought with his emotions, part of his brain was thinking rationally. "Um… was there evidence of his unit having been searched?"

"Yes. It had been taken apart very comprehensively. His computer was taken, but there were other valuable items that were not."

"So the killer, or killers, were searching for something."

"It would appear so, sir – probably something related to his research. Mr. Kuznetsov was working on something fairly secret, evidently. The Defense, Science, and Technology guys are involved." The inspector paused. "I don't suppose he talked to you about his work?"

"No. Caleb didn't mention it at all, although…"

"Although what?"

"Although I think he wanted to." Julian shrugged. "The trouble was, he was always so secretive. Sharing thoughts never came easily to Caleb."

The inspector got up from the table. "Or maybe he decided he didn't want to get you involved."

It was Sunday, and the responsibility he felt to do all he could to ensure that the parishioners of St. James had an authentic experience of God weighed heavily upon him. Julian therefore did what had become a habit most Sundays: He rose early whilst it was still dark, picked up his staff, and walked the creek path to the slab of rock where he often sat to pray. Showery weather had meant that it had been a few days since he'd been there.

Julian loved these times of quiet. They were occasions when he was overwhelmed by two realities. The first was the privilege God had given him of representing him. And the second: his utter dependence on God for being able to do anything significant. In these moments when he sat still with God, he knew himself to be standing in the 'thin' place, where heaven almost touched earth. But today, he also needed to show God the wound in his heart caused by Caleb's death.

Scudding clouds meant there was little moonlight, so he was particularly glad of his staff. But, by dint of long practice, he found his rock – and sat down.

As time kissed eternity in the stillness, dawn broke and peeped over the hills behind him, spilling its morning light into the valley.

All too soon, it was time to return to the cottage. He reached beside him for his staff, but did not pick it up. Something was wrong.

He frowned and examined the rock surface.

Then he worked it out. The limestone rock was deeply pitted in places – presumably by some sort of erosion eons ago. He'd always enjoyed the deep little craters because they sometimes filled with rain and looked, for all the world, as if God was providing him with his own 'holy water'. The biggest of these pits was about eight inches in diameter – but someone had filled it with soil. They'd even taken the trouble of transplanting some grass into it.

Julian tried to think who would do such a thing.

Then he remembered. Caleb. He had taken a walk to this rock, at Julian's suggestion, whilst lunch was being prepared.

Not at all sure what he would find, Julian dug down into the soft soil.

It didn't take long before his fingers touched something hard.

With a sense of incredulity, he pulled out an oblong object that had been wrapped in plastic and sealed with duct tape. It took a moment for him to realize that it was a computer hard drive.

What did it all mean? Julian massaged his forehead. Caleb had left this in a place where he knew Julian would find it. He was obviously trying to hide it from other people, but why?

Julian turned the plastic package over in his hands. What on earth should he do with it? Should he give it to the police? But why hadn't Caleb given it to them? Obviously, Caleb had wanted Julian to find the hard drive – presumably because it contained something that he would appreciate the significance of.

Possessed by the conviction that it was wise to give as much thinking time to a problem as possible, Julian re-buried the hard drive. In truth, he could not think of a better place to hide it.

When he got back to the cottage, he was surprised to see that Dillon was not only awake, but that he had put the kettle on the stove to boil.

"You're up early."

Dillon was hunched over, sitting in his anorak by the fire. "The blasted parrot things screeching and squawking – they woke me up, like they have every morning."

"Ah, the cockatoos and galahs; they do make for a rather raucous dawn chorus. They'll become background noise after a few days."

Dillon grunted. "I doubt it. No one could sleep through the racket they make."

Julian made porridge for them both. As they sat down at the table to eat, Julian broached the subject of what Dillon was going to do whilst Julian was conducting the morning service at St. James. "You're welcome to come if you wish, but there's no pressure."

Dillon snorted his derision. "There's no way you're going to get me to church. I'll walk down to the beach café and buy some chips."

"Good idea. Enjoy the walk. Let's meet back here for lunch at 12:30."

Dillon looked at him suspiciously. "You don't mind?"

"Of course not. For as long as it's helpful to you, this place is your home. Sure, there are things I've asked you to help me with in the garden, but there are freedoms too."

Two hours later, Julian unlocked the door to the porch of the church. He always enjoyed that delicious quiet moment before people turned up. Julian laid a hand affectionately on the old stone font. It had been shipped out from England when it was already hundreds of years old... so it had stories to tell.

As he turned to go up the aisle, he frowned. For the second time that morning, something he saw was not right.

He inspected the walls and the windows, searching. And then he saw it. The piece of lead-light in the side window had been repaired. Whilst the larger hole remained untouched, the small round hole that had once contained the drop of blood from the sword that killed St. James, now had a piece of red glass in it. In the last week, someone had repaired it.

Julian inspected the repair closely. He discovered that the repair had not been done well. The glass hadn't been cemented into place, and he was able to move it slightly within its lead sleeve. As he looked closer, he could see light reflecting from what looked to be a metallic flake set in the middle of the crimson disc.

Julian steadied himself against the wall and tried to think.

Who could have been responsible for this?

Again, the answer came quickly enough.

Caleb.

Chapter 6

At 11am, Julian drove down the road toward the beach and the little settlement of Second Valley. There was only one person he could think of who might help him solve the conundrum he had come across at St. James' church. Julian was still struggling to come to terms with the fact that Caleb must have returned sometime before his death, let himself into the church, and gone to the bother of repairing one tiny piece of glass in a lead-light window. One thing was certain, if Caleb had gone to such trouble to be secretive, Julian needed to be careful about who he reported this new finding to.

When he arrived at Second Valley, he parked outside a quirky looking house. A winding path took him past miniature castles, pottery fantasy figures, and wind chimes made with bent spoons and forks. The tines of the forks were bent so they held colored glass marbles.

A brass bell hung by the door.

He rang it, and as he did, he heard the deep bark of Duke, Leah's dog.

Leah came to the door. Her generous figure was dressed in a

caftan, and her long hair, died purple and pink, hung free over her shoulders.

"Julian, how lovely to see you." She kissed him on the cheek. "Come through to the workshop."

Duke, the black-faced German Shepherd pushed through and gave Julian a lick. They were old friends. Julian patted the dog's head as he followed Leah through the house.

Leah chuckled. "Your opposition has moved into town."

"Do you mean the witches?"

"Oh, you've met them, then."

"Not really. I accidently disturbed one of their ceremonies as I was walking the coastal footpath at sunset. Three of them were standing on top of a grassy hill. One was holding a branch. She was wearing an overcoat. I'm afraid my presence disturbed them a good deal. It certainly surprised them."

Leah laughed. "It would. I doubt that she was wearing much under the overcoat. She was probably preparing to go 'sky clad' at sunset."

Leah had set up her workshop in the large conservatory at the back of her house. As she perched herself on a stool, Julian handed her a small drawstring bag. She opened it and tipped its contents on the bench. Pebbles of every shape and color spilled out. Julian had collected them from the beach over the last month. The stones were not intrinsically valuable. They were mostly quartz, marble, and metamorphic pebbles that had colored intrusions flowing through them. Amongst her many other talents, Leah made jewelry from polished stones and titanium.

She handed the bag back to Julian. "These look great, Julian. Thanks."

"Leah, do you still do lead-lighting?"

Leah's answer was to point to some dainty, lead-light jewelry boxes and a terrarium that stood on a shelf behind her.

Julian nodded. "I've got a conundrum which I hope you might help me solve." Giving only the essential details, Julian told her about the mystery of the martyr's glass. He finished, saying, "I was hoping you might be able to remove the piece of glass, so I could examine it."

Leah nodded. "How intriguing."

Julian continued. "Leah, could you keep this secret… as in really secret… until I know what's going on?"

She looked into Julian's eyes and seemed to study him for a few minutes. "Yes," she said.

That was good enough for him.

Leah raised a cautionary finger. "Removing a piece of glass in situ is not an easy thing to do. I'd need access to a power-point."

"What for?"

"For my mini rotary saw. It's got a diamond-cutting wheel. I'll need it to cut the flanges of the lead."

"There is one, but you'd have to use an extension cord." He paused. "Is it possible to replace the glass with another piece of red glass?"

"Of course – if I knew how big it was."

"It is one-and-a-quarter inches in diameter. Perfectly round… plus what's hidden under the edge of the lead."

Leah screwed up her nose. "I'll have to have a look at it so I know what thickness of glass to use." She paused. "When did you want to do this?"

Julian shrugged. "Now?"

Leah laughed. "How am I going to live this down, Julian?" You've finally got me to go to church on a Sunday." She picked up a pencil, a piece of paper, and a ruler. "Come on then. Run me to the church. I'll do some measurements then come back and cut the glass while you get lunch for us both. After lunch we'll go back and fix it all into place."

Julian nodded his thanks. "I've promised to have lunch with my new house-mate, Dillon. But I can come straight back after lunch."

Leah raised her eyebrows. "Who's this Dillon fellow?"

"A street-kid from Adelaide."

"Don't tell me: You're trying to straighten him out."

Julian nodded. "Something like that."

Leah shook her head. "You and your lost causes."

As they drove up the valley in Julian's pick-up, Leah looked at Julian coyly. "You know I tried to seduce you when you first came to Second Valley, don't you?"

Julian said nothing.

"You didn't respond. I may be a good few years older than you, but there are not many who can resist my assets. Did you even notice?"

Julian smiled. "I didn't fail to notice, Leah. There's nothing wrong with my hormones."

Leah leaned back in her seat. "But I sense some tragedy… or do you have a misplaced sense of integrity?"

"My girlfriend died of cancer… and I like the simplicity of being a monk. It keeps me focused on the important things."

Leah shook her head. "There are not many men like you, Julian. I'm not sure if that's a good thing or a bad thing."

Leah was able to prise up the lead lip with a nail file and ease out the circular piece of red glass. "I'll take this home so I've got the exact measurement. It was badly set, so it came out easily." She held the glass up to the light. "There's definitely something in this glass. Here, take a look."

Julian took it from her and examined it. "I suspect we were meant to get it out easily."

Leah looked up at the image of St. James. "Let's get your martyr's blood back home where we can have a good look at it."

Julian dropped Leah back at her house and then drove back to his own cottage, where he made lunch for Dillon and himself. It was a fairly rudimentary affair – fried cheese and tomato sandwiches on homemade bread.

When he was back in Leah's workshop, she flicked through the colored panes of glass that she kept in a magazine rack. "The trouble is, glass thickness has now gone metric. I'm pretty sure I've got clear glass that's near enough the right thickness for the large diamond-shaped hole, but I've not got any red glass the right thickness for the small one."

Julian grunted. "Just use anything you've got. Clear glass, if you have to."

Leah held up a finger. "I've got an idea." She started to rummage in a drawer that had boxes full of different kinds of stones. "I went to the gem market at Christies Beach a few months ago and bought some stones. I slice them up and put them in my leadlighting – particularly if I'm making things which wouldn't normally have natural light behind them. They add color and interest in any light." She paused. "Ah, here we are. Heliotrope… and it's pretty much cut to the right thickness."

Julian looked at the stone she was holding. It was dark green but had vivid streaks of red running through it. One side of the stone was slightly undulating. The other was smooth from where it had been cut.

Leah looked at it approvingly. "The ancient Babylonians carved this stuff into amulets."

Julian looked at her with a frown. "It doesn't look as if it will let any light through."

"You'll probably get a bit coming through the red iron oxide, but that's not the point."

"What is the point?"

Leah handed him the slice of stone. "Another name for this stone is 'bloodstone' – or 'Martyr's Stone'. In the Middle Ages, it was seen as being representative of Christ's blood shed on the cross."

Julian nodded. "Well… that would certainly make it appropriate." He examined the stone. It had an old-fashioned feel and evoked images of Arthurian legends. It was a stone that told stories.

Leah sat herself down at her workbench. "Right. Hand it back, and I'll shape it to size."

She opened a flat wooden box to reveal a set of miniature cutting tools that fitted onto a tiny electric drill. Soon, she was trimming the stone with a mini cutting wheel. It didn't take long before she held up the finished result. "That should do it." She paused. "Now, let's have a look at what's inside the glass we took out."

Julian took it from his pocket and handed it to her.

Leah got up from her workbench. "I'll get my digital microscope. I use it for making jewelry."

She plugged the microscope into her computer and fiddled with the focus on the microscope pen. "We can zoom to times 500 magnification, so we should... woah!"

Julian was watching the image on the laptop computer. "Woah indeed," he echoed.

The one-millimeter cube of metal in the center of the red glass resolved itself into a highly miniaturized piece of something that looked like sophisticated technology. Julian didn't recognize what it was, but he knew it was something Caleb wanted him to find... and keep secret.

"How do we get it out of the glass to see what it is?" Julian spoke the question out loud before he'd realized it.

Leah picked up the glass and examined it. "I think this piece of glass might be a composite. The base is three millimeter glass, but a glassy-type of liquid has been puddled into the center of it, making it look like old-fashioned bottle glass." She handed it to him. "Here, have a look."

Julian couldn't make anything out at all, but was beginning to feel a prickle of concern about involving Leah in something that was probably related to Caleb's death.

"Leah. This is all getting pretty weird, and I'm scared of involving you in something that might be dangerous. Do you mind if I take it on from here – alone?"

Leah put her hands on her hips. "Don't be stupid. I'm too far into this to step back now." She busied herself in a cupboard and came back clutching some small bottles. "Here, we've got meths, ether, and acetone." She lined the bottles up in front of Julian – then put the piece of red glass in a metal dish.

"Wash the top of the glass with these solvents. Start with water, then work your way successively up to stronger solvents until you find one that works." She grinned. "I'll go and get us both a glass of wine." A furrow crossed her brow. "You do drink, don't you?"

He nodded. "I'm an Anglican."

She laughed.

Julian brushed the glass with water, then ether. Neither made an impact on the glassy material imprisoning the tiny metal object. Then he turned to methanol… and instantly, the reddish glassy material began to dissolve.

It wasn't long before he was able to use a small paintbrush to nudge the metal chip onto a piece of paper.

Leah called out from the kitchen. "I'm nipping down to the beach cafe to get some biscuits for the cheese. Make yourself at home."

Julian was again having misgivings about involving Leah in something that could be dangerous. But what on earth should he do? Whatever else he did, one thing was certain: he had to keep the miniature chip hidden in a place no one would think to find it.

His eyes fell on the martyr's stone.

Moments later, he had used Leah's drill set to drill a two-millimeter wide hole part way through the stone. Then he brushed the metal chip into the cavity. He leaned back from his work. All he had to do now was to cover it in a way that didn't compromise the chip, but which kept it hidden.

His saw a tube of super-glue on the workbench… and the tiny pile of stone dust caused by Leah's cutting wheel. After a brief foray in the kitchen, he returned with a sheet of grease-proof paper. Julian squeezed a tiny puddle of glue onto it and mixed in the stone powder. Minutes later, the glue had set.

Julian stared at the shiny cap of colored glue. Its green hue perfectly matched the martyr's stone. He used a paper-clip to dab a tiny amount of glue next to the cavity containing the micro-chip… and slid the green cap over the top.

He'd done it. The micro-chip was now invisible.

Leah returned – all generosity and irreverence. "We've got cheese and booze for when we get back. But first, let's return to the church and fix your window." She grinned. "Church twice on Sunday... No one's going to believe me."

Back at St. James, Julian watched Leah at work with a good deal of interest. She had not only cut the martyr's stone to insert as the saint's drop of blood, but also a clear diamond-shaped piece of glass to fill in the larger hole. Julian was grateful. That should mean no more bird droppings on the lectern.

Leah fitted each piece of glass into place, and then folded down sections of the lead lip to hold it in place.

After painting the joints with flux, she soldered the gaps with a soldering iron. Finally she brushed putty into the cracks and rubbed off the excess. Julian's job was to go outside, stand on a ladder, and press a wooden board against the window so it wouldn't bend and break when Leah pushed on it.

Using the solder and soldering iron on a vertical surface was not easy, and Julian heard language from Leah that had probably never been uttered before in St. James' church.

When all was done, Julian expressed his thanks. "Leah, you're a blessing. That was a repair that should have happened a decade or so ago. How much do I owe you?"

Leah waved a dismissive hand. "Just say a prayer for me and my many sins."

Julian smiled and nodded.

She looked around the church and shook her head. "What on earth is the function of a place like this today?"

Julian followed her gaze, and said with rather more vehemence than he intended. "The church's voice is not heard much today. Society doesn't want to hear it, and the church seems unable to speak it. It's still hanging its head in shame at the abuses that have gone on within its institutions. The fact that it can't agree on moral issues... or even the fundamental truths of the gospel, means it has no clear message." He pursed his lips. "Its clerics have become poorly paid social workers. They dispense motherhood statements and air opinions about justice – safe in the knowledge they will never have the responsibility of doing anything about it."

Leah looked at him with surprise. "Wow! It sounds as if you've been needing to say that for a while."

Julian smiled apologetically. "Yes. But I probably shouldn't have."

She turned back and collected her things together. "I can see how you would sit somewhat awkwardly in the ranks of the church." Leah smiled. "It makes you very attractive."

As Leah was packing up her equipment, Julian's phone rang. When he answered it, he recognized the voice of Geraldine. She was purser for the *One and All* sail training ship based at Port Adelaide.

"Hi Gerry. What's up?"

"G'day Julian. We need you. One of our watch leaders has gone down with shingles. We've got a five-day voyage beginning Tuesday. Can you fill in?"

"Whoa!"

"Yeah. Sorry for the late notice. I've rung you because we've got a dozen kids on probation on the trip. You're our top 'teen-whisperer,' so we need you."

Julian pinched the top of his nose. "Possibly. But I've got a complication."

"What?"

"I'm looking after my own teenager-on-probation. He's seventeen years old, and he's called Dillon."

"Can you bring him along with you?"

"Have you got room for him?"

"Yes. We haven't quite got a full complement."

Julian was delighted. "Okay. It's a deal."

"Great. When can you join the ship?"

"Why don't you pick us up from Second Valley when you sail down the gulf? Pick us up from the jetty in the Zodiac."

"Right-ho. Easy done. See you about lunch-time on Tuesday."

He put his phone away and carried Leah's box containing the mini-drill set back out to his pick-up.

Leah got into the front seat and rubbed her hands together. "Time for a glass of red and some cheese."

Julian grinned. "You've certainly earned it."

As they turned off the main road and headed down the valley toward the beach, Leah turned to Julian with a questioning look. "I never asked. What did you do with the little metal thingamee?"

Julian smiled. "I've hidden it."

"What? At my place?"

"Possibly."

Leah grunted. "You are a man of secrets, Julian."

Jade thought that the galleries of the Mortlock Library were one of the most beautiful places to be in Adelaide. It was Victorian architecture at its best. Two levels of galleries hung under a glass-domed roof, and they were lined with old books – all without dust-covers. The peace of the place demanded that you walk its parquetry floors with reverence.

Jade was not, however, feeling very peaceful. In fact, she was feeling downright mutinous. She was sitting with Wang Lei at a table in one of the side booths

"I will not," she said.

Wang Lei tossed his head contemptuously. *Bèn dàn* (stupid egg). "You will."

"Why?" It was a ridiculous question, for she knew the answer full well.

Wang Lei spelled out the brutal reality of her situation – and seemed to do so with some relish.

"Let me remind you of our glorious 'Golden Shield Project'. It is our national public security project – our criminal information system." He pursed his lips. "You really don't want to get on the wrong side of that."

"Your Golden Shield Project is a military thing. I'm a civilian," she retorted.

"No. It is *your* Golden Shield Project. Censorship, surveillance, and cyber sovereignty are essential if China is to become great." He sniffed. "It is the duty of every Chinese citizen to assist."

"No!"

"Perhaps I also need to point out the realities of our 'Social Credit System.'"

Jade rolled her eyes.

Wang Lei continued, unabashed. "It is used to assess every business and individual's economic and social reputation. In other words; to assess their trustworthiness." He paused, to let his words sink in, and then continued. "The system is linked to our Skynet mass surveillance system that incorporates facial recognition. As you know, we use it to regulate social behavior." He pointed to her. "Let me assure you, your face is on file."

"But that is just used to punish dishonest behavior – and stupid things like violating traffic rules, or jaywalking."

"Or being conspicuously unpatriotic." Wang Lei wagged a cautionary finger. "You really don't want to be black-listed by our Social Credit System. You won't be able to buy an airline ticket and visit your parents. You will have to earn credit by paying large sums of money… and it will take you five years to get free of it." He smiled unpleasantly. "You will also be banned from university and effectively become unemployable." Wang Lei leaned back. "Is that what you want?"

Jade knew she was beaten. She slumped back in her chair.

"What exactly do you want me to do?"

"You will join the ship, the *One and All* tomorrow morning."

Chapter 7

D illon stood half way down the wooden jetty guarding the shopping bag at his feet. His feet were bare – only because he was copying Julian. The trouble was: Julian seemed to feel no pain, whereas Dillon's feet were soft and felt every crack, groove and bolt head on the jetty. But he hoped he looked as cool as the monk, who typically, was not looking like a monk. He'd swapped his woolen shepherd's shirt for a sun-bleached canvas smock-top. The monk had rolled his jeans up to his calves and was looking very nautical. His possessions were stuffed into a duffle bag.

The view from the jetty was impressive. A sandy cove nestled alongside the stone sea wall. The pathway on the top of the sea wall led on to the jetty. Behind it was an impressive backdrop of cliffs. It was odd that he'd never appreciated the beauty of the place before. He'd seen it earlier when he'd been driven down to Second Valley by his friends to go fishing. Dillon had tagged along, but behaved so badly that his 'friends' simply drove off and left him stranded. Their actions resulted in him putting into effect the dreadful plan he had been contemplating for weeks.

Seeing the scene now he was in his right mind made everything look different. The little island at the end of the cove on the other side of the jetty begged to be explored. But that must wait, because for the first time in his life, he was going sailing.

He'd had enough misgivings about the prospect to pepper the monk with questions – even as recently as that morning.

The monk had listened and said, "Dillon, most of the people on the ship will have not sailed before. They'll all be learning, just like you. But a few things will make life easier. First, I will not respond to you unless you call me by my name, Julian. Second: your hands will get raw… so protect them as much as you can. Third: you will feel overwhelmed by the number of ropes – we call them lines – there are on the ship, but you will work it out. Fourth: you will be faced with a decision on how to behave every hour you're awake, and every four hours when you are asleep."

"Why four hours?"

"Because that's the maximum amount of time you'll be allowed to sleep."

Apprehension again gripped his heart.

Julian had finished by laying a hand on his shoulder and saying, "You'll discover things about yourself you never knew."

The ship, the *One and All*, was now clearly visible in the distance. Slabs of sail hung above her sleek white hull. When she was about a mile offshore, the ship seemed to stop, even though all her sails were still up. Minutes later, an inflatable dinghy sped away from her side and came buzzing toward the shore in a shallow arc. As it came closer, Dillon could hear the boat slapping though the waves.

A bearded, shaggy-haired man piloted the inflatable to the wooden steps that led down from the jetty into the sea.

Julian gave the man a wave and picked up his duffle bag.

Dillon made his way down the steps, handed his shopping bag to Julian, and half fell into the boat. It was not the dignified start he'd hoped for.

Julian made the introductions.

"Dillon, this is Mick. Don't let appearances fool you. He's the bosun on the ship. Do what he says if you want to stay alive."

Dillon could have wished for more comforting words.

Once the inflatable had been manhandled aboard and lashed down on top of the coach-roof, Julian made his way aft where Teddy Allen, the skipper, was getting the ship underway once more. He had backed the foresails against the mizzen so that the sails were trying to sail against each other, resulting in the ship being stationary, or 'hove to'. When the *One and All* was again pushing its way through the water, the captain turned to Julian.

"You're a welcome sight, Julian. You've got more than your fair share of the kids on probation on your watch. Two of them have already tried to copulate in one of the double bunks. You've got the starboard watch." He glanced across to the rocky coastline. "The wind's from the west, so the sooner I'm off this lee shore, the better I'll feel."

"Where are we making for?"

"We'll try for American River on Kangaroo Island." The skipper cast his critical eye over the sails. "Middle watch is currently on deck. Your lot are up next at eight bells, so I suggest you get them all on deck and show them the ropes while you can."

The call went through the ship. "Starboard watch – muster on the foredeck."

A few minutes later, Julian surveyed those gathered round him on the sloping deck. Two-thirds of them looked to be aged between sixteen and seventeen. That meant there would be excited chatter down below in the bunks – which would frustrate the seasoned sailors who had learned to grab every opportunity to sleep whenever they could.

The last person to join the group was a strikingly beautiful Chinese woman who looked to be in her late twenties or early thirties – it was difficult to tell. Her hair was bound up in a ponytail. It swung well down her back like the tail of a wild horse. Her limbs looked strong and lissome and she moved with an easy grace. She nodded to Julian in what might have been a bow and said, "I saw that you had many young girls in your watch." She smiled. "I suggested to the captain that maybe I should join your watch to help." She paused. "He said, 'Yes.'"

Julian raised his eyebrow. "Are you one of the volunteer crew?"

"No. I've not sailed before. But I am a woman."

Julian pieced together the logic and nodded his thanks. "What is your name?"

"My name is Jade Zhou."

Julian noticed that she was wearing a red ribbon in her hair.

Soon Julian was leading his charges around the ship, familiarizing them with the things they would need to know when they took over the watch. From the corner of his eye, he could see Dillon tagging along with every appearance of reluctance.

"The *One and All* is a 130 foot long, 121 ton brigantine. Her foremast carries square sails, and her mainmast carries fore and aft sails. In all, twelve sails are carried, and this, together with her two lifting center-plates, means that we have lots of things to play with to balance the ship."

He led his watch to the foremast. "You will learn that the lines controlling the sails on the jib-boom and foremast are led to the belaying pins at the base of the mast standing behind it. When we set sail, we normally begin with the staysails and then work up and out." He pointed to the ratlines running up the side of the foremast. "Each of you are free to climb those ratlines if you wish and get out on the yards. But before you do, you must let me know. And when you go, always climb with the wind blowing on your back – with the ship leaning away from you."

Dillon spoke up. "I thought that was something only the real crew should do?"

Julian could hear the fear in his voice. He tried to give a reassuring reply. "You'll be wearing a safety harness, but you won't be able to clip it on until you get over the crosstrees and out onto the yards. Until you do, just trust yourself." He smiled. "And relax. We haven't lost anyone yet."

He had two safety harnesses looped over his arm. "Who wants to be the first to go up?" He found himself looking at Jade. She exuded physical competence.

Jade picked up his signal. "I will," she said.

One of the young girls, emboldened by Jade, also volunteered. Julian was not surprised. It was often the girls who went first.

He talked the two of them through the procedure.

Jade stood on the gunwale, gripped the shrouds, and went up the ratline with fluid ease, treading lightly on the ropes. The other girl followed next, going considerably more slowly.

Julian was just behind her. "Take your time. Enjoy the view."

"It's the view I'm scared of," she wailed.

Julian chuckled, hoping to turn her incipient fear into something worth laughing at.

Jade was already at the point where the ratlines ended under the crosstrees. A mini set of ratlines then splayed out backward to the end of the crosstrees – from which another set of ratlines ran toward the top yard of the mast.

Julian yelled instructions. "Take hold of the shrouds of the backward ratlines, and walk your hands out until you can grab the base of the next set of shrouds. You'll be leaning back, so this is definitely the point you don't want to let go. Haul yourself up, then wait for me."

Jade managed it easily… and after many cries of anguish, so did the other girl.

Julian didn't give them any respite. He stepped past them onto the footrope that ran along the bottom of the boom holding up the lower topsail. Julian pointed to a steel cable – the jackstay. "This is what you clip your harness on to." He grinned. "When you've done that, you're safe."

Ten minutes later, all of them were back on deck.

Julian turned to Jade. "Thank you for setting an example." He paused. "You did well."

She lowered her head demurely.

Eight members of Julian's watch managed to get their "buttocks over the futtocks" as the skipper called it – and get themselves aloft.

Unfortunately, Dillon wasn't one of them, and the consequence of this was beginning to play itself out. He sought to protect his ego by becoming loud and obnoxious. More worryingly, he began to assert himself sexually with the girls in his watch by making inappropriate comments and suggestive advances. The danger was that some of the girls understood his language only too well. They had grown up with it.

Julian saw it all and knew it must eventually come to a head. His immediate response was to move his sleeping quarters from the focsle where the crew slept, into the main cabin where the paying guests slept. Here, every person had a narrow enclosed bunk, each with its own light and curtain. As both sexes shared the main sleeping area and the showers, some sexual tension at the start of the voyage was inevitable. After a few days, however, weariness engendered by an unforgiving 'watch system' usually dampened people's sexual ardor.

Julian had little doubt that his presence in the sleeping cabin would also curtail the worst excesses being plotted by some in his watch.

He enjoyed sleeping in a bunk. It gave him the chance to be still and 'feel' the ship. The *One and All* felt like a living thing. She vibrated with tension as she pitched and rolled – and creaked and shuddered as she leaned to the wind. They were noises that told Julian exactly what the ship was doing. Just occasionally, there was a bump and a crash as the ship met a big sea. In the background, the sound of bilge water sloshing about could be heard above the hum of the ship's generator.

He also enjoyed the culture of the *One and All*. The permanent crew had weather-beaten features, bare feet, and their ankles and wrists sprouted fancy rope-work bangles. They combined competency with humor – a culture perfectly suited to a sail-training ship.

With the wind on its beam, the ship surged its way out of Gulf St. Vincent and thrashed its way across the stormy waters of Backstairs Passage to Kangaroo Island.

Both the light and wind began to fade as the ship nosed its way into the calmer waters of the wide estuary of American River.

Julian, who was aloft, paused from his task of furling the lower topsail to gaze at the peaceful scene around him. The wide estuary was dotted with boats and flanked by trees. Pelicans, black swans, and a host of other seabirds swam in its shallows.

From his unique vantage point, seventy feet above the deck, he observed a disturbing scene. It was over in a flash, and he almost missed it.

Jade was at the base of the foremast, coiling a brailing line when Dillon, presumably in an act of bravado, tried to put an arm around Jade's waist. Her action was swift and dramatic. She dropped the coil of rope and chopped his hand away before the rope had hit the deck. An instant later, she was crouched with one arm back ready to punch. From Julian's vantage point, her reaction looked instinctive. But it was over in a moment. Jade stood up and turned away… while Dillon slunk away nursing his hurt pride – a slightly wiser man.

Julian resolved to speak with the boy after dinner.

The ship's cook, a fearsome-looking Dane called Sven, had decided to delay dinner until the ship was docked. In reality, Sven was a gentle giant, but most of the new crew had yet to work that out.

Whatever else the little altercation on deck had taught Julian it was that Jade was not a woman to be messed with. She had been trained to fight.

As it turned out, Julian was so busy that he didn't get a chance to catch up with Dillon until next morning after breakfast, and all hands had been mustered to clean the ship. Teams were put to work cleaning the toilets – much used by those suffering sea-sickness on the passage over – scrubbing the decks and polishing up the 'bright-work.' The skipper decided to wait for an hour in order to catch the tide that would take them out of the estuary. This gave time for the permanent crew to play 'hacky sack.' They stood in a circle kicking a small leather sack to each other, keeping it in the air using only their feet. Some of the new crew joined in. Jade Zhou was one of them.

As he watched her, Jade's behavior began to puzzle Julian. He could tell that she had a deft touch with her feet and superb timing – yet she miss-kicked the 'hacky sack' fairly often. It took a few minutes for Julian to come to the realization that she was deliberately underplaying her ability.

His immediate concern, however, was Dillon. Julian had asked him to sit with him on the quay, and he had done so with ill grace.

For a while, Julian contented himself with pointing to the crabs that could be seen climbing amongst the sponges and seaweed on the pylons. The water was crystal clear.

When Julian judged that Dillon's mutinous hubris had calmed somewhat, he said: "Dillon, I'm going to tell you a secret which I hope you will remember for the rest of your life. It's one that may even save your life."

The comment succeeded in getting Dillon's attention.

"What?" he demanded.

"Picture in your mind's eye a group of people in a room. Tell me: who is the most powerful person there?"

"Dunno," said Dillon irritably.

"I'll tell you," said Julian, unruffled. "The most powerful person there is the person who serves."

Dillon looked at him, making no attempt to hide his derision.

Julian continued. "It's true. It's the person who gives out the food; the person who pours the drinks; the one who cleans up the spills. The way they do it sets the mood for everyone in the room. It's the one who is considerate, the one who turns a bad question into a good one, the one who is kind… these are the people who are truly powerful. They don't brag. They serve. And it is these people who are remembered with fondness." He paused. "In the brief time you've been aboard the *One and All*, what do you think most people think of you?"

Dillon lowered his head and said miserably, "They think I'm a chicken and a dickhead."

Julian nodded. "And what would you like them to think?"

58

Dillon shrugged.

"Differently?" suggest Julian.

"I suppose."

"Then act differently." Julian paused. "Here's my challenge to you. Shock people with your kindness, but don't be showy. That's vital. Be the person who collects the dirty plates, who wipes down the tables, who gets the least popular person a mug of coffee. This," he said, "will make you powerful." He breathed in deeply... "And that is the secret I want to share with you."

Dillon looked gloomily in front of him. "But it's too late. They know I'm a dickhead."

"There is a way to fix that."

"How?"

"Apologize. Go to everyone you have been offensive to, and say that you're sorry."

"But what will I... actually say?"

Julian looked at Dillon, trying to assess the boy's level of conviction. Eventually he said. "Tell them you are sorry for behaving badly, and you did it because, deep down, you were scared."

"What! I can't say that."

"You can."

"Why?"

"Because it's true... and because those you speak to will never forget your words." Julian snapped his fingers. "Your reputation will change like that... and you will discover real power – the power of being a servant."

Without waiting for Dillon's reaction, Julian changed the subject. "How are your hands?"

"Sore."

"And your feet."

"Really sore."

"Put your training shoes on when you get back on board." He smiled. "You'll find it's easier to be nice if you are not in pain."

Chapter 8

Jade left the galley counter with her plate of food and looked for somewhere to sit. She chose a table that was nearly empty and sat near the far end – close enough to the two others on the table to be sociable, but not close enough to be socially presumptive. Being a Chinese person in another culture had taught her to be cautious. The fact that she was on board a ship, playing a role that was not her real self, made her doubly so. But she had only herself to blame for the awkwardness she felt. Jade had intended to play a role that was wholly false... but she found legitimate delight in being on board the *One and All*. She loved everything about ship, its clouds of sails; the extraordinary view from up aloft; the joy of lying in the netting under the jib boom and watching the dolphins showing off as they surfed the bow-wave.

It caused her pain to remember that she was on board the ship primarily for one reason – to win the confidence of the man called Julian – to deceive him. It was a role she hated. As she thought about it, she discovered that she had crushed the bread roll she was holding in her hand. Realizing what she'd done, she broke it apart and put it on her plate. She was now back in perfect control.

The food on board was surprisingly good, although it was

nothing like Chinese food. The giant shaggy-haired cook had a great fondness for making sauces – always with cream.

Her mind turned to Julian. She had inveigled herself into his watch, but had not yet managed to attract his attention. Perhaps she wouldn't be able to. The thought of that sent a frisson of fear down her back.

Julian was an enigma. He was striking to look at, although he appeared totally ignorant of the fact. He had strong facial features and soft brown eyes that were dangerous to look at. They invited a level of understanding she couldn't afford. Julian appeared totally guileless, but seemed to be able to read people and situations with a perception she'd seen in no one else. She'd watched him covertly and seen his ability to both understand and manage disrespectful teenagers. It had seemed that he'd only been on board the ship for a few minutes before the boys wanted to be with him, and the girls had begun to fall in love with him. The magnificent mane of graying hair falling down his back certainly helped. She wondered if it was a vanity. But she wasn't confident that was the case.

As she pondered these things, a shadow fell over her. She looked up, and instinctively put a hand to her throat. Julian was standing before her.

"May I sit here?" he asked.

She interrogated his features for some clue as to his motive… and saw nothing. She cleared her throat. "Yes."

He sat down on the bench opposite – but slightly diagonally from her. He had positioned himself so that he was not fully in her face.

"Why have you chosen to sit with me?" She said the words before she'd realized it.

Julian looked around the deck cabin. "Because there was space."

"Oh." She wasn't sure if she was disappointed or not.

Julian continued. "And because you are conspicuously the most beautiful woman on the ship." He smiled. "I say that as fact, not to chat you up. So I hope you will now relax."

Jade was appalled that her misgivings were so transparent. She shook her head. It was all so ridiculously ironic. Her role was to get

alongside him – using feminine guile if necessary… and here he was
– already frustrating that option.

"Is anything the matter?" he inquired.

"No. No." She looked down at her plate.

"Are you managing to find your way around the ship?"

She shook her head. "No. I doubt I ever will. The number of
ropes… sorry, 'lines,' is crazy.

Julian nodded. "Some people cope with the ship. Others endure
it. Some learn from it… and a few are changed by it." He looked at
her with his disturbing brown eyes. "But only a few truly love it."

How did the man do it? He had the ability to move from the
superficial to things profound with total ease – as if it were the same
language. She was disorientated.

"The food is excellent," she said. *Lame, lame. Do better.* She
gripped her hands into a fist and chastised herself. Aloud, she said,
"But I see that you don't have meat on your plate."

Julian grunted. "I'm not a strict vegetarian. It's just what I've
become used to." He shrugged. "Perhaps I am not naturally ideo-
logical."

"Somehow, I doubt that." *Woah. Far too personal.* She hurried on.
"We Chinese kill and eat anything. We've learned to in order to
survive." She summoned a smile. "Nothing is safe from us."

Her double-entendre was not lost on herself.

He smiled. "Don't you enjoy your Chinese heritage?"

"Oh yes. I am very proud to be Chinese. But hardships over the
centuries have made us pragmatic."

"How so?"

He was inviting her to go deeper – to unlock things she'd never
voiced before. It dawned on her that deep thinking was his language
– and she'd better learn to speak it if she wanted to get alongside
him.

"We Chinese have had to fight for survival, but somehow in the
process, we have lost our soul. Personal survival and the wellbeing
of those close to us, is everything. We've been schooled by history
not to waste our cares on much else."

Julian raised a questioning eyebrow.

Hoping she wasn't imperiling her soul, she continued. "A Chinese woman will sweep the dust, leaves, and rubbish from her yard into the street – where it becomes someone else's problem." Struck by a pang of conscience Jade continued. "But the Communist Party are changing this. They are punishing anti-social behavior and rewarding behavior that is good."

"So I've heard."

Further conversation was forestalled by the approach of Dillon. He stood two yards away from Jade, wringing his hands together. After looking around nervously, he took one pace closer.

"Er, excuse me miss... Jade."

Jade looked up warily, her countenance carefully neutral. "Yes?"

Dillon continued to wring his hands. His eyes flicked momentarily to Julian. "I want to apologize for being rude to you today."

Jade pushed herself back from the table.

Dillon continued. "The truth is: I was trying to show off... because... um, I was scared."

Jade looked at the boy, and then at Julian.

He appeared to be concentrating on his food.

When she turned back to the boy, he'd gone.

"What...?"

Her look of bewilderment was met with a smile. "Would you like me to get you a mug of coffee?"

The wind had turned during the night and was now light but strengthening from the South. The *One and All* was bowling along at nine knots. With the wind coming over her rear quarter, she was being driven along primarily by her square-rigged sails. Julian didn't give his watch much rest. He drove them from task to task, teaching them how to furl and unfurl the topsails, coil, belay and sweat up ropes. It was heartening to see that Dillon was now more engaged. He was doing well – although he still looked far from confident. He hadn't yet managed to get aloft.

Julian told his watch to have a break, and then ducked into the deck cabin to pick up two safety harnesses. He stepped back out on deck and tossed one to Dillon. "Put that on and follow me."

The boy started with surprise, but obediently put on the harness.

Julian gave him no time to think. "Stand on the gunwale and hang on the base of the shrouds." He clapped his hands. "Quick. Chop, chop."

Before Dillon had time to think he was standing at the base of the shrouds.

Julian rapped out the next instruction. "Climb up three steps on the ropes and stop. Keep your eyes level and concentrate on what you're doing. I'm coming up behind you."

Dillon did so. When he stopped, Julian said, "Go up four more steps and wait for me. I'm older than you, and I'm not as fast."

It took very little time for Dillon to reach the top of the shrouds.

Julian chivvied him along. "Reach up to the shrouds that are angling back over your head. I bet you've done this a thousand times on the monkey bars in the playground when you were a kid. Trust your hands, and haul yourself up onto the crosstrees."

Tentatively, Dillon reached out… and in no time at all, he was standing on top of them. He held onto the second set of shrouds and gave a yell of triumph.

Julian shook him by the hand. "Congratulations. You've officially made it aloft. Enjoy yourself and look around. Have a look at that massive iron swivel that holds the main yard. We call the boom holding up the sail a 'yard' just to confuse land-lubbers."

It was a weak joke, but it kept Dillon's mind busy.

"Clip your harness onto that iron bar and stand next to me on this bolt rope."

Dillon did so.

"Now lean your body over the yard – because that's what you'll need to do to furl the sail once it's brailed up. When you lean over the yard, your feet will kick the bolt rope up so it's level with you. When that happens, relax. It's quite normal."

"Oh, I don't feel so good. Get me down. Get me down!" cried Dillon.

Julian could hear the rising panic, and responded straight away. "Sure. Getting down is easy. Follow me. Don't rush."

When they made it back to the deck, Julian took the safety harness from Dillon, and said in a voice loud enough for those standing round the deck-house to hear, "You did well up there, mate."

That afternoon, the permanent crew organized a 'line finding' competition. Members from different watches competed to find various lines on the ship, and tie a bowline in the end of them. Various complications were gradually added to this. One included having an arm and a leg tied to someone else who was blindfolded, whilst the other person had an egg in their mouth. Dillon was very much part of it, although he did not play a starring role.

By nightfall, the *One and All* was anchored off a beach on the north-east coast of Wedge Island.

That night, the ship's permanent crew put on some entertainment in the form of skits. Australian literature was currently the vogue, and a number of the crew could quote from the Australian poets, Banjo Patterson and Henry Lawson. Julian thought this was probably because their poems had a significant anti-authoritarian streak – which perfectly matched the Aussie larrikin culture.

The skit by the bearded bosun, Mick, was particularly good. He had painted two eyes and a nose on his chin. When he lay upside down over a table with a sheet over his eyes and nose, a comical little face appeared which recited poetry.

Julian didn't stay to the end. He made his way to the ratlines, climbed the foremast… and sat on the crosstrees, staring at the starry night. He needed a place to be at peace.

―――――――――――

Next morning, the inflatable ferried most of the crew to the beach for a game of beach cricket and a Bar-B-Q.

Julian was one of those who elected to stay aboard. Again, he needed the peace. One of those who also chose to stay aboard was

Jade. She was leaning over the taffrail at the back of the ship when a storm petrel fluttered down and landed on the rail just beside her.

Julian, who was speaking to the bosun, Mick, paused to watch her move slowly toward the bird with her hand extended.

To his great amazement, the bird allowed Jade to pick it up. She spoke to it softly, before putting it back down.

Julian smiled at her. "That was pretty special."

"Yes, it was," she said.

Jade turned round and looked at the water. "It's so amazingly clear. I've never seen water like it."

"Do you want to go for a snorkel? There are masks and fins in the lazarette. I can get them if you want."

She nodded.

Mick volunteered to sit up on the crosstrees to watch out for sharks. Julian was grateful. The islands in the southern Spencer Gulf were a favorite haunt for the ocean's most fearsome predator – the great white shark. They came to feed on the local seal colonies.

It wasn't long before Jade and Julian were swimming in the water along the length of the ship. Jade duck-dived down to get a look at the ship from below. Julian followed her. He never failed to be in awe of the sight of the darkened hull of the ship suspended above him.

When they surfaced, Julian said, "Do you want to see if you can swim under the ship and come up the other side?"

Jade took up the challenge.

Down they went. Julian equalized the pressure in his ears and kicked himself along, keeping beside Jade.

Seeing Jade in the water was more unsettling than Julian would have liked to admit. There was almost nothing to hide her stunningly beautiful body in her one-piece bathing costume. Her dark hair floated over her back like a mermaid. However, although she was obviously fit, she was not a great swimmer. When they kicked up through the water on the other side of the ship, she was on the edge of panic. Jade grabbed hold of Julian and thrashed furiously for the surface.

If Julian's sensibilities had been tested by the mere sight of Jade, having her cling on to him like a limpet as she gasped for breath, completely shattered them.

"Take your time. I've got you," he said. He sculled with one arm and wrapped the other round her waist.

Neither of them said anything as they climbed the boarding ladder back up to the deck.

The wind had backed and freshened to a point that made the *One and All* pitch uncomfortably as she rode at anchor. Teddy Allen, the skipper, decided to 'up anchor' and sail through the night, seeking to make for the relative shelter of Gulf St. Vincent.

Julian's team had the Middle Watch – midnight to 4am. Whilst Julian enjoyed sailing at night, it was a novelty for the rest of his watch. Certainly, sailing at night made navigation easier. The various lighthouses and beacons located at strategic points on the coast all had unique flashing sequences, making identification easy. And it was just as well, for the limestone cliffs on the southern coast of Yorke Peninsula made for a ship's graveyard. If that wasn't enough, little rocky islands stood like sentinels across the stretch of water between the rocky coast and Kangaroo Island – ready to trap the unwary.

The *One and All* had its fore-topsail brailed up and the big mizzen sail reefed. She was jogging along nicely, sailing as close to the Easterly wind as she could.

Julian was at the wheel and most of the rest of his watch were huddled down around him, sitting on the deck behind the gunwales, hiding from the wind. Some were nursing mugs of cocoa.

The sails glowed eerily in the moonlight, and Julian was watching them closely. Now and then, he glanced at his crew. As he did, he caught Jade watching him.

He smiled. "Would you like to have a go at steering the ship?"

She got up immediately.

Julian made way for her in front of him and put her hands on the spokes of the wheel.

"The ship is sailing 'full an' bye', that is to say, she's sailing as close as she can get to the eye of the wind – which is about 45 degrees." He pointed to the compass on the binnacle. "That's our course, but don't try and sail to the compass. Pick a star that's sitting by the edge of a sail, and keep it in that position. You'll find it easier. Just refer to the compass occasionally."

Jade moved the spokes tentatively and then frowned. "The ship is not moving."

"It will, but there is a lag time of about ten seconds. You have to think ten seconds ahead. It feels weird initially, but it will become second nature with practice."

Julian stood on the helmsman's grating just behind Jade, acutely aware of her presence. She was only an inch away, and he could feel her body heat. He dared not move.

But Jade did. She eased herself back by the tiniest amount until she was resting lightly against his chest.

When the bell rang to signal the next watch, Jade did not feel ready to climb into her bunk. Instead, she walked up the ship to the tiny triangular piece of deck right at the front, and sat down out of the wind.

Julian followed her, but elected to stay standing. He leaned over the bow, as the ship plowed its way through the inky black seas. It was as if he were trying to say something, but hadn't got the words.

Eventually, he broke the silence. "Come here and look at this."

Jade got to her feet and stared at the water. It glinted with phosphorescence as it tumbled, crashed, and cascaded. Then suddenly she saw it – streaks of phosphorescence slashed the water. Dark shapes with pale undersides were weaving, diving, and leaping through the water at the bow. As they broke the surface, they left a trail of phosphorescence. It was a magical display. And then, just as suddenly, the dolphins were gone.

They both sat down together.

Jade was now very sure she'd captured Julian's attention. Somewhat alarmingly, he had also captured hers. Her heart was a storm of emotions. For the moment, however, she was just glad he was beside her.

Julian cleared his throat. "Jade. I don't want to mislead you. You may not know, but I'm not a full-time member of the crew." He paused. "I'm actually a monk." He looked at her. "Do you understand what that means?"

She stared straight ahead. "You do not marry."

"Yes. I've made a vow of poverty, chastity and obedience." He smiled wearily. "I've already broken the vow of obedience – several times actually, and I'm borderline on the poverty thing… but I would like to keep my vow of chastity."

Jade lowered her head, aware of a pain, a deep regret. Then she lifted her head and said defiantly. "Why do you tell me this?"

He looked at her for some time before saying. "You know full well."

Gāisǐ! (damn). He saw into her soul.

For a long time, nothing was said. The uncomfortable reality of Wang Lei's threats and demands played on her mind. She would have to do something to win Julian's confidence so he would confide in her… and perhaps find the intellectual property Wang Lei wanted so badly.

She cleared her throat. "I am finishing off a doctorate at Adelaide Uni."

Julian turned to her and waited for her to say more.

"I need a quiet place where I can write undisturbed – for about a month. You've told me about Second Valley, and it sounds like a peaceful place. Is there somewhere I could rent?"

Again there was a long silence as the ship pitched and crashed through the waves. Jade wanted to scream. *Say something!*

Eventually, he did. "Is that wise?"

It wasn't the reply she'd hoped for… and she grappled to find an answer. "I'd like to find out," she said, ambiguously.

"Give me your phone number, and I'll see what I can do." He looked up at the foremast as the staysail and jib began to flutter and drum. Jade had the sensation of the ship turning slightly, and the drumming stopped.

"What is your PhD about?" he asked.

"Electrical engineering. I'm researching electrical locks for computer systems."

"So, you're working in the Braggs Building of the University."

"Yes. Do you know it?"

"I did a PhD and worked there for about eight years before I studied theology."

Jade feigned surprise. "Really? That's a coincidence."

"Hmm."

More silence followed. Julian seemed to be lost somewhere deep within himself. Eventually, he seemed to claw his way back to reality and said, "Jade, I'll see what I can organize for you. The voyage will end in two days… and Dillon and I will be dropped back at Second Valley. I'll get back to you within 24 hours of that."

Jade's heart raced. *I've got you.*

But somehow, she didn't feel very joyful.

Chapter 9

D illon walked with Julian up the road from the beach clutching
the shopping bag that contained all he had taken aboard the
One and All. He reflected ruefully that the few days on the ship had
changed him, but he couldn't quite put it into words.

He glanced across the paddocks to the hillside rising steeply on
the far side of the valley. The hillside was dotted with cattle. Dillon
had only lived with Julian in his cottage for a week, but against all
expectation, he couldn't help but feel affinity with the place. It was
as if he was waking up from a coma, and seeing things he'd never
seen before.

He frowned and tried to make sense of it.

Dillon had never been so imprisoned, yet felt so free. No other
captor had ever been so ripe for scorn, but Julian was impossible to
hate. Julian's life was so crazily simple, yet profound. Dillon shook
his head. Nothing made sense.

They crossed the road to the small clearing next to the bridge
that led to their cottage.

Julian interrupted his musings. "Have you discovered our secret
springs?"

"No."

"They're just over there under that giant fig tree. Have a look."

Dillon dropped his shopping bag on the ground and ducked under the low branches of the tree. He immediately saw a small rock pool. It looked inviting.

Julian came up behind him. "You can almost picture water nymphs and fairies bathing here, can't you?"

Dillon didn't know what a water nymph was, so he said nothing.

Julian pointed beyond him. There's another pool a bit further on, and you can actually see the spring water filling it." He smiled. "Only locals know about this place. A few of them bring trailers down and fill up their water tanks from here."

A warm feeling came over Dillon. He couldn't work out why until it hit him: this made him a local. It was a good feeling.

The mood changed when they got to the cottage. Julian was frowning.

Dillon felt compelled to ask, "What's the matter?"

Julian shook his head as if not wanting to bother Dillon with his concerns.

"What is it?" insisted Dillon.

Julian rubbed his stubble. "Someone's been in here and had a very thorough look around."

Dillon laughed. "You don't even lock your door, Julian. And Ellie comes and goes…" He shrugged. "What do you expect?"

Julian shook head. "No. This is something else entirely. Everything has been investigated – moved slightly, but nothing has been taken. It's very odd."

Dillon was not convinced. "I'll put the kettle on."

Julian didn't raise the subject again, and after lunch, took Dillon to his workshop.

"With everything that's happened, I've not had the chance to show you how to build a stick chair." Julian pointed to the one he'd half built. "Why don't you begin by finishing this one?"

Dillon was embarrassed at the memory of his wanton vandalism, and regretted doing it. He was also far from sure that he wanted to attempt anything that would show up his incompetence and make him feel any more of a failure. In fact, he was regretting ever asking Julian to show him how to build a chair, and was about to say so when Julian handed him a strange wooden hand-tool.

"That's a travisher. It's a type of spoke-shave but, as you can see, it has a curved blade. I use it for hollowing a seat pad after I've roughed it out with an adze." Julian looked at his pile of wood. "Making chairs out of local wood here is very different from how they do it in England, where they've been doing it for centuries. There, they can use green beech, sycamore, and yew – all of which carve easily. But our local Australian trees are brittle and very hard. They blunt any instrument you attack them with. So, you've got to adapt. You've got to let the shape of a piece of wood determine its purpose. Don't try and fight it."

And before Dillon realized it, he was being instructed in the use of the ax, draw-knife, and the hand drill. After an hour, Julian left him alone.

Feeling surprisingly content, Dillon got on with his work.

As the light began to fade, and the chill of the evening announced itself, Julian came to the workshop and inspected Dillon's work. He laid a hand on his shoulder briefly. "You're going to be good at this." He smiled. "I appreciate your help."

Dillon frowned, as if not comprehending. Appreciate! It was extraordinary. He was appreciated. The very notion that he could be appreciated was ridiculous.

After an evening meal of vegetable stew and dumplings, Dillon began to feel tiredness creep over him. Every muscle in his body had been abused by the physical demands of working on board the *One and All*... and working in Julian's workshop.

Julian went outside to throw the kitchen scraps to the chickens. As he came back, he stayed at the entrance of the kitchen door and said, "Come outside, and have a look at this."

Dillon was most reluctant to leave the warmth of the fire, but he donned his anorak and followed Julian outside. Julian was wearing his shepherd's shirt, seemingly impervious to the cold. They both sat down on a garden bench in the dark.

Dillon shivered. "It's cold. What are we doing here?"

"We're letting our eyes get used to the dark. I want to show you something?"

"What?"

"Randalsea is one of the best places in South Australia to see the night sky."

Dillon rolled his eyes in disbelief and hunched himself over. Julian was weird. Before he realized he'd said it, he blurted out. "I don't believe in God. How come you do? You used to be a scientist."

Julian laughed softly.

His reaction made Dillon cross. "Seriously. Why aren't you an atheist?"

"Because I know too much."

"What?"

For a long while, Julian said nothing. Eventually he said, "If you are wondering whether you have significance, or whether your existence was intended, you've got to look for evidence." He pointed to the night sky. "A good place to begin is by looking at the cosmos, because if that shows signs of design, it's a fair bet you were designed to exist too."

Dillon grunted in contempt. It was rubbish.

The mad monk continued. "There are four forces that build the universe. Two of them are the electromagnetic force and the gravitational force. If the ratio of the relative strengths of these two forces had differed by one ten-thousand trillion-trillion-trillionth… there would be no life on planet Earth." Julian turned to Dillon. "That's just one of a number of similar statistics. You can shrug your shoulders and say that's not significant, but I think that's simply bloody-minded, intellectual laziness."

Dillon blinked. He'd never heard such things – or such strong language from Julian.

Julian pointed to the sky. "Our eyes have got used to the dark. Look up and tell me if you see anything that looks like a star moving across the sky.

The sky was looking brilliant, millions of diamonds shone with exaggerated brightness, and the drama of the Milky Way swept across the heavens in an arch. After a few minutes a star glided across the night sky. It had gone from east to west in just a few seconds. "I see it," he cried.

Julian laughed. "You've seen your first satellite. I've sometimes seen as many as ten in an evening."

"Wow."

Julian pointed to the Milky Way. "Do you see the dark bits in the Milky Way?"

"Yeah."

"That's the 'Dark River.' It's a cosmic dust cloud containing plasma and dust. It weighs more than a million times the weight of our sun."

Dillon let out an expletive.

Julian pointed away from the Milky Way. "And can you see those two fuzzy white blurs?"

"Yeah, I think so. What are they?"

"They are the Magellanic Clouds, which are, believe it or not, two dwarf galaxies."

"Wow!"

Julian stood up from the bench seat. "Let's go inside and get warm."

Dillon followed him inside. "What are we doing tomorrow?" he asked.

"Tomorrow, I introduce you to a wonderful story."

"Oh yeah. What story?"

"Your story." Julian smiled. "Sleep well."

Julian was on his own, having dropped Dillon off at the Women's and Children's Hospital so he could keep his appointment with the psychiatrist. Normally, if he were alone in a city, being in the Botanic Gardens would be one of the best places to be. He loved wandering amongst the trees and flowerbeds. But on this occasion, he had things to do.

He made his way to a stern-looking Victorian building that stood in the middle of its grounds. It was the Museum of Economic

Botany, and no matter what inventive things its curators did to make it contemporary, it always looked as if it had traveled by mistake in a time machine to sit, rather strangely, in the gardens of a twenty-first century city.

He climbed the stone steps and entered into the gloom of the museum.

After making an inquiry of the attendant on duty, he was introduced to the curator, Dr. Eunice Jenson.

Julian fished in his haversack and retrieved the small metal dish he had washed the Martyr's stone in. All the ethanol had evaporated away leaving behind a dark red, brittle substance. He showed it to Dr. Jenson.

"I was wondering if you could tell me what this is."

The curator took the dish, examined the contents and sniffed it. "What can you tell me about it?" she said.

"It barely dissolves in water. Doesn't dissolve in ether, but is soluble in methanol."

Dr. Jenson nodded and took out a pen. She used it to crack a piece of the brittle glass-like substance off and, much to Julian's alarm, put it in her mouth.

Almost immediately she pulled a face and spat it out on her hand. When she had composed herself, she said. "It's just as I suspected – astringent. What you've got here is kino."

Julian signaled his lack of comprehension with a frown.

"It's the sap from a blood-gum, or some other eucalypt. It oozes out when the tree is wounded – as it often is by boring insects." She pointed to a cabinet near the far side of the display hall. "We've got a display of these types of resins over there. Some were used for commercial purposes."

Julian nodded. "You don't happen to know a Dr. Caleb Kuznetsov, do you? I know he was a frequent visitor to the Botanic Gardens."

The curator's face immediately lit up with a smile. "Of course; a very pleasant fellow, if a little strange and awkward in company. Caleb quite often came in here. Why do you ask?"

"I regret to tell you that he died recently."

"Oh. How sad." She furrowed her brow. "What's the connection between him and the kino?"

"He, er… gave it to me as a curio not long before he died." He shrugged. "I wondered what it was… and did some experiments."

"So you're a scientist too."

"I used to be."

After some polite pleasantries, Julian took his leave and made his way to the kiosk on the edge of the lake. Julian had enjoyed going there ever since he was a child.

He saw Jade straight away. She was sitting under the bare limbs of a giant oak tree. Two ducks were standing at the foot of her chair, hoping to be fed. He sat himself down, trying not to look at her legs. They were on full display, catching the spring sunshine.

"I've confirmed your retreat for you," he said without preamble." He handed her a piece of paper. "That's the phone number of Ellie Tremelling. She's a near neighbor of mine. Ellie is the booking agent for the holiday cottage." For no reason he could think of, he added. "It's about half a mile down the valley from me."

"Oh. Thank you. What's the place like?"

"It's about one-hundred-fifty years old, but has reverse-cycle air-conditioning, a wood stove, a luxury bathroom, and a hot tub on the decking. The view down the valley to the sea is fantastic. It's a popular place for honeymooners."

She gave him a wry smile. "It sounds as if you know the place well."

Julian hoped he wasn't blushing. "One of my jobs is to maintain the place and keep it stocked." He paused. "Would you like some potato wedges?"

She shook her head. "But I'd love a coffee."

Before long, they were both nursing a coffee and pretending to be relaxed. Julian wondered for the umpteenth time why he had acceded to Jade's request to find her a retreat where she could write up her thesis. So far, it was a question that he couldn't answer.

He stirred his coffee, even though it had no sugar.

Jade interrupted his thinking. "Why did you become a monk?"

Julian smiled, hoping to keep the weariness he felt out of his voice. It was not the first time he'd heard the question. That was the trouble with cities. There were just too many curious people. He shrugged. "Rather unexpectedly, I discovered the story of Jesus – and it won my heart."

Jade frowned. "Christians are not in favor in China. They create trouble."

Julian spoke carefully. "I take it, you are referring to the riots that happened in Hong Kong."

She lifted her chin. "Yes."

"Hm. As I recall it, the only offense the protesters committed was to carry umbrellas."

Jade waved hand. "Pah! They vandalized shops and threw Molotov cocktails. I saw it on television."

Julian nodded. "Political hotheads did join the protest and cause damage, and that is very much to be regretted. But that can't be laid at the door of Christians." He shook his head. "It's not what faithful Christians do."

"Our government makes no distinction between people in a riot."

"No, it doesn't."

An uncomfortable silence hung between them.

Jade looked at him defiantly. "You can be a Christian without being a monk. Why did you become a monk?"

Julian began stirring his coffee again. "I guess it was a sense of not belonging to anything else that was worthwhile." He tried to smile. "I'm a 'wandering Aramean.' This place is not my home."

"What is a wandering…?"

Julian raised a hand. "Forgive me. It's a quote from the Old Testament. What I'm trying to say is that I feel a bit disconnected with the world… as if I've woken up in some sort of parallel universe." He glanced up at her. "I'm a person who doesn't belong, but who nonetheless tries to do some good… before returning to the place where I really do belong."

Jade tried to press him further, but Julian changed the subject. "When will you come down to Second Valley?"

"In two days..." she looked at the piece of paper Julian had given her. "...If it's all right with Ellie." Jade picked up her bag and stood up. "I should go," she said.

Julian got to his feet.

For a moment, the two of them looked at each other.

"Do take care of yourself," he said.

She nodded.

Even as he watched her leave, he wasn't sure why he'd said it. He just knew that he was profoundly sad.

Chapter 10

D illon hated hospitals. In fact, he hated anything to do with
doctors. You went to doctors when you were weak and in
pain. Neither affliction bothered him today, but he was required to
visit the shrink for the third time, because they feared he was sick in
the head. He'd endured the first two visits without any great drama.
A kindly old man called Dr. Mackenzie had seen him. Dillon had
answered his questions using the fewest words possible. The old man
had nonetheless expressed pleasure at Dillon's progress and had
planned to see him today.

It seemed that it didn't matter what you did to a psych ward in a
hospital, it always had the feel of a psych ward. It wasn't just the
vacant stares of the other patients, some rocking back and forth
compulsively, it was the small things – the locks on the doors, the
over-emphasis on cheerful posters, and the lack of medical gowns.
There was that faint feeling that despite the cheerful attitude of the
staff, they were having to work at it. And everything felt just a bit
tired – as if hope was hard to find.

And, of course, there was the waiting. Nothing ran to time.

Eventually, he was called into a consulting room. He was
surprised to see another person sitting in the chair… 'THE' chair…

beside the coffee table. Dillon wouldn't have minded a coffee. The psychiatrist seeing him was not his usual psychiatrist. He was faced with a middle-aged man, running to fat, who had a mustache.

"Who are you?" Dillon demanded.

"Watch your tongue, young fellah. My name is Dr. Haslip. I'm standing in for Dr. Mackenzie."

Dillon sat himself down and resolved to get the whole business over with as soon as possible.

Haslip's opening questions were pretty much what Dillon was expecting.

"How are you feeling?"

"Alright."

"You haven't felt depressed… or felt that everything you do tires you out?"

"I'm tired alright. There's lots of physical work at Julian's place."

"Do you think this fellow Julian is taking advantage of you?"

The thought made Dillon laugh. Julian didn't force him to do anything… which was crazy because he ended up doing a heap of things he would have normally objected to doing. "No. I like doing what I do."

Haslip folded his hands together. Dillon had the feeling that he was being closely watched. It was not a nice feeling.

Haslip broke the silence. "I have the power to have you incarcerated in here, or let you go back to Mr. Julian Alston. It all depends on you giving me the answers I want."

Dillon sat back in alarm. "You can't do that. I'm not sick in the head. I'm gardening and making furniture." he ran out of words. The very thought of not going back to Second Valley was shocking.

Haslip steepled his fingers. "If you want to go back, then I need to know a whole lot more about Julian Alston."

Dillon was at a loss. "What is there to know? He lives in a crazy way, but he's a nice guy." He paused. "He's a mate."

"He's not talked about sexually explicit things to you?"

Dillon laughed. "Julian is as straight as anyone can be."

"What do you talk about?"

Dillon didn't know where to begin. "Um… did you know that the 'Dark River' in the Milky Way contains stuff that's a million times the weight of the sun?"

The doctor blinked. "Does Mr. Alston do anything that is secretive? Do you get a sense that things are happening which he doesn't tell you about?"

Dillon rubbed the back of his neck. This was not the sort of conversation he normally had with Dr. Mackenzie… and he wasn't sure what was going on. Instinctively, he recoiled.

He drew a breath. "Look, mate; Julian is okay – a good bloke. So just bleedin' leave him alone." He let out a mild profanity. "The guy doesn't even lock the door to his cottage. He says that if people need anything, they can take what they want." Dillon slumped back in his chair and folded his arms. "I ain't sayin' nothing more."

"You will Dillon, or you'll find yourself incarcerated in here."

The doctor's comment succeeded in pulling Dillon up short. "What do you want to know?" he asked sulkily.

"Does Mr. Alston have friends with whom he does things that he's secretive about?"

"Of course he's got mates. But I don't know everything."

"Who?"

Dillon let out a sigh of exasperation. "Well, there's Ellie. She helps in all sorts of ways, including doing the washing. She's harmless." He paused. "And there's Leah. She makes jewelry at Second Valley. Julian spends a bit of time with her – but she's not his girlfriend. They're just mates." Dillon wrinkled his nose. "They've been getting up to something a bit mysterious recently. I don't know what."

The doctor nodded and jotted something down in pad. Then he stood up. "That will be all for today. Just mind you keep behaving yourself."

Dillon was at the door in a flash. Before he left, he turned to the doctor. "Mate, do you know something?"

"What?"

"You're an asshole."

Julian was not due to pick up Dillon for another thirty minutes, so he sat himself back down at the table Jade had just vacated. His conversation with her had stirred up all sorts of emotions . Some of them were delicious, some deeply disturbing. For a man who sought out peace as surely as a compass needle sought out North Pole, he was in unfamiliar emotional territory.

In order to give his hands something to do, he went to the kiosk and ordered a bowl of wedges. He'd not eaten such a thing for years but remembered them as a childhood treat. Julian knew he was reaching back for the innocence and simple pleasures of the past.

The girl serving at the counter smiled at him. "What size would you like? Normal?"

Julian had no idea what normal was. "I suppose so."

Ten minutes later, he was rewarded with an impossibly large bowl of wedges. They were scalding hot, as he discovered when he dipped his first one into chili sauce... and then sour cream. They were also very good – just as he remembered.

The comfort food manifestly failed to stop his mind going over his conversation with Jade... and every one of his other encounters with her.

He'd eaten about a quarter of the wedges before his stomach refused to accept any more, and with a sense of guilt at allowing such waste, he pushed the bowl away. The two hopeful ducks had waddled up and were standing near his feet, but there were signs on the table asking patrons not to feed the wildlife.

Julian looked at them apologetically.

Somehow, Jade had pierced his defenses. It was as simple as that. What was even more disturbing was that Julian was deeply suspicious of her and her motives for making contact with him. There had to be a connection between Caleb's death, Julian's discovery of Caleb's intellectual property, and Jade seeking to develop a connection with him. The very thought that Jade could be associated with those responsible for Caleb's murder was abhorrent. Instinctively, he knew she was innocent of any involvement, but she may not be innocent of any connection. He tried to think of an analogy that explained his convictions. It was, he decided, as if each of them had been invited to a dance that both were unwilling to attend, and they had been forced to dance together. And on dancing together, both had discovered a mutual attraction – one that had surprised them. What had happened was against the unwritten script each had been operating by, and now neither of them knew quite what to do.

Julian massaged his forehead. What was it about Jade that so attracted him to her? What was it that caused his spirits to lift at the sight of her?

Her physical beauty was an obvious answer. She was outrageously beautiful and carried herself with a demure elegance that was entrancing. But it was more than that. Julian had met a number of beautiful girls, and some of them had even tried to flirt with him. He was long practiced at gently fending them off. Letting it be known that he was a monk usually did the trick.

During his four years of theological training and two years at Second Valley, he had never had cause to doubt his calling. He felt settled in his soul and was content. But meeting Jade had unnerved him, and he wasn't sure why.

The thought of her caused him to reflect back on the one woman who had absolutely won his heart – Tansing. She had been full of joy and sweetness… and her soul pulsated with life. They had met at University, fallen in love, and were engaged to be married. However, an aggressive brain cancer, a glioblastoma, had robbed them of the future they dreamed of, and she had died eight years ago.

What would Tansing think of Jade? Would she be pleased? Or was he betraying her memory by allowing his heart to be vulnerable?

He was most certainly imperiling the vows he'd made when becoming a monk. That, perhaps more than anything else, was what disturbed him.

He tried to kid himself that the affection he felt for Jade was something only he was aware of. It was his secret, and he wasn't jeopardizing anything other than his own sensibilities. He could contain it and just watch from afar... hoping that his infatuation would dissipate with time, and that a cool head would again prevail.

But even as he thought it, he knew it was a lie. He was experiencing something surprising and something quite new. He shook his head. Allowing his heart to be vulnerable to Jade was wrong at every level. If his recent meeting with Jade had taught him anything, it was that she was spiritually in a different place, ideologically on a different planet, and culturally from a different universe. There was also the disturbing probability that she was engaged in something subversive.

It was all too much... and Julian knew what to do when he felt overwhelmed. He closed his eyes, stilled his heart... and showed himself to God, inviting him to see everything, and be Lord of everything.

When he opened his eyes again, twenty minutes had passed, and he was late for picking up Dillon.

Chapter 11

J ade looked with some guilt at the old woman as she heaved open the farm gate. She felt it was a job she should be doing. Ellie beckoned her to drive through, which she did obediently, before pulling up beside the tiny stone cottage.

She loved it straight away. The windows peered at her curiously from underneath a steeply sloping roof. They were deeply recessed into the stone walls. The cottage seemed to be inviting her to let it enfold her in its protective arms.

Ellie unlocked the door and led Jade inside. It was immediately apparent that the cottage was built in two halves. The old section comprised a bedroom, complete with a queen-sized brass bed, and a study with a desk and bookcase. The back of the cottage, however, was a completely new extension. Glass and crisp-looking corrugated iron featured amongst balks of timber that looked as if they'd come from an old jetty. The entire back of the house was an open plan kitchen, dining room, and lounge.

Ellie pointed to the wood-burning heater. "The cottage has reverse-cycle air-conditioning, so you don't have to use that. But having a fire to sit by, is a wonderful thing in the evenings."

Jade looked out of the glass sliding doors that led out to the decking. The view was spectacular. She could see a broad sweep of the sea between the two headlands of the valley. It wasn't hard to imagine why the cottage was so popular with honeymoon couples – particularly given the added attraction of a spa on the edge of the decking.

"Whoever renovated this place has done a great job," she said.

Ellie smiled. "Yes, the boy has done well."

"The boy?"

"Yes. Julian."

Jade's mouth dropped open with amazement. "Julian did this?"

"Yes. He owns it." She looked around her. "It's crazy actually. This place is about as different from the cottage he lives in as it could possibly be."

"But I thought he was a monk... and he couldn't own anything."

Ellie laughed. "Oh, Julian lives the poverty thing very faithfully, I can assure you. In fact, I don't know how he does it. But even a monk needs something to support him. The Anglican Church only pays him for one day a week, which is not enough to cover rates, power bills, and basic essentials. So, he renovated this place and lets it out. He maintains it, and I do the admin." She smiled. "He pays me in chairs."

Jade didn't understand what she meant, but chose not to pursue the matter. She was still in shock. Julian was indeed a dark horse.

Ellie put a card on the table. "That's Julian's number. Ring him if anything's not working, or if you need some more firewood."

Jade didn't let on that she already had Julian's number, but she nodded her thanks.

After Ellie left, Jade wandered through the house, seeing and feeling Julian's taste and creativity all around her. It was a good feeling.

But she wasn't there to feel good. She had a task to do – however onerous that might be. Her very survival depended on it.

After setting up her computer on the desk in the study, she went to the bedroom. Jade stared at the red ribbon lying on the dresser, and tried to sort out her stormy emotions. Eventually, she snatched the ribbon from the dresser and tied it around her hair.

Then she rang Julian.

Jade thought she was ready for him. She was wearing tight leggings and a halter-top that showed off her bare midriff. But when she saw him at the door, she felt somewhat foolish.

He was dressed in his shepherd's smock. The leather lacing at the neck was loose and showed off his brown chest.

She swallowed. "I've got a proposition for you," she stammered.

Julian nodded. "Have you settled in okay?"

"Y… yes." She paused. "You didn't tell me you owned this place." Jade had meant it to be a comment, but it sounded more like an accusation.

Julian shrugged. "I bought both cottages with my savings and some inheritance money, when I was a research scientist. My father was a marine pilot for Port Adelaide. It paid quite well."

"Ah," she said. "Hence your love of boats."

He nodded.

The evening chill was beginning to be felt through the open door. Julian continued. "Would you like me to light the combustion heater? Then you can see how to do it for yourself."

She nodded and tried to recalibrate what she might say.

It didn't take long before the fire was alight, and both of them were seated in armchairs either side of it. From where she sat, she could see outside to the flanks of one side of the valley. The lowering sun was bathing it in golden light.

For a while, she didn't want to break the spell… and pollute the occasion with any tawdry scheme.

Julian seemed to embrace the silence and appeared very much at ease.

Eventually, she said. "Could you proof-text my thesis? English is not my first language…and you have technical training as a scientist."

He smiled. "Your English is better than mine."

"But I'd have more confidence in it if you would check it over." She wrung her hands. "I'll pay you."

"What subject is your thesis in?"

"Electrical engineering. What area did you do your doctorate in?"

"Quantum physics."

"Why quantum physics?"

"Because miniaturization was fast coming to an end with conventional physics."

She frowned. "What do you mean?"

"Circuit boards were getting so small that the electrons forming the electrical current were starting to burn holes in them." He shrugged. "If we were going to get truly small, we needed to embrace a whole new generation of technology – hence quantum physics."

Jade had the absurd notion that Julian was attacking her branch of science. "So your life was once dominated by quantum wierdness." It was an unfair comment, and she regretted saying it straight away.

Julian appeared unruffled. "There's certainly a lot of mystery."

"What do you mean?" Her voice still had a combative edge to it.

"How much do you know about quantum physics?"

"Very little," she conceded.

"Then let me tell you the story of how one mystery was first uncovered."

Jade crossed her arms protectively in front of her.

Julian began to speak softly. "Imagine a ray gun shooting photons at a barrier. This barrier has two vertical slits cut into it. And behind the barrier is a wall that stops the particles that pass through the slits. This back wall has the ability to measure where these particles hit."

"So?" she demanded.

Julian held up a placating hand. "When all was in place, the scientists fired the ray gun... and the results amazed them."

"Why?"

"The scientists discovered that the electrons didn't behave like tiny marbles, but behaved like waves. When the electrons passed through the slits, they fanned out in semi-circular ripples. These two sets of curving ripples – one from each slit – interfered with each other, before hitting the back wall in a wave pattern."

"So what?"

Julian continued. "The scientists then wondered what would happen if they fired the particles one at a time. Doing this meant there was no chance the particles could interfere with each other to form a wave pattern. But when the photons were fired one at a time, a wave pattern still formed on the back wall." Julian gave a soft laugh. "The scientists were stunned. Each particle had apparently split itself into two, gone through two slits simultaneously, and then interfered with the other – before hitting the back wall. And as particles don't do this, it was concluded that each particle must exist as a 'wave of probability' that allowed it to pass through both slits."

Jade was amazed. "Wow!"

Julian nodded. "And if that wasn't strange enough, things soon became even more complicated. Scientists placed a measuring device near the slits so they could observe which slit the individual photon actually passed through." Julian drew in a deep breath. "This is where it gets really interesting. "When the photons were being observed, they stopped behaving like a wave and began behaving like tiny marbles. The photons now hit the wall behind the slits in two vertical lines."

Jade furrowed her brow. "So when the photons knew they were being observed, they changed their behavior. That's crazy."

"Julian grinned. "Welcome to the bizarre, non-intuitive world of quantum physics. It's a world where sub-atomic particles don't exist as physical particles until they are observed." He leaned his head back. "And all this has rather a lot of relevance to theology."

"Why?"

"Because the Bible says God saw something in his mind's eye... and this caused everything to exist."

Jade waved her hand derisively. "Pah! Christianity is a Western religion – a tool for Western imperialism."

To her mortification, Julian laughed.

"What?" she demanded.

"Jesus was born a Jew in the Middle East… and the earliest Christian missionaries traveled to Africa, the Balkans, and India, as well as to Europe. All the West has done is to institutionalize and commercialize Christianity – and occasionally done a bit of good." He shook his head. "The West doesn't define Christianity."

"What does?" she retorted.

"A love story."

Julian closed his eyes, making it clear that he didn't want to pursue the matter further.

Jade was happy enough to allow silence to reset the conversation. She wasn't sure she'd come off very well so far.

She was grateful when Julian threw her a lifeline.

"You've seen the place where I live – Second Valley. Tell me about your home in China."

Jade raised her eyebrows in surprise. "Er, my home is very different from this place."

Julian's silence invited her to say more.

She attempted to marshal her thoughts. How on earth could she describe something that was so foreign? With some surprise, she discovered that she wanted him to understand… to know more about her.

"I come from Shanxi province. That's south of the Mu Us desert. The whole area – the Shanxi, Shaanxi, and Gansu provinces – is a Loess Plateau. It is hundreds of feet of volcanic dust… and it blows and blows and blows. And it's high country, typically 5,000 feet."

Julian expressed surprise. "It can't be an easy place to live."

Jade laughed. "It's not. But it is an important place, and very fertile. Some say it is the cradle of Chinese civilization. But it is difficult to live there. Massive canyons that have been cut thousands of feet down by rivers, dissect the Plateau. The water eventually empties into the Yellow River. Their sediment is what makes it yellow."

"How do the locals live in such a place?"

Jade shrugged. "There are cities and towns, but the peasants dig big holes in the ground – as large as a courtyard. Then they burrow into the side walls to make their houses. Extended families live in different caves."

"Wow!"

Jade smiled. "We call them *yaodongs*. Chairman Mao lived in one once. Some are quite nice and have brightly painted doors. But when earthquakes come, they collapse – and people die."

Julian shook his head in apparent disbelief. "Is anything being done about the erosion?"

"Oh yes. Planes bomb the sides of the gullies with seeds of quick-growing vegetation. Then they bomb it again with deeper rooted, slow growing vegetation – such as pepper trees."

"Do your parents live in a…."

"*Yaodong*. No. They live in a city – a small one by Chinese standards. My father is a teacher – quite poor. My mother can't work because she is arthritic."

"Do you have any brothers and sisters?"

"My parents were allowed to have another child, because I was their first child… and was only a girl."

"Only?"

Jade shrugged.

Julian remained quiet for a long time, and then got to his feet. "Thanks for sharing your story, Jade." He paused. "It's a remarkable one."

He made for the sliding door that led out to the decking. Julian pointed to a stick chair that stood by the spa. "Dillon helped make that. He finished it this morning." Julian smiled. "He wanted you to know."

Jade nodded.

He looked at her with those dangerous brown eyes. "Is Jade your Chinese name?"

His question startled her. "N, No," she stammered. "It is the English name I gave myself when I came to live here."

"May I ask what your Chinese name is – your real name?"

She lowered her head. "Please don't ask me."

He slowly reached out and touched the red ribbon tied around her ponytail.

With her head still bowed, she said. "Please be careful... whenever you see that red ribbon."

What he did next scandalized her. He slowly undid the ribbon, then handed it to her.

"Good evening, Jade Zhou. I hope you will be happy here."

———

Julian and Dillon sat on the bench at the back of the house and drank soup from their mugs. It had been a good day, and Dillon had worked well. The trouble was, he knew it, and was getting a bit cocky.

Julian didn't mind at all. He was listening to him with half an ear as he watched some yellow-tailed black cockatoos wing their way to their evening roost. They always seemed to be flying as if they were tired – flapping their wings just enough to stay aloft whilst calling out to each other with their raucous cries.

Dillon was giving Julian a bit of cheek regarding the idiosyncrasies of Second Valley.

"The Parananacooka; the Anacotilla..." Dillon shook his head. "Crazy names."

Julian inclined his head. "You've not heard anything yet. We've got a road just a few miles from here called 'No Where Else Road.'"

"You're kidding."

"Dead set. And another not far from it called 'Yo Ho Road'. It runs to Yo Ho Station."

It was the wrong thing to say to Dillon. He immediately started to sing: 'Yo, ho ho and a bottle of rum'. Fortunately, they were the only words of the song he knew, so the boy got tired of his own voice fairly soon.

When Dillon did speak again, he was thoughtful.

"I turn eighteen next month."

"You'll be an adult."

Dillon lowered his head. "Yeah."

"Are you worried about the future?"

"Sort of."

"You've got a real feel for wood. You seem to understand it."

Dillon shrugged.

"Why don't you do an apprenticeship as a cabinet maker up in Adelaide?" Julian looked him in the eye. "Do you think you could stick to that?"

"But where would I live? I just squatted and couch-surfed before."

"We could find good people you could board with."

"Yeah, but how would I get to work?"

"Bus or train. Same as anyone else." Julian paused. "Have you got a driving license?"

"No."

Julian clapped him on the shoulder. "Then your first driving lesson starts tomorrow."

"Serious?"

Julian nodded. "And one more thing: if you stick at your apprenticeship, your reward will be coming down here on weekends. This place can always be your home… if you want it."

Dillon's eyes began to well up, and he lowered his head quickly. "Yeah," he grunted. "I'd like that."

———

At 4am, Julian's phone rang.

Julian clawed his way to consciousness and groped outside the hammock for the seat where he'd left his phone.

"Julian here," he said – injecting enough energy into his voice to give the illusion that being phoned at 4am was a perfectly normal occurrence.

He could hear sobbing on the end of the line… then Leah's voice – broken and pitiful.

"Julian. I've been attacked… and they've killed Duke."

Chapter 12

B lood was everywhere – dark and sticky. Leah had trodden it all over the floor of her bedroom. The blood belonged to Duke. The dog's great body lay on the floor amongst shards of glass. Leah was stroking his head and weeping. "Duke was in his kennel out the back and heard me scream. He just flew at the window, crashed through, and started mauling the attackers." Leah sobbed. "One of them must have had a knife."

Julian reached over and placed his hand over hers. "But you're okay?"

She nodded dumbly.

Julian got to his feet, unhooked a dressing gown from behind the door and handed it to Leah. Her nightie was not providing much modesty. "I've called the police and they're on their way."

"There were two of them," she sobbed. "It was difficult to see in the dark. One covered my face with a gloved hand, and another spoke to me with an eerie electronic-type voice."

"A voice synthesizer."

"I suppose so. He kept asking: 'Where are the things Julian Alston is hiding.' He kept saying it over and over. I managed to shake free of his hand and screamed. Then Duke came in through the window" She reached for the great dog's ruff and stroked it. "He was magnificent... and then they ran for it."

The sickening hand of guilt lay heavy on Julian's heart. This was his fault. He should never have involved Leah. But for the life of him, he couldn't work out how anyone could possibly know Leah had been involved – even in a minor way, in the mystery surrounding Caleb. The 'not knowing' was deeply distressing. He put his arms around Leah's shoulders and hugged her.

She gripped his shirtfront, buried her face into his chest and wept deep, shuddering tears.

Julian was heartbroken for her... and angry. Anger was not a sensation he was particularly familiar with, and he was shocked at its strength. He tilted his head back and breathed deeply. What was not in debate was that the whole affair had to be taken to the next level – a level significantly higher than that of the local police.

Dillon listened with an increasing sense of guilt, appalled at what had happened to Leah and her dog. He'd only met her a couple of times, but he'd liked her instinctively. She was naughty, but good.

Julian finished speaking. "So Dillon, now you know. A friend of mine has been murdered, quite possibly because of information he left for me to find. People have searched this home trying to find it, and have now attacked a dear friend, because they've found out that she knows something about what's hidden." He paused. "Although for the life of me, I don't know how they could have found out."

Dillon lowered his head. "So you want me to leave?"

"I think it would be safer for you, yes."

"But do you 'want' me to leave?"

Julian shook his head. "No. If things were normal... safer... you'd be very welcome to stay. You've fitted into the rhythm of things here pretty well."

The gnawing feeling of guilt meant that he couldn't enjoy what he heard. In the end, he couldn't bear it any longer.

"Julian, I might have been responsible for Leah being attacked."

Julian's head jerked up. "What?"

"Um… yeah. It's the only thing I can think of that makes any sense." Using as few words as possible, Dillon recounted the conversation he'd had with Dr. Haslip. When he'd finished, he hung his head, waiting for Julian's outrage.

But it didn't come.

"Thanks for telling me that, Dillon. It might be useful."

Useful! Is that all you've got to say. Bawl me out, for goodness sake. I deserve it. But Dillon said nothing out loud.

Julian continued. "You could have had no idea of the significance of what you said… and this Haslip guy was trying to milk you for information." He reached over and laid a hand on Dillon's shoulder. "You were bright enough to pick it up, and that may have given us our first breakthrough."

"So, you don't want me to leave… really?"

"No. But staying may be unsafe."

Dillon grinned. "I can't go. I haven't finished the kitchen chair."

Julian held up a cautionary hand. "Are you sure?"

Dillon's answer was to get up and set about cooking breakfast.

"Mr. Alston, my name is Edwina Stanthorpe. I'm from ASIO. I'd like to see you tomorrow, if that's okay."

Julian wasn't sure if Ms. Stanthorpe was asking permission or giving a directive. He was nonetheless relieved at the thought of someone helping him shoulder the responsibility of managing the increasingly complex web of events he found himself caught in.

"That should be fine. When?"

"I'll fly in from Canberra to Adelaide tonight and drive down in a hire car tomorrow. I should be with you mid morning."

Julian gave her the usual instructions to park in front of the Institute, and then to ring him.

"And Ms. Stanthorpe, I will need some evidence…" he trailed off, unsure of how to express himself."

Edwina Stanthorpe rescued him. "I will show you my identification papers and invite you to ring my boss: the Federal Minister for Home Affairs."

Julian's head was spinning. What sort of world had he strayed into? "Thank you."

"Until tomorrow, then." Ms. Stanthorpe rang off.

Julian had been proof-reading the first two chapters of Jade's thesis. She'd given him the text on a memory stick and he was reading it through, suggesting changes, using the computer's 'Track Changes' facility. She'd written the chapters well, but had made the mistake that many clever people make of not always making the logical sequence of her arguments clear.

His computer was on the kitchen table. He'd come to think of the study as Dillon's domain, and didn't want to intrude.

He closed the computer lid and pocketed the memory stick. What he needed now was some quiet... the very special quiet that came from sitting in the presence of God. Over the years he had become used to picturing himself standing before God. It hadn't always been so. In the early years, he'd not dared to lift his head... until he'd felt a divine imperative that he should. *A child should always be able to look at its father.* He'd kept his head up ever since... and saw the brilliance of love – soft, but glorious.

An hour later, he went out to the workshop to check how Dillon was going. Having satisfied himself that all was well, he walked along the track beside the creek to the cottage where Jade was staying. His thoughts turned to the attack on Leah and the grisly murder of Caleb. He clamped his mouth in a straight line. If he'd hoped for peace in his Second Valley retreat, he was not currently finding it.

As he approached the cottage, he noted the thin plume of smoke coming from the chimney. Jade had managed to get the combustion stove alight. And it was just as well; it was a chilly day.

He knocked on the door.

Jade met him, ran her eyes over him, frowned slightly, and led him through to the back parlor. "You look tired... and stern," she said without preamble.

Julian did not doubt it. He'd tried to hide it, but Jade had seen through his façade.

He handed her the memory stick, but didn't talk about its contents. Instead, he said: "I had a friend, Caleb Kuznetsov. He and I shared a laboratory in the Braggs Building at Adelaide University."

Jade nodded. "I didn't know him, but I read in the papers that he had died." She paused. "I'm very sorry for you. Was he a close friend?"

Julian ignored the question. "What the newspapers didn't report was that he had been murdered... tortured to death, actually."

Jade's mouth dropped open. There was legitimate horror in her eyes.

Julian pressed on brutally.

"He was murdered, quite possibly by people who had an interest in his research. Since then, a dear friend of mine, Leah, a local here, was attacked by people who wanted to know if she had connived with me to hide something Caleb might have given me."

Julian watched Jade closely. The horror in her eyes had given way to something else – fear.

He gave her no time to recover her wits. "You are Chinese, scientifically literate, and very beautiful. You found a way to join my 'watch' on the *One and All*... and you dressed provocatively when I visited you two days ago." He shook his head. "That wasn't the real you, was it?"

Only a log shifting in the stove broke the silence.

Eventually Jade raised her head. He could see tears in her eyes. "And who is the real me?"

For a long time, Julian said nothing. Then he spoke. "She is the woman who can pick up a weary storm petrel; a woman who can delight in life and be amazed."

"Do you think she really exists?"

Julian nodded. "But if you are involved in any way with the death of Caleb or the attack on Leah, I will see to it that you are handed to the police." The brutality of his own words surprised him... and the shock of what he said seemed to linger in the air.

Jade straightened up. She looked statuesque… and very beautiful.

"I know nothing of the murder of your friend, or the attack on this woman, Leah. That is simple fact."

Julian interrogated her with his eyes, then nodded. "I believe you… but I think that you are part of the context of this whole bloody business – whether you know it or not."

For a long while, Jade said nothing. Then, having seemingly come to a conclusion, she said, "I am Chinese… and I'm proud to be Chinese. I'm proud of our government, well… mostly proud." She looked at him defiantly. "I am proud of the order and prosperity they have brought." She paused, and seemed to deflate a little. "But sometimes I am not allowed to be me. Pressure is brought for me to do things for the benefit of my country." She dropped her head. "I have parents who are vulnerable."

Julian nodded. "So you have been given the task of getting alongside me – seducing me if necessary – to find out any information I might have concerning Caleb's work."

He saw her wince at his words.

"Yes."

He nodded.

Jade raised her hand slightly, "But…" she was unable to finish the sentence.

"…You found yourself more human than you thought," finished Julian.

She nodded and reached out to him, but changed her mind at the last moment and let her hand drop back down to her side.

"Where… where does this leave us?" she said quietly. "I would not like to lose your… friendship."

Julian bit his lips – his mind was in turmoil. He decided to keep her at bay with philosophical banality. " We are two pilgrims on a journey, whose paths have crossed. We've both been surprised and beguiled… and we can't undo that. Nothing can be the same. According to Heraclitus, you can't step into the same river twice… because the river is forever changing."

Jade waved a hand irritably.

Her action caused him to reevaluate his approach. "Is there danger for you and your family if you do not give them any information?"

She nodded, keeping her head bowed.

Julian continued. "Then I will tell you some things, all of which are true." He sat down on a kitchen chair and gestured for Jade to do the same. When they were seated, he said: "Yes; Caleb Kuznetsov and I worked together in the Braggs building at Adelaide Uni. No: we did not work together on the same projects. He worked with an American team from Michigan University. No: I hadn't seen him for six years until the other week. No: he didn't talk about his work, or share anything in confidence… other than to express some misgivings about the culture of his workplace. He gave no details. I had the sense that he wanted to share something, but in the end, he felt unable to do so.

"When he came to visit me the other week, he spent the morning with me and left after lunch. I heard nothing more from him, or about him, until a few days later when I heard he had been tortured and murdered."

Julian saw Jade wince, yet again.

He continued. "Will that be enough to keep the dogs at bay?"

She furrowed her brow. "Dogs at bay?"

"Keep those who are pressuring you, happy."

Jade nodded. "Perhaps."

Chapter 13

J ade looked at him angrily. "Is it true?"

Wang Lei waved a dismissive hand. "Of course not." He sniffed. "How dare you suggest it."

Wang Lei had turned up at the cottage in his black Audi hatchback that afternoon. Jade was with him in the parlor of the cottage sitting at the table where she'd sat with Julian, just hours earlier.

"But you are engaged in espionage."

Wang Lei shrugged. "Espionage is such a strong word."

"I would have thought it's meaning was pretty clear. At the very least, it is malicious action designed to hurt a host nation."

"Pah!" Wang Lei spat the words out with a savagery that surprised her. "The West is complacent. It has allowed us into the world game. We are hungrier than they are for strategic influence, strategic resources, and strategic ownership."

"And if other nations object…?" she left the question unfinished.

"If a dog disobeys, you beat it until it learns who the master is." Wang Lei closed his hand into a fist. "You must control the narrative – and the information you want people to know."

Jade made no effort to hide her disdain. "Like the 'nine dash line' and the South China Sea?"

Wang Lei shrugged. "If you make the claim often enough, loud enough… and link it to national pride – people will believe it."

"The United Nations does not."

Wang Lei laughed. "You mean America." He waved a hand dismissively. "We pay them no heed. But if an individual nation challenges us, we will counter-punch harder than we have been hit."

"Concocted outrage and ruinous trade sanctions that are blamed on some pretended fault." Jade snorted. "They are false-hoods that no one believes."

Wang Lei did not respond to Jade's contempt. He smiled. "The trick is to use aggrieved rhetoric that tells the story you want people to believe. We don't greatly care if the West doesn't believe it. The important thing is that our own people believe it. And they will, because they want to. We appeal to national pride. Our people see us delivering on what they want: greater wealth, political security, and state-of-the-art infrastructure. It's a game the West does not play well. They are locked into a ruinous adversarial political system that stymies growth and gives no leadership." He waved a hand. "They are weak and risk-averse. It is now our time in history to be strong."

Jade shook her head. "I very much fear that we have just become the new bully in world politics – a bully without principle, whose only aim is to thrive at the expense of others." She sighed. "I can't see it ending well. An emerging power has never taken on the top dog without it resulting in war. And with nuclear powers now involved, I shudder to think what the outcome might be." She looked down into her lap. "It's a high price to pay for wanting your name to be written large on history's page."

Wang Lei scowled. "You need to be very grateful that I do not report your unpatriotic views to the officials of CCP, but the cost of my silence is your total obedience." He scowled at her. "Do I make myself clear?"

Jade said nothing.

Wang Lei got up, pushing the chair over so that it banged on the floor – and walked to the sliding door.

Jade was not ready to let him go. She followed him out onto the decking.

"But what about truth," she said. "Is truth now meaningless? It was once a noble trait that was revered." She nearly added, *by the Shaolin monks*, but stopped herself in time.

Wang Lei's answer was to spin round and give her a slap across the face with the back of his hand.

Jade staggered under the blow, but had the presence of mind not to retaliate.

Wang Lei pointed at her with a quivering finger. "Obey, or face the consequences." He stalked off around the side of the house to his car.

Jade listened to him leave... convinced of one thing: Wang Lei had been very much involved in the murder of Caleb Kuznetsov... and the attack on Leah.

Dillon had been dawdling along the creek path heading toward the beach café to reward himself with an iced coffee. He'd left Julian reading by himself in kitchen. It had been too cold to sit outside. Dillon sometimes sat with Julian when he was reading, and whenever he did, Julian would start reading aloud in his soft voice. Dillon heard stories about a man he'd previously thought didn't even exist... but whose words now warmed his heart and disturbed him.

He was a hundred yards away from Jade's cottage when he spotted her standing on the decking with another man. Dillon was too far away to make out the details, but he was close enough to see the man spin round and hit Jade across the face. The action was so quick, unexpected, and brutal that it left Dillon momentarily bewildered. Then he yelled out in protest and anger, "Oi," and started to run, but moments later, the spinning of the car's tires drowned out his cries of protest.

A few minutes later, he was on the decking, knocking on the glass door. From where he stood, he could see Jade bending over the sink, pressing a wet towel against her cheek. He opened the glass door and let himself in without waiting for permission.

"Who was that bastard who hit you?" he demanded.

Jade waved a dismissive hand. "No one you need to worry about. It is a personal matter."

Dillon was full of fury. "I don't care what it was. It was wrong. Bloody wrong."

Jade surprised him by saying. "Dillon, I have something to ask you."

Dillon picked up the chair that had been upended on the floor and sat down.

"What?" he demanded. In truth, he would have done anything for Jade, for he knew himself to be a little bit in love with her. Most certainly, he was in awe of her.

Jade stayed by the sink pressing the wet towel on her cheek. "Dillon, can I ask a favor?"

"Anything," he said quickly.

"Can you make me a staff, like the one Julian has?"

Dillon grinned with delight. This was exactly the sort of thing he did best. "Of course. How big do you want it?"

"About six feet tall, or a bit under. But can it be lighter than Julian's staff – strong but a little bit flexible?"

Dillon furrowed his brow... then brightened. "Yeah. Julian's got some yew that he cut from the trees at the churchyard. That should do it." He paused. "When do you want it?"

"Tonight, if possible."

"Wow." Dillon rubbed the back of his neck. "I'll get straight back to the workshop then."

Edwina Stanthorpe was, by any measure, small. She had iron-gray hair – fairly long, pulled back into a ponytail, and she wore a navy business-suit. Julian couldn't see much of it because she kept her overcoat on. A chiffon scarf put her just on the right side of looking severe. The most remarkable thing about her was that she was visually unremarkable.

It caused Julian to instantly be on guard.

On meeting him, she said, without preamble: "Text-message the Federal Minister for Home Affairs on this number. Don't send a message. Type in this number. He will ring you back. Once you have spoken, I will watch you erase his number from your phone… and if you are ever reported using it, I'll have your guts for garters." She fixed him with her bright eyes. "Is that clear?"

Moments later, Julian had the surreal experience of listening to a voice he vaguely recognized from news reports. On hearing Julian's request, the Minister gave a pithy, if unflattering description of Ms. Stanthorpe. "I'm due in the House," he said, and rang off before Julian could thank him.

Julian handed his phone to Edwina. "Erase it yourself. The Minister wasn't exactly complimentary about you."

"That's because I've got his balls in a vice over a very silly misdemeanor."

Julian couldn't think of anything to say, so he led her across the bridge and up the grassy slope to his cottage.

She sat at the kitchen table and glanced around. "A far cry from a science lab."

"And this place is a far cry from Canberra."

"It certainly is," she said. "Is there a place we can sit outside?"

"There's a fallen log at the end of the garden."

Edwina rolled her eyes, but followed Julian out of the house. When they were seated on the log, she hunched herself forward and pushed her hands deep into the pockets of her overcoat. "Tell me everything."

Julian had to make a decision about how much to divulge. He could think of no reason to withhold anything, so he told the entire story, although he did not mention anything about Jade.

Edwina did not write down a single note. Julian suspected that she had a photographic memory. When he mentioned Dillon's experience with Dr. Haslip, she nodded, as if to herself.

"Ah, Dr. Haslip. He's been to China eleven times in the last two years – always as a guest of one Chinese organization or another." She smiled. "There are so many interesting things to see there, aren't there?"

Julian didn't know whether she was being serious.

He pressed on and finished by recounting the attack on Leah.

"Hmm, nasty? Is she well?"

"As well as can be expected."

"Where have you hidden the micro-chip and the hard-drive?"

"Somewhere safe."

"Can you give them to me now?"

"No."

"When, then?"

"I would probably need a few hours notice."

"I don't have a few hours." She paused. "Are they well hidden?"

Julian thought briefly of the Martyr's stone embedded in the lead-light window. "Yes, I can assure you of that."

"Then keep them safe. I'll send people to collect them." She cocked her head sideways, like a sparrow. "You haven't had a look at what's on the hard-drive, have you?"

Julian shook his head. "No. But I'd appreciate it if you could tell me the gist of what this is all about."

Edwina nodded, and after a few moments during which she presumably assessed his request, she said: "Our American cousins are none too pleased about the death of Dr. Kuznetsov. He was very important to their work."

"What work?"

"Dr. Kuznetsov and the research team at the University of Michigan have worked to create the world's smallest computer. They've developed a complete, functioning system. A key characteristic of this computer is that it does not lose its programming or data when it is turned off. The device was originally designed to be a precision temperature sensor for use in medical research. It can measure to an accuracy of 0.1 degrees Celsius, evidently."

Julian frowned. "Why would that be so interesting to the Chinese?"

"Because it can also be used in espionage – particularly, for surveillance. We can fit it on a mechanical mosquito and get real time images."

Julian was amazed. "Wow."

Edwina smiled. "I'd be grateful if you kept that information to yourself."

"...or you'll have my guts for garters."

She smiled. "You understand perfectly." Edwina continued. "Mr. Alston…"

"Call me Julian."

She looked at him with her periwinkle blue eyes. "You may call me Edwina." She paused. "Not many people are invited to do so."

Julian nodded his thanks.

After a pause, she said, "Julian, you are in danger here. Your house has been searched; a known associate has been attacked…" she pursed her lips. "The next logical step is to attack you in order to extract information as to the whereabouts of the micro-computer and hard-drive. I shall send people down here this evening to watch over you."

"No, thank you."

Edwina pulled herself upright. "Why not? It's not just your safety or personal preference that is the issue; it is protecting information that is of national significance."

Julian inclined his head. "Yes, I do have a personal routine which is sacred to me, but that is not the reason I don't want a bodyguard."

"Then why?"

"I already have one." Julian smiled. "He's young, fit, and already lives here."

"Is he trained?"

Julian skidded round the edge of perjury by saying, "He's been used to looking after himself – and has done so for quite a few years."

Edwina shook her head. "It's more than my job's worth. I can have two of my agents with you within two hours."

"Not necessary. They'd simply get in the way and attract attention. The local newshound for the Yankalilla Regional News is already peppering me with questions. And besides, if you're going to pick things up soon, there's no point." He paused. "How long before you can retrieve Caleb's technology?"

"Longer than I would like. The Yanks are flying in a scientist to collect it." She sniffed. "They are insisting we don't touch anything. Despite the ANZUS treaty, they are pretty cagey about who gets to look at their toys."

After some intense questioning and assurances, Julian prevailed. It was with some relief that he changed the subject. "Can I interest you in some mint tea?"

She looked at her watch. "I'll have to leave in twenty minutes. Perhaps that's time enough for you to tell me about your work on the sail-training ship, the *One and All*."

Julian nodded – aware that he'd never mentioned the *One and All* to her. Edwina Stanthorpe was not a woman to be underestimated, and she was signaling that fact to him.

Chapter 14

They came on the second day.

Jade was almost relieved when they did. Staying awake all night behind a bush beside Julian's gate was a miserable business. She allowed the chill of the night to keep her awake – but dared not let herself get too cold. When people came, she needed to be ready...and she was in no doubt that they would come.

Jade was dressed in a long black padded jacket and padded pants. She wore a black balaclava and had pulled the hood of her jacket over her head. Currently, she was sitting down behind the bush with her back resting against an old wooden fence post. Her *gun* was leaning on the fence wire.

Dillon had done a great job. She'd tested it as best she could within the confines of the cottage. The weapon was marginally heavier than the *gun* she was used to at the *guan*, but that was probably a good thing for what she had in mind. Importantly, the weapon came to hand very readily.

There was a half moon, and the moon-glow gave the open grass area on the other side of the bridge a ghostly glow. Some moon-glow even found its way through the treetops to leave eerie dancing patterns on the bridge.

The black car pulled off the main road and made its way a hundred yards down the road, before pulling into the grassy area by the bridge. The lights of the car switched off... and for a moment she saw no movement inside it. Jade was grateful. She was now on her feet and using every second to warm and stretch her muscles. There could be little doubt that the men in the car had already scoped out the whereabouts of Julian's cottage – probably the day before. They would know what they were doing.

When the car door opened, the interior light showed four men. Three of them got out. All were Chinese, heavy set, and each was wearing an earpiece. One of them was carrying something in his hand. It took a moment for Jade to recognize it as a blowtorch. It had been screwed onto the top of a small gas canister. The sight of it told her all she wanted to know. It enraged her. But she was careful to harness the anger – to let it motivate rather than sabotage. The man leading the group held a low-powered flashlight with a red filter.

By the time they stepped on the bridge, Jade was standing bolt upright at the other end of it. With her head slightly bowed, she watched from under her hood. Her *gun* was upright behind her right arm. She had little doubt that she must look like the angel of death. Her face became expressionless – for that's exactly what she was.

The red light played on the uneven surface of the bridge, and then lifted slightly to reveal Jade – motionless and deadly.

An instant later, Jade's *gun* whirred through the air, and she charged forward. She brought it down on the forearm of the person holding the flashlight with such a force that she knew that both radius and ulna bones would have snapped like rotten wood. The flashlight dropped into a crack in the bridge's surface, cutting its light in half.

By this stage, Jade had reversed her *gun* so that it flashed upward between the same man's legs. As he doubled forward with a yelp of anguish, Jade brought the *gun* crashing down on the man's head.

He collapsed instantly.

Watch your footing.

Jade stepped over the body, moving the *gun* left and right in a hypnotic blur. Her eyes were on the man at the back. He was reaching into his jacket. She had no doubt as to the reason. But first, she had to disable the man between them. He was the one carrying the blowtorch.

There would be no mercy.

She moved to keep the man with the blowtorch between her and the man drawing his gun. Jade crouched low and jabbed her *gun* upward in a lightning-fast strike. It hit her opponent square in the throat. He made a gurgling sound and spun away. As he did she jabbed him again, but this time in his side… where his spleen was. The man arched his back in agony… and she dispatched him with a *coup de grâce* blow to the head.

Everything was happening in slow motion. *Too slow*. Jade flicked the blowtorch into the creek with the end of her *gun*.

She would be shot. *Move. Move.*

Then an absurd thought. Perhaps dying was okay.

The remaining man stood in front of her, both arms extended, holding a pistol in a very competent manner. As he braced himself to fire, his foot twisted in one of the cracks in the bridge. It put him off balance for barely an instant.

It was enough.

Jade was on to him.

The trouble with holding a gun with two hands is that it leaves both sides unprotected. Liver and spleen are vital organs – and very vulnerable. Jade drove her gun into the man's solar plexus. He doubled over and had no chance of seeing, let alone warding off, the next two blows to his exposed side.

As the man retched, Jade brought her *gun* up so that it smashed into the middle of the man's face. Before he'd dropped to the ground, she had flicked the man's pistol off the bridge into the creek.

The fight that had seemed to last for hours was over in seconds.

Everything was quiet.

What of the man in the car?

Jade bent to switch off the flashlight, and tossed it into the creek. Under the cover of almost complete darkness, she crossed the bridge and circled round the grassy area in which the car was parked.

She approached the driver's window. The man was looking away from her toward the bridge.

The first he knew of Jade's presence was when she drove the end of her *gun* into the side window, shattering it. Her second jab smashed the man's jaw.

Before he could recover himself, Jade had opened the door and hauled him out so that he lay prostrate on the ground. She patted him down to check he was not armed then prodded him in the back.

The man got to his feet, groaning.

Jade pushed him from behind, marching him to the bridge.

When the man saw the carnage on the bridge, he stopped in apparent disbelief. Jade prodded him sharply in the back, pointed to the bodies, and then pointed to the car.

For the next few minutes, she supervised the driver as he hauled the bodies by the jacket collars to the car. He laid one of his colleagues along the back seat, another in the trunk of the car, and the final one in the front passenger seat. It was only the seat belt held the man upright.

Jade watched the car drive away with a dawning realization of what she had done. She felt sickened. She bent over and retched into the bushes – again and again.

When some semblance of normality began to reassert itself, she walked back over the bridge and tossed her *gun* over the gate with a sense of distaste. It was defiled, and she never wanted to touch it again.

Her final act was to remove her balaclava and untie her red ribbon – not easy to do with gloved hands. She looped the ribbon around the rusted top rail of the gate in a half-hitch… and walked back to her cottage.

Julian looked at the van with 'Crime Scene Investigation Unit' written on its side, and the two cars parked beside it. There would be no way of keeping anything hidden from the locals. He sighed. His only consolation was that he knew nothing about what had happened and couldn't tell them anything.

Dillon had found the staff he'd made for Jade that morning when he was heading across to Ellie's with a newly made chair. He'd come back and expressed his bewilderment at finding it to Julian.

When Julian had gone out to investigate, he saw the red ribbon straight away. It didn't take long before he also discovered blood spilled over different sections of the bridge. The flies had found it and were crusted around the edges of the dark red puddles. He looked around, trying to make sense of what had happened. A rising sense of concern for Jade rose up within his gullet. This was in no way dispelled by the sight of something metallic lying under the water in the creek.

He climbed down into the creek bed and waded into the water. In fifteen minutes, he'd retrieved a blowtorch, a pistol with a silencer attached, and a flashlight. He lined up each item on the bridge, trying not to handle them – using twigs to move them whenever he could. They made for a macabre collection.

Dillon saw them when he came back from Ellie's. He looked at the objects with wide eyes. "Bloody hell!"

"Try not to tread in any of the blood."

Dillon nodded dumbly.

Julian then text messaged Edwina Stanthorpe with a six-digit number. She rang back straight away.

"What?"

It wasn't the most forthcoming of acknowledgments. "A person or people unknown tried to attack me last night. I've recovered a blowtorch, a pistol, and a flashlight. There's a lot of blood. I know nothing about the attempted attack and only discovered the scene of an apparent fight this morning. What do you want me to do?"

His blunt summary of his findings succeeded in making the taciturn Ms. Stanthorpe more voluble. "Touch nothing. I'll get forensics down there straight away. Protect the scene as best you can." She paused. "You are quite sure no one is hurt?"

"As far as I know."

"What about your bodyguard. Are you quite sure he wasn't involved?"

"Yes, he was in the house all night, sleeping in his hammock."

"His hammock?"

"Yes."

"Leave it with me." With that peremptory command, she rang off.

Julian made one more call. It was to Jade.

"Are you all right?"

"Yes."

"Good." He paused, unsure of what to say next. In the end, he opted to say, "Well, have a good day," and rang off.

Two people from ASIO interviewed him and then Dillon. The interviews were brief, for the simple reason that neither of them had seen or heard anything.

Julian was intrigued that Dillon, like himself, made no mention to the authorities of Jade's staff. And Julian made no mention of the red ribbon in his pocket. He had been winding it around his fore-finger all day, and letting it slide off.

It was mid afternoon when the forensic team finally left. Julian was pleased to see them go… because he was eager to make a visit.

"Is your name Leah?"

"Yes dear, it is. And who are you?"

"My name is Jade. I have some information that you might like to hear concerning the people who attacked you the other night."

The woman in front of her blanched and stiffened. Jade instinctively reached out. "It's good news," she said. "Honestly."

Leah looked at her for a moment and then held open the door. "Come in."

Jade followed Leah into the kitchen. The woman was wearing Persian pantaloons, a white shirt, and an embroidered waistcoat. She looked formidable.

"Would you like some tea? It's about morning tea time."

Jade nodded and elected to open the conversation. "I'm a friend of Julian's… a fellow scientist. We met on the *One and All.*

"The ship?"

"Yes." She paused. "Julian told me that you had been attacked, and that your dog was killed."

Leah lowered her head and wiped away a tear. "Yes. Dear old Duke."

Jade drew a deep breath. "I'm so sorry." She drew a deep breath. "I hope that what I'm about to say will help ease some of that pain, but I would ask you to treat what I say as confidential."

Leah turned a quizzical eye on her. "How mysterious. Do go on."

"Three men came to attack Julian last night."

"Is he all right?" Demanded Leah.

"He's fine. In fact, he didn't even know about it. What I can tell you is that the three men were beaten severely and will be in no shape to do anyone any more harm." Jade secretly wondered if any of them were even alive. She hoped she would never find out.

"Why are you telling me this?"

Jade did not admit to the main reason – that she felt a degree of responsibility for what had happened to Leah because she'd allowed herself to become complicit in Wang Lei's schemes. She passed off the question with a shrug. "I thought it might be helpful to you to know – to bring closure."

"And who was this night watchman, this minder… this mysterious bodyguard?"

"I'm afraid I can't tell you. Let's just say that it is someone who has Julian's best interests at heart."

Leah nodded. "Are you and Julian lovers?"

The question brought Jade up with a start. "No. Although I find him…" *what?* She thought frantically. 'Very interesting,' was pathetic. 'Beguiling,' was better. She elected to say, "…different from any other man I know."

Leah laughed. "He's certainly that. I tried to seduce him, but to no avail. The boy has some very troublesome principles." She smiled at Jade. "Would you like him to be your lover?"

Jade stammered, "I don't know."

Leah smiled and nodded.

There were still two hours of daylight left when Julian made his way by the back track to Jade's cottage. He had the advantage of seeing her for a full minute before she noticed him make his way to the decking. He had seen her in an armchair. She had her legs pulled up like a little child and was chewing at a fingernail.

All was obviously not well in Jade's life. He wasn't the least surprised. Julian drew in a deep breath and stepped up onto the decking.

Jade saw him straight away. She got to her feet and opened the sliding door for him.

Julian was surprised to find that the room was cold. The wood stove must only be barely alight.

For a moment, the two of them faced each other, neither seemingly wanting to break the connection.

Then Jade reached out tentatively, reached round his neck, and cupped his ponytail. Then she eased the ponytail forward and laid it against her cheek.

Julian thought it was the most sensual thing he had experienced since the death of…

Jade then pushed herself away from him and kept her head bowed.

Without a word, he handed her the red ribbon.

As she took it, Jade started to breathe deeply. It took a moment for Julian to realize that she was hyperventilating.

Jade whimpered as she fought for breath.

The sight of it broke Julian's heart. He lifted a hand. "Stop." It was said as a command. Then he softened his voice. "Hold your breath, be at peace… and breathe slowly."

She did as he said, and then she began to cry.

Wondering if he was doing the right thing, he put his arms around her.

Jade clung to him.

Gradually, the tears subsided.

Julian eased himself away from her, brushed an escaped lock of hair from her face, and led her to an armchair.

When she was seated, he put the kettle on and set about getting the fire going. He could see that it was almost out. It was as if hope itself was nearly dead.

He was conscious of her watching him as he went about his tasks.

As he handed her a mug of tea, he said, "Thank you for protecting me, by the way." It was difficult equating what must have been extraordinary violence with the girl curled up on the armchair with a tear-stained face.

"There were three of them… and a driver," she said in a small voice.

Julian sat down in the other armchair and waited for her to say whatever she needed to say.

"I gave them no mercy… and I may have killed them."

At this point, Julian felt obliged to say, "The forensic team found a blowtorch and a pistol. You stopped a terrible evil… and I'm more grateful than I can say."

Jade closed her eyes as if trying to block out the memory.

Julian continued. "The police have not connected you with anything. Only Dillon and I know."

"And Leah," she said. "I visited her this morning – when I still had courage." Jade sniffed. "She doesn't know I was involved in the actual fight, but I think she suspects." Jade's face crumpled and she started to cry again. "I… I… thought I'd feel better as the day went on, but it's got worse… the shock… the realization."

Julian again lifted a hand in something that was half way between a benediction and a command. "Shhhh. Peace."

He allowed the silence to do its work.

The wind was beginning to increase in strength. He could hear it sighing around the chimney.

Somewhere in the distance, a dog barked.

He waited for peace to reassert itself.

Eventually, it did.

He cleared his throat. "Would you like to have dinner with Dillon and me tonight... or perhaps we could bring dinner to you."

Jade shook her head. "No. Just you. Please stay."

So he did.

Nothing was said for the next hour.

Julian embraced the silence and watched the daylight surrender to the night. He fervently prayed that Jade's fears would similarly surrender to peace.

After an hour, Julian got to his feet. "I'm going back to check Dillon is okay with dinner, then I'll be back." He looked around the kitchen and opened the fridge. There wasn't much inside.

"I'll come back and make you a fried cheese and tomato sandwich." Julian grinned. "I've found it seems to fix most things."

He was pleased to see her smile.

Jade had never eaten a meal of red wine and toasted cheese and tomato sandwiches before. She finished the meal with deep contentment, and promised herself that she would make the meal for herself sometime soon.

The demons that had plagued her all afternoon had been quieted, at least for the moment, and the two of them were seated by the fire again. Weariness was beginning to tug at her.

Seeing Julian in the armchair apparently very much at peace, caused her to wonder what philosophy could be so strong as to generate it. Jade remembered the words she'd used to challenge Wang Lei: "What about truth?" She winced at the memory of it, and her hand instinctively went to her face.

She decided to test Julian with the same question.

"What do you understand about truth?"

Julian came instantly awake.

"It is a precious thing, a sacred entrustment."

NICK HAWKES

"It's not something that is simply expedient?"

Julian shook his head. "Lies are parasitic on truth. A lie requires a background culture of truth-telling in order for it to be believed."

She looked at him with a hint of challenge. "How can you be sure that what you believe is actually true?" Jade shrugged. "Isn't truth just a relative thing?"

"Truth is something that authentic Christians have to be passionate about – because they know that God requires it, defines it, and embodies it." He paused. "Jesus said, 'I tell you the truth' about eighty times in the gospels."

Jade screwed up her nose. "Christianity is Western philosophy." She lifted her hand and corrected herself immediately. "Okay, it's not Western."

"Neither is it a philosophy."

Jade frowned.

"The 'Jesus story' is not a philosophy that gradually came into being as a result of someone meditating somewhere, or because of centuries of thinking. It exploded on the world scene, fully formed, two-thousand years ago… and it did so because it is based on historical events."

"So what?"

"So if it can be shown that any of the essential truths about Jesus are false, Christianity collapses like a pack of cards."

"But it *has* been shown to be false."

Julian closed his eyes. "Not by those who value truth."

She couldn't think of a rejoinder, so she stayed quiet.

Why had she challenged Julian? In part, she knew it was legitimate curiosity about what he believed – and what could be believed. It was some shock to her when she realized it was resentment – resentment at a belief that was foreign to her… and which kept him from her.

At some stage, she fell asleep.

When she woke up, Julian was gone.

120

Chapter 15

Julian cut an apple into two and handed one half to Dillon. They were just finishing breakfast. "Do you want to take me for a drive this morning – to build up your log-book hours?"

"Serious?"

"Deadly."

Dillon grinned. "Yeah."

Julian had been nursing an ongoing concern for Jade and was keen to find ways to distract her from living with the trauma of two nights ago. "Why don't we invite Jade to come with us? Then you can show off your driving skills."

Dillon managed a sheepish grin. "Yeah."

Julian glanced up at him. "Which means, your driving has to be smooth, careful, and wise."

"Wise! You use the weirdest words."

"They're good words."

Julian pulled out his phone and rang Jade.

She agreed to the proposal readily enough, and they organized to pick her up in half an hour.

Dillon piloted the aged pick-up through the gates to Jade's cottage where it squeaked and bounced its way to a halt.

She came out to meet them almost immediately.

Jade gave Julian a shy glance, then, without a word, stepped up into the cab.

Julian climbed in after her.

There wasn't much room on the bench seat, and Julian was acutely aware of Jade's presence. Her thigh was necessarily pressed against his.

Dillon crashed the gears, apologized, then reversed out of the driveway. Once his nerves were settled, he did a passable job of his driving – which considering this was only his third time, was pretty good.

When they got to the main road, Julian cautioned. "Trucks come barreling down the hill round that corner at a rate of knots, so when you see it's clear, get across to your lane quick smart."

Soon they were making their way along the winding road through the valleys and along the hillsides of the Fleurieu Peninsula. When they passed through Delamere, Julian pointed to the church.

"That's St. James, where I lead the church on Sunday."

Jade leaned forward and craned her head around. "It looks old and very English."

"I think that's what it was intended to look like."

She sat back. "I've never been in a church."

"Me either," added Dillon.

They climbed up past the huge wind generators on Starfish Hill until they crested the rise.

"Turn left here," said Julian.

They didn't stay on the bitumen road very long. Julian directed Dillon to drive down a dirt track through the stringy barks, blue-gums, and yucca bushes with their dense fans of spiky leaves.

"Why are we driving here?" asked Jade. She was holding onto the handle on the dashboard as the pick-up bounced and jolted its way over ruts and potholes.

"Because my ancestors came from here. You've told me about your family's home in Shanxi; now I'm showing you mine."

Dillon stopped at a tired-looking farm gate that blocked their path.

Julian opened it and beckoned them through.

They hadn't got going for many seconds before Jade exclaimed, "My goodness! Look at that."

Her comment caused Dillon to bring the vehicle to a halt. He too was looking at the vista before him in amazement. "Wow!"

The rutted track they were on was cut into the side of a steep hill. The valley fell away beside them to the sea: and there, across a deep blue stretch of water, lay Kangaroo Island. Its coast and hills could be seen clearly, despite it being ten miles away.

Jade lifted her hand. "I feel as if I can almost touch it."

Julian smiled. "The air is pretty clean here, and the sea is too. There's nothing beyond where we're standing other than Antarctica."

"Where did you ancestors live?" Asked Jade.

"I'll show you. It's only a few hundred yards further on."

Following Julian's direction, Dillon brought the pick-up to a halt beside what looked to be the ruins of a stone stable.

Jade frowned. "They didn't live there, surely?"

"No. Climb out, and I'll show you where."

He helped her climb over the barbed-wire fence on the up-hill side, and trudged fifty yards up to the top of the hill. When he got there, he turned. "Here."

Dillon looked around. "You're kidding me. Who would live here?"

It was an understandable comment. The almost bare, steeply rounded hill was fully exposed to any southerly wind – which was most of the time. Julian pointed to a grassy mound. "My great, great, great grandparents lived in a wood-slab house right there. You can still see the stone hearth if you look carefully. And there's even a fruit tree in what must have been their front garden."

"What's that?" asked Jade. She was pointing to a stone structure that was embedded into the hill.

"That's the water tank my ancestor made. He built it into the ground. I might say: he took a great deal more care building that than he did his own home."

Jade looked at him with puzzlement.

Julian pointed to the stables. "His job was to water the bullocks that hauled the silver and lead from Talisker mines to Fisheries Beach down on the coast. It was loaded onto ships from there in lighters."

"But how did he get the water? The place is on top of a hill."

"He cut channels on the hill which funneled the water into this sediment trap – which overflowed into the tank."

Jade raised her eyebrows. "Ingenious." She peered over the wall of the tank at the car tires and rusted wire that had been dumped at the bottom. "Pity about the rubbish." She fingered the rebate running along the gable ends of the water tank. "You can see that it used to have a roof. But look: the water harvesting system is still working. There's a bit of water in there."

"Can I get down there?" said Dillon.

Julian raised an eyebrow. "I suppose: if you really want to. There's a rope ladder in the back of the pick-up. Hook the end over the steel spike by the sediment trap.

It didn't take Dillon long to fetch the rope ladder and tentatively make his way down the inside wall of the tank.

It was an experiment that didn't last long. Dillon stepped down into what he thought was nine inches of water – and sank down to his knees in glutinous black sediment. Then he saw the skeleton of a long dead sheep. Some of its bones were lying bleached in the sun.

He wasted no time coming back up the ladder.

Julian saw Jade smile and lift her gaze across the sea to Kangaroo Island. "Wow," she said. "Fancy looking at this view every time you woke up in the morning."

Julian was delighted with her reaction. "Yes," he said. "The lure of the Island eventually proved too strong for the children who lived here, and they migrated to the Island." He smiled. "I'm related, in some way or another, to about half the population there."

Jade pointed to a mob of kangaroos that could be seen on the flanks of the hill on the other side of the valley. "Look!"

"You'll see plenty of those on the Fleurieu. They're Eastern Gray kangaroos – and they've played hell with my garden."

Jade turned to him. "From someone who waters teams of bullocks, to a research scientist and a monk – that's quite a story."

"You'll have your own story, Jade."

He helped Dillon climb over the parapet. The boy looked at his filthy jeans. "Geeze, I don't want to that again." He looked up at Jade. "What story are you talking about?"

"And you will have your own story too, Dillon. The question is: What would you like to add to it… for future generations to read?"

Dillon looked at him derisively. "You're starting to sound like a preacher."

Julian laughed. "I'd like to think you'd know what a preacher sounds like."

Jade looked back up the valley. "How far away is the mine site from here? I've seen no evidence of anything that looks like a mine so far."

"I'll show you." He turned to Dillon. "I'll take over the driving until we get to the mine site."

"Mate, it's all yours. It gave me the heebie-jeebies looking at the drop-off at the side of the road. Jeesh!"

Julian drove the pick-up back up the valley, through the gate, and threaded his way along a dirt track until they came to a sign, 'Talisker Mine.' Beside it was another sign warning people to beware of walking off the paths because of mine shafts. Julian pointed to it. "Most mine shafts have been covered, but the wood's rotted and they've been hidden by undergrowth, so that sign is no idle warning."

The three of them spent the next hour climbing about the ruins of the mine site. Most of the wooden structures had rotted away, and there wasn't much left of the stonework. Julian guessed that locals had taken the stone and repurposed it. He led them up a steep track to what remained of the manager's house. Being the highest house set on top of the hill, it too had commanding views across Backstairs Passage to Kangaroo.

Julian turned and looked back over the mine site. He could see a rusting steel wheel lying in a creek-bed; the old crusher site, and the brick kiln. He pointed them out.

"Believe it or not, this mine was once the largest silver and lead mine in South Australia. A bloke sent some ore to England for assaying, and as a result of the report, Talisker Mining Company began working in 1862."

Jade looked around her. "You said there was a town here. I can't see where it could have been. Everything is so steep and rugged."

"Yes. They called the town Silverton. It was built on the flatter plateau… and it was a fair size. At its peak, 300 people lived there. It had a resident doctor, a bank, an Institute, and even a school."

Dillon looked toward the coast. "So they hauled stuff from the mine all the way down to the coast. Gee, I hope they had good brakes. That's a lot of downhill."

Julian nodded. "Yeah. 1,600 tons of ingots were transported that way over ten years."

Jade looked at him questioningly. "How come you know all this stuff?"

Julian shrugged. "This was my playground when I was a teenager. My parents used to bring me here to the Fleurieu for holidays whenever they could. They thought of the place as home, even though they lived in Port Adelaide." He smiled. "I think it was their way of keeping me out of trouble around the wharves."

"There's got to be some dark secrets you know about this place," said Dillon. "C'mon. Tell us."

Julian laughed. "Well… rumor has it that there is a cavern underground that served as a dining hall."

"Wow! Can you show us?"

Julian shook his head. "It's a secret only known by a few." He looked up at the sun that was now well down in the western sky. "Time to get back." He pointed to Dillon. "You're driving."

Julian escorted Jade to the front door of her cottage, and made to return to the pick-up. She held up a restraining hand. "I need some wood chopped," she lied, then smiled sheepishly. "Or perhaps a glass of Shiraz that needs attending." Jade hastened on. "I really enjoyed today. It made me forget." She shrugged. "I guess I'm not yet ready to let it go."

To her great relief, Julian smiled. "I'll get the fire going."

She was conscious of nervousness as she poured the wine. There was a distinct shake in the ruby-red flow as it poured out of the bottle. Affecting a normalcy she didn't feel, she handed a glass to Julian. "Cheers," she said.

He smiled. "For a good Chinese girl, you have picked up our vernacular and our bad habits very well. How long have you lived in Australia?"

"My father taught me English when I was growing up. He said I must learn it if I wanted to do well. I've been studying seven years in Adelaide now – four years doing a science degree and three years doing a doctorate."

"Nearly finished, then."

"I suppose so."

"Then what?"

She lowered her head. "I don't know."

Nothing was said for a while.

The room was beginning to warm up, and the wine was already going to her head. She'd eaten almost nothing for lunch. It made her less guarded with her speech than she might otherwise have been. Gnawing at her soul was what had become the perennial question for her. Where was their relationship going? Where did she want it to go? She frowned. The questions were too hard. Everything was too hard. There were cultural differences, political differences and, of course, religious differences.

Jade wondered idly what it would it be like to wake up in the morning and see his kind, weather-tanned face; to feel his magnificent mane of hair falling across her own body?

She shook her head, cross at herself. Before she could stop herself, she'd blurted out, "Christianity doesn't belong in China."

She didn't mean to say that for a moment. Jade knew that she was giving voice to her frustration that Julian didn't belong in her world. But he was just a man… and didn't know that.

Julian held up his wine glass and allowed the light to play through the blood-red contents, twirling it slightly this way and that.

"Are you familiar with Emperor Shun? He was the last of the legendary 'Five Emperors', Tradition has it that he lived around 2,200 BC."

Jade frowned. "What about him?"

"Confucius records that he worshiped *ShangDi*, the Emperor of Heaven – in other words, he worshiped the one God who is over all." Julian again twirled his wine glass. "Indeed, for most of China's history, your emperors sacrificed a bull to *ShangDi* at Mount Tai once a year. It was known as the 'border sacrifice' because it was near the northern border of the nation. But then the kings got carried away by their lust for control and power."

What do you mean?" Said Jade crossly.

"They wanted to share in the title of God so, in 220 BC, the first emperor of the Qin dynasty incorporated the word *Di* into his own title *huangDi* which literally means 'king-god' – which we interpret today as 'emperor'. Then, 700 years later, the emperor of the time moved the border sacrifice from Mount Tai to his own city, the Forbidden City, to reinforce his link with God." Julian sighed. "It is the oldest sin in the world – trying to domesticate God to suit your own purpose." He smiled, "But that doesn't negate the fact that worship of *ShangDi* has been integral to China for most of its history."

"How do you know this?" She said crossly.

"Because of you."

"Me?"

He shrugged. "Knowing you prompted me to do some research."

"Am I that important to you?"

"Yes."

Jade blinked. Had she heard rightly?

"Oh."

She didn't trust herself to say anything more. For the moment she was simply content to have him near her... to have him to herself.

The evening wore on, and Julian eventually rose to go. She stood up with him, hating the idea of him going. They faced each other on the hearthrug.

He reached out and touched her ponytail. There was no ribbon in it today.

Jade let Julian caress her hair with his fingers.

"Why do you sometimes wear a red ribbon?" he said.

"It is a distraction. When people see the ribbon, they see a woman, not a warrior." She looked him in the eyes. "Only I know it is my battle-flag… and now you do too."

Chapter 16

Jade had to steel herself to cross the bridge. It was absurd. The place looked so benign – even idyllic. The trees leaned over the bridge, protecting it from the full glare of the morning sun, and light danced on the water as it chuckled and gurgled its way between the rocks.

She stepped across the bridge, quickly, but not so quickly that she couldn't search the place for visual clues to terrible things that had happened just a few days ago. She saw nothing that disturbed her. The place had been well cleaned.

Jade pushed open the metal gate and made her way across the closely cropped grass to the cottage.

From the front, the cottage looked very much like hers, the big difference was that this one had no modern extension on the back.

She made her way around the rainwater tank to the back of the house where she could hear noises of industry. Julian was out the back chopping up kindling. He gave her a wave. She could also hear scraping sounds coming from the small stone barn that stood ten yards from the cottage.

The kitchen door leading out to the garden was open, so she peeped inside. What she saw was a scene that belonged to another era. To say that it was rustic and simple would be an understatement. She was shocked to see a canvas hammock strung between the walls.

Julian came behind her with an arm full of kindling.

She pointed to the hammock. "Who sleeps there?"

"I do. I haven't stowed the hammock away yet. The British navy would have me flogged." He eased past her and dumped the kindling in a steel bucket. "Have a look around. He pointed to the other room. "Dillon sleeps there in the study."

"No four-poster bed, I see," she said wryly. However, when she saw the bathroom, she was surprised. The bathroom was minimalist, certainly, but it was functional and stylish.

Julian must have seen her look of surprise for he said, "Never compromise on the bathroom."

"You're a strange man, Julian." She faced him. "We need to talk."

He gestured toward the kitchen table and kicked the back door shut so the warmth of the fire could make some headway against the morning chill. "Tea?"

She nodded.

It wasn't long before she was nursing a mug of mint tea. "I will have to get you some Chinese tea."

"That would be nice." Julian sat himself down on the other kitchen chair. "What's on your mind?"

"Wang Lei. He is the man who organized to… er, put me on to you."

Julian waited for her to say more.

She cleared her throat. "If he runs true to form, he may try to bring pressure on you to give him what he wants, things related to your friend Caleb, by threatening to hurt me."

Julian's head jerked up. "Would he do such a thing?"

"Oh, he'd make the threat sure enough. It's what he does. He's a bully. But I want to assure you that he would never hurt me." She paused. "So if the time comes when anything like this plays out – please call his bluff. Give him nothing. I'll be quite safe." Jade looked at him. I'm guessing you've found something Caleb left for you – although I believe at the time he was here, you had no idea he was leaving you anything to find.

Julian raised a questioning eyebrow.

She nodded. "You told me as much earlier, and you are a man of your word." Jade reached out and put a hand over his. "Just make sure that whatever you've hidden – if you've found anything, is well hidden, and stays hidden."

Julian nodded. "If I find anything, I'll make sure it is."

Jade glanced round the kitchen and shook her head. Everything was so minimal that there didn't seem to be a place to hide anything.

Julian guessed what she was thinking, for he gestured through the window. "How many rocks did you see outside?"

She couldn't remember seeing any.

He continued. "There are plenty of places I can hide things."

Dillon came in through the door. He'd been sitting on the back step taking off his boots.

"Any tea left?"

Julian smiled. "There's plenty of water in the kettle, mate. Go for it."

Jade gave Dillon a wave. Inside, however, she was in turmoil. Her nerves were jangled. She knew enough about Wang Lei to know that things must necessarily come to a head again. He was not a man who gave up.

Back in her own cottage, she stood in front of the dresser in her bedroom – and tried to come to terms with her sense of unease. Every nerve within her screamed.

Whatever was about to happen, she had to be ready. She shook her head. Julian had no idea what he was up against. How ironic. The very man she'd been sent to seduce and deceive was the man that she now felt fiercely protective of – to the point of pain. She was also aware that her days of living at Second Valley were almost half over. Those days had been some of the most dreadful and most wonderful of her life.

As she looked at the red ribbon lying on the dresser, she reflected on her years of training, both in China and in the *guan* at Adelaide. That too, in its own way, had come to a head. A month ago, the *Shifu* had invited her into his room in the *guan* and unlocked a safe. It was full of terrible items used to kill. There were four pointed stars, disks with razor sharp edges, a nunchuck, and knives of every shape and size.

She'd recoiled in horror.

The *Shifu* saw her reaction and nodded. "The Shaolin do not kill. But a warrior must be ready to do so." He pointed to her. "You must choose which path you tread. I can train you in either, as you wish. This is the ultimate step. But to take it, you must understand the meaning of life, and the reality of death." He paused. "I don't think you have yet opened your eyes to either."

One by one, he had taken the items from the safe and laid them out on a bench so that their obscene savagery was on full display. "One of these items will fit you better than the others. Whatever it is, please pick it out and keep it with you until we talk again of this matter." He glanced up at her. "See if you can live with it."

"I do not wish to take any," She'd stammered.

"And you probably won't, long term. I suspect that you will take the path of *Ch'an* philosophy – but be warned, that too may not give you what you seek.

Jade picked out one item, almost with irritation. She had done so because it was the least offensive looking of them all. It was a length of thin, flexible wire – faintly serrated. The wire was now laid out next to the red ribbon in front of her, and she wasn't at all sure she had the courage to do what she had in mind.

Then she remembered the blowtorch.

The memory of it caused her to pick up the wire … and begin to thread it through the ribbon.

She would be ready.

"Do you think you will get another dog?"

Leah smiled sadly. "Not yet, Julian. We'll see how I feel in a few more months."

Julian nodded. He and Dillon had driven down to the beach settlement to check on Leah, and to see how she was going after her ordeal. Dillon never passed up an opportunity to visit Leah. Not only was it obvious that he enjoyed her personality, but she also offered him real coffee to drink. Julian approved of their friendship, even though the two of them sometimes conspired to poke fun at his monkish idiosyncrasies.

Was he idiosyncratic? he wondered. To him, his chosen lifestyle was perfectly logical… and he was very content with it. Julian frowned. Something was jarring in his spirit. It only took him a few moments to realize what it was. It was the word 'content'. He'd used the word often when explaining his chosen life-style. And it was true… until recently.

The reason everything had been thrown up into the air again was not hard to determine. It was Jade. Over the last few weeks, she had found a very special place in Julian's heart. Theirs was, of course, an impossible relationship – at least impossible to take any further… and the thought of that was hurtful. The realization of it came as a shock.

What was it about her that so attracted him? She was absurdly beautiful. Jade had a stately elegance that he suspected she was quite unconscious of. Her body was slim and, he had to admit, compellingly alluring. It had caused him several uncomfortable nights. But it was something deeper within her that really caught his attention. She had a soft spirit, a seeking spirit… and a gentleness that enabled her to pick up an exhausted storm petrel. And yet, she had an uncommon ability to unleash violence on evil when necessary. She was obviously a woman of strong principles. Julian shook his head. Jade was in every way, a contradiction.

"…and Julian complains about the roos pushing the wire to get at his cauliflowers… but then I see him deliberately leaving the vegetable scraps out for them." Dillon shook his head. "I asked him why, and he said that two of the female roos were carrying joeys."

Leah's laughter was enough to bring Julian back from his musings. His direction of thought had been prompted, needless to say, by a suggestive comment from Leah about his relationship with Jade.

Before he could defend himself from the friendly ridicule, his phone rang.

When he heard the voice, his blood instantly chilled. An electronically synthesized voice said, "Mr. Alston, your friend Jade will be drowned in a water-tank in exactly one hour, unless you give us what we want. Do you understand?"

"Yes," croaked Julian. The word caught in his throat.

'You will leave Caleb Kuznetsov's material – all of it – in a bag, and place it in the rubbish bin in the lay-by at the Garnett Kelly reserve. Do you know it?"

"Yes." The reserve was just seven minutes' drive north of Second Valley.

The phone cut off.

Leah looked at him with a frown. "What's the matter?"

"Yeah," added Dillon. "You look as if you've seen a ghost."

Julian only half heard them. "Someone's kidnapped Jade and they're threatening to kill her if I don't give them what they want."

Dillon's mouth dropped open, and he let out an expletive. "What do they want?"

"Things my murdered friend Caleb left here for me to find."

Dillon frowned. "But…"

Julian didn't allow him to get any further. He lurched to his feet. "I've got to get somewhere quiet to think." He rubbed his forehead. "But I must be ready." Julian turned to Leah. "Leah, can I borrow some of your acetone?"

"Of course." She went off and fetched it.

When she handed it to Julian, he nodded his thanks and made for the door.

Dillon called after him. "Where are you going?"

"A little way along the coastal path. I've got to think"… *and pray*, he added silently to himself.

To say that Julian was in turmoil was a gross understatement. He was seething with emotion. The very thing that Jade had so recently warned him about had happened. It was surreal… and terrible. Julian was quite unprepared for the emotional shock to his system. He was struggling to function. The dreadful threat had brought into sharp focus a truth that he had been hiding from. The thought of losing Jade was impossible to contemplate. Even the risk of losing her was impossible to bear.

He glanced down at the foaming, swirling sea sucking its way back to the ocean, to gather its strength before surging forward again to crash against the rocks a hundred feet beneath him. Their violence and confusion perfectly matched the mental storm going on within him.

After twenty minutes, he came to a conclusion. Nothing must be allowed to threaten Jade. Even though she had assured him that no harm would come to her in a scenario such as this, he simply couldn't trust it. Evil, he knew, could never be trusted.

He headed back to his vehicle. Picking up the hard-drive from the stone cavity would only take ten minutes. The rock by the creek was only a few hundred yards from the road. That would give him thirty minutes to drive to St. James, dissolve the cap hiding the cavity in the martyr's stone with acetone, and then drive to the Garnett Kelly reserve. It was only ten minutes away, but even so, he had no time to waste.

As he drove up the valley, Julian reflected bitterly that the demand had been cleverly made. By giving him just sixty minutes to make the exchange, he had no time to involve the police, Edwina Stanthorpe, or anyone else. Second Valley was over one-and-a-half hours drive from Adelaide where the nearest ASIO office might be.

Julian brought the pick-up to a savage halt beside the road. He got out, vaulted the farm fence, and sprinted down to the creek. The sheep that had once watched him with curiosity, now fled to the other side of the field.

Julian sloshed through the creek and climbed up to his rock.

Without ceremony, he dug his fingers into the soft earth of the cavity… and found nothing.

With a sense of unbelief, he realized that the hard-drive was missing. Someone had taken it.

He rocked back on his heels in anguish and looked around him. There was simply no possibility of any mistake. There was only one cavity filled with soil and grass – and it was empty.

As he ran back up the field to his pick-up, his mind was working furiously. Perhaps Jade's captors would be content just having the micro-computer. But what could he put it in?

When he got to the pick up, he rummaged in the glove compartment and found a box of matches and some red insulation tape. That would do. He'd stick the micro-computer to a piece of red tape, put it in the matchbox, and tape it closed with more red tape. Julian stamped on the accelerator, and the pick-up lurched up the road, protesting noisily at the unaccustomed haste.

Julian swerved dangerously onto the Main South Road and drove frantically toward Delamere.

A few minutes later, he skidded to a halt in the dirt under the yew trees and ran to the church. After retrieving the key and fumbling it into the lock, he pushed his way inside.

The benign figure of St. James – facing his own appalling reality, looked down on him in multi-colored glory, as Julian's eyes fixed themselves on the martyr's stone.

It only took him a second to see that his cunningly disguised green cap had been removed. The tiny cavity that had been hidden behind it was now fully exposed.

And it was empty.

Chapter 17

J ade was furious with herself and she only had herself to blame. First, her kidnap had been so easy, so casual, that it was ridiculous. Wang Lei had simply driven up to her cottage, knocked on the door, and ordered her to get into the car. She would have fought him off and overpowered him easily had it not been for the two men with him. They both stood by the car with their hands inside their jackets, making it clear that they were armed.

Her second mistake was probably worse. She had made it plain by her protestations and questions, that she was concerned for Julian's welfare. Wang Lei immediately seized upon the fact. It did not take him long to determine that Jade was not the loyal Chinese person he could once bully into doing her duty. She was someone who had truly lost her heart to Julian. The fact amused Wang Lei greatly, and he'd taunted her. "*Too Bee-eh* (ground beetle) has lost her heart to a 'foreign devil'. They make a good match. Both need to be trodden on."

Jade chided herself. Was she really that transparent? Could she really have been so stupid? She should have played along with Wang Lei and looked for an opportunity to frustrate his plans when she could.

She was certainly in no place to do so now. Jade had been tied hand and foot, and dropped inside a huge, empty, polyethylene rain-water tank. She estimated that it must hold over 5,000 gallons. Fortunately, it was new and was probably waiting to be plumbed in to the new corrugated iron house standing next to it. Unfortunately, the tank had been made in one piece with an integral roof. There were no sharp edges she could use to attack the ropes that bound her hands and feet.

The inside of the tank smelled of plastic – which was, she conceded, better than a rotting sheep carcass. It was a small mercy that the access-hole near the edge of the roof of the tank had been left open. At least some fresh air would reach her.

What was very evident was that she needed to escape, and do so very quickly. She shivered at the memory of overhearing Wang Lei's ransom demand to Julian. Whilst she had warned Julian to call Wang Lei's bluff, her warning sounded completely hollow when she put herself in Julian's situation. She would have given in to his demands in a heartbeat.

There was one advantage to having her hands tied behind her. She knew herself to be extraordinarily supple. Jade arched her back, until her hair fell over her wrists… and her hands touched the ribbon.

She pulled it free, and it fell to the floor of the tank.

Having her hands tied behind her back was now a distinct disadvantage – but not one that presented any great obstacle. Jade folded herself forward and moved her hands under her bottom, then under her thighs… and then moved them completely free of her legs.

Her hands were now in front of her.

She reviewed her situation.

There was absolutely no way she could use the wire in the ribbon to cut herself free from her bonds. She needed another hand to do that… or a mouth.

Jade twisted her arms sideways and pulled her handkerchief from the pocket of her jeans. She stuffed it into her mouth. Then, picking up the wire, she put one end of it into her mouth, biting on it, but protecting her teeth from its serrated surface with the hand-kerchief.

Jade gripped the other end of the wire between finger and thumb… and rocked the wire over the rope with tiny back and forth movements.

The wire cut through the rope with disturbing ease. She shud-dered to think what it could do to human flesh.

In short order, both her hands and feet were free.

But she was still imprisoned.

Jade inspected the wall of the tank. It was ribbed around the sides to give it extra stiffness and stability. However the ribs were shallow and sloped, and impossible to use as steps. But they could still be used to achieve a momentary purchase for her feet.

She backed herself against the far wall of the tank opposite the access-hole, and drew a deep breath. Then she ran at the opposite wall, leaping at the last moment to place a foot on one of the ridges and push, so that she bounced back and up into the air.

His hands flailed forwards and gripped the edge of the access-hole. She allowed herself to feel a small degree of triumph as she swung there, but again, she dared not linger. The serrated wire had cut into the back of her thumb and it was bleeding, making one hand quite slippery.

Jade pulled herself up until she was able to support herself on her elbows. She looked toward the house. It was only a few yards away but the tank had been placed, as most tanks were, at the gable end where there were no windows. The new home had been built at the head of the valley that gave Second Valley its name. With a shock, she realized she must only be half a mile from Julian's house. But she dared not run directly there. She needed to remain unseen.

Jade set off across the fields, keeping the rainwater tank between herself and the house.

Jade ran down the hill toward the creek that ran along the northern boundary of the old stone mill. The gnarled and twisted giant red-gums that sheltered her with shade gave her the brief illusion of safety.

The thought came to her that Julian's cottage could very well be under observation. How could she get to it without being seen? And even more concerning: would Julian even be at the cottage?

She paused by the roadside until she saw a delivery van wait for a cattle truck to pass, before it turned down the road to the beach. Jade snuck between them, so she couldn't be seen, then dived down into the creek bed on the other side of the road. However, she was not so quick that she failed to notice Julian's pick-up parked near the bridge to his cottage.

Was it being watched?

She didn't have time to think, because she could hear someone approaching from the cottage. Jade hunched herself down behind a bush and peered between the leaves.

Her heart leaped when she realized it was Julian. He looked appalling – grim and aged.

She waited until he had pushed through the gate and was on the bridge, then she called out to him as loudly as she dared.

His head snapped round, and his mouth dropped open.

In the next instant, he plunged down the embankment, blindly pushing past bushes and stumbling through the water, until he could wrap his arms around her – hugging her to himself, kissing her on the top of the head and brushing her tear-stained face.

She was weeping both with joy and grief at the torment she'd so recently experienced. But when he kissed her hair again, Jade allowed herself to experience a giddy feeling of delight. She gripped him fiercely.

"Are you all right?" he asked huskily. Julian released her and ran his hands down her arms.

Oh how she wished he was running them down her body.

"I'm fine." She lifted her head.

It was all too much for Julian, as she knew it would be. With just a moment of hesitancy, he kissed her – long and deep. She could feel the warmth of his passion, and it was thrilling. Jade arched her body and pressed it into him.

The moment of madness passed all too soon.

Julian said gruffly, "I've got to get you somewhere safe."

Julian couldn't believe it. Jade was safe... and he'd let his emotions run wild – unchecked. He'd deal with the bewilderment of that later. Right now, he had a fierce determination to get Jade, Dillon, and Leah – all who were closest to him – to a place that was secure. Nothing, he vowed, must be allowed to harm them. The thought of losing Jade again was unbearable.

There was just one place he could think of where he could keep them safe.

The reality of the appalling danger they were still in came home to him when Jade whispered, "Julian. I don't know if your cottage and pick-up are being watched."

He did some rapid thinking. "Stay here," he said. "I'll get Dillon and a few things together." Julian hated leaving her.

He climbed out of the creek and ran back to the cottage, letting himself into the kitchen by the back door. Dillon was sitting where he'd left him, at the table, disconsolately drinking a mug of tea.

"Jade has escaped and is waiting for us by the bridge. Quick! Get packed. I'm taking us all to a safe place."

Dillon's mouth dropped open.

"Go, Go!" said Julian, propelling him out of the chair.

Julian pulled his phone from his pocket and rang Leah. He wasted no time with lengthy explanations.

"Leah, Jade has escaped from her captors... and I'm taking her, Dillon, and you to a safe place. Pack some gear. I'll pick you up in five minutes." He put the phone down without waiting for a reply.

Julian threw some personal belongings into his duffle bag and walked with Dillon to the bridge. He noted idly, that Dillon's belongings had now expanded to three shopping bags. Julian told him to wait at the gate until he had backed the pick-up onto the bridge, under the cover of the trees.

The bridge creaked and groaned at having to bear such a heavy burden.

Julian was beyond caring.

Jade scrambled up from the creek and dived into the cab.

Julian picked up a hessian sack from the back of the pick-up and covered her with it.

He and Dillon climbed in, and Julian drove to Jade's cottage, dropping her right by the door.

"Pack quickly while I collect Leah."

She nodded.

To his intense relief, Leah was waiting in front of her house with a multi-colored carpetbag at her feet. She climbed into the cab and favored Julian with a questioning look. "Are we in danger?"

"Possibly."

She gripped the handle above the door to steady herself as Julian turned the pick-up around. "You may be a man of peace, Julian, but you've brought a lot of drama in your wake in the last few weeks."

Julian was all too well aware of it.

When he was back at Jade's cottage, he threw everyone's luggage into the trunk of Jade's car and climbed in next to Jade in the front seat. She gripped the steering wheel. "Where are we going?" she asked.

"To Adelaide, but via a circuitous route that won't take us past places where they may be watching for us. When you get to the main road, turn right to Delamere. From there we'll take the Range Road to Victor Harbor... but we won't be staying on it long."

"Why?"

"I'll take you back to the Main South Road via some back roads – some of them dirt."

"I suppose it's no use me telling you this car was not built for dirt roads."

Jade's car was a demure, cream-colored Corolla. He managed to smile. "None whatsoever. We're going places people won't expect to see you."

The trip to Adelaide was mercifully uneventful. Leah had asked Jade to drive up Brighton Road on the western side of the city, so she could be dropped off at the Glenelg tram stop.

Julian tried to assure her that he could provide accommodation for her, but she was adamant. "I think it safer, dear, if I distance myself from you as much as I can. If you drop me at the tram stop, you won't know where I'm going, or who I'm staying with." She smiled. "I'll be free to have coffee in cafés, walk in the park, and paint butterflies on the faces of the children in the house."

Julian couldn't fault her logic.

When she was dropped off, Leah became curiously formal. She shook Dillon by the hand, holding it briefly in both of hers. She gave Jade a hug and Julian a kiss. Julian smiled at the sight of her as he turned in his seat to wave goodbye – a highly colorful friend with a carpet bag at her feet. He hoped fervently that she would stay safe.

Their next stop was a barber's shop. It had taken all of Julian's guile to persuade Dillon to get his hair shaved off. "I don't want anyone to recognize you," he said. "And besides, a shaved head is a pretty cool look."

With some reluctance, Dillon agreed.

Julian used the time Dillon was getting his head shaved to ring Edwina Stanthorpe. It was not a call he was looking forward to."

She rang him back, almost immediately after he messaged her the prescribed number code.

The ASIO agent didn't waste words. "The American has arrived, and we are due to meet you mid morning tomorrow. I trust there are no complications."

Julian massaged his forehead. "Ah… slight complication."

"What?" she demanded.

"Caleb's micro-computer and the hard drive… have both been taken."

"What do you mean, taken?"

"They've been removed, stolen, before I could recover them."

There was a moment's silence. "You are not playing silly games with me, are you?… Have you given them to another party? Because, if you have, that's treason."

"No… no, nothing like that."

"Are you having pressure applied to you?"

Julian shook his head in irritation. "No. Nothing like that." He paused. "It's just that someone's found out where I'd hidden the items and taken them."

There was a slightly long pause, and then Edwina Stanthorpe. "You incompetent idiot. You assured me that they were well hidden – extraordinarily concealed. Where did you leave them, under your front door mat?"

The conversation continued in much the same vein for the next few minutes. At times, Julian was obliged to hold the phone some distance from his ear. He was left in little doubt about her feelings.

"What are you going to do now?" she asked brusquely. "I suppose there's no chance of you retrieving the lost items."

"I doubt it," he said.

"So, what are you going to do?"

Julian drew a deep breath. "I'm going to hide."

"Hide!"

"Yes. All this has become a bit much, so I'm going to ground. I'm hiding."

"Not from me, you won't"

"Even from you. I'm sorry Edwina. Good bye."

He ended the call before he could hear the retort he was sure would come. Julian had made no mention of Jade. He was keen to keep her out of the whole tawdry affair.

Dillon came out of the barber's shop looking sheepish and self-conscious with his shaved head. "Pretty cool, eh," he said. His eyes still had a slight look of pleading in them.

"Wow! You look great – quite 'the man.'"

Dillon nodded, apparently assured. "Where are we going now?"

Julian opened the door for him. "I'm taking you to my home town."

"Where's that?"

"Get in, and I'll show you."

Chapter 18

Julian had a love/hate relationship with Port Adelaide… mostly love. He loved its rich maritime culture… but hated the modern utilitarian ugliness that was beginning to encroach. The center of Port Adelaide was largely built of local blue-stone and stone that had once been the ballast of sailing ships that had traded there. There were huge, forbidding-looking warehouses, mills, and lofts. Narrow laneways ran between them, some with aerial gantries running over the top.

In the main part of the town, you could still read faded signs advertising anything to do with ships.

But the Port looked tired, as if it was unable to find a future direction. Its glory days were behind it. Now, ugly modernism was trying to encroach. Working class hubris was determinedly holding back the process of gentrification. The recent development was anything but gentrified. It seemed as if no one had yet come up with the imagination to marry the past with the future.

It was a pity, because Julian thought that the area would take off like a rocket when that marriage happened. The Port must be the only marine waterfront in Australia that was so chronically underdeveloped and underappreciated.

In the main part of the town, there was a pub on almost every corner. Those not built of stone looked seedy. Those built of stone had wide, second floor, covered verandas – giving shade to the sidewalk underneath and a capacious drinking platform above. The balustrades of these verandas were made of intricate, cast-iron, lace-work. Sadly, the pubs were not busy. It was as if they too were waiting for the ships to come in. Even so, Julian was pleased to see them. The pubs still retained a degree of dignity, much as an elderly matron commands respect.

He guided Jade down Commercial Road, over Black Diamond Corner, toward the red lighthouse that had been relocated at the wharf as one of the attractions of the Maritime Museum.

Jade parked the car behind the customs house. The stately building looked as if it had been designed more for India than Australia. In fact, there was a rumor that the plans for it were swapped by mistake... and that somewhere in India, was a very Australian-looking customs house.

At some time in his youth, Julian had explored almost every inch of the port. Some of it had been in the company of his father. He had taken Julian to visit the tugs, the Maritime Academy, shipping agents, and any visiting ship. In later years, he took Julian to the town's old pubs. Wherever they went, his father always had a story to tell.

Julian had also explored the port with his school-friends and got into his fair share of mischief. If they weren't goofing about near the wharves, they were on the water, sailing patched up boats of every description.

They got out of the car, picked up their luggage, and walked alongside the loading platform of a huge corrugated-iron warehouse, toward the lighthouse. Julian noticed that the end of the warehouse had recently been divided into shops – all of which appeared to be overawed by the building they were in. One of them sold doughnuts.

"Look!" exclaimed Jade. "The masts and spars I see above the roof-tops... they have to belong to the *One and All*."

Julian nodded. "Yes." He turned to Dillon. "And that's where you'll be staying, Dillon. She's in her home berth alongside Queen's Wharf for three weeks – for maintenance. You can stay on board if you pull your weight and help with the work." He put a hand on Dillon's shoulder. "Do you think you can manage that?"

Dillon nodded.

Julian approved. If the last few weeks had shown anything, it was that Dillon was good with his hands. He would be an asset.

Dillon felt a bit self-conscious as he walked across the gangplank and stepped down onto the deck. Julian and Jade followed him as he made his way aft.

Mick, the bosun, was sitting cross-legged on the aft deck behind the ship's wheel doing something with rope. The man gave Dillon a friendly wave but almost immediately turned back to his work. "Almost didn't recognize you, Dillon. Stow your gear. Then come and give me a hand."

Dillon nodded and made for the main cabin hatchway.

Mick called after him.

"Not there, Dillon. You're crew. You bunk in the focsle."

Mick's comment drove away any lingering misgiving he had.

A few moments later, he returned to Mick, having first dug into one of his bags for his beanie. A shaved head, he discovered, was not treated kindly by a chilly spring wind.

"What do you want me to do?" he asked.

"I want you to put a back splice in the ropes of every fender. The ropes are starting to unravel."

"How do I do that?"

"Sit here and watch. First you make a crown knot, and then you weave the strands under and over the layers of the rope."

It didn't take long for Dillon to learn the basics.

Mick nodded approvingly. "Once you've cut the ends and burned them to stop them unraveling, roll the back-splice on the deck with your foot to even it all out."

Dillon became so absorbed in his work that he almost forgot the nagging concerns he had about Jade and Julian. Perhaps his time aboard the *One and All* might help clear his mind and indicate the way ahead.

He reached for the knife and cut the excess strands from the back-splice. Next, he flicked a cigarette lighter and lit the frayed ends. It caught fire, melting the strands. The smell from the burning rope was faintly reminiscent of celery. Dillon snuffed the flame out with a wet spatula. Mick had warned him of the danger of getting the molten fibers on his skin. "It sticks on to you and burns like hell."

So Dillon was careful.

When the evening meal was served in the galley, Dillon felt he had earned the right to it.

"So this was your home." Jade looked around her with interest. Although Port Adelaide was only eight miles from central Adelaide, she'd never been there before.

Julian nodded. He had hoisted Jade's rucksack onto his back and was carrying his duffle bag. "It made for an interesting playground."

She looked round at the old stone buildings and tried to imagine the stories they could tell. Jade also noted, with sadness, that many of the shops had been vacated.

"Where are we going?" she asked.

"You're going to a pub."

She raised a quizzical eyebrow. "A pub?"

Julian grinned. "Sadly for you, it is no longer operational. Friends of mine, who have been friends of the family for as long as I can remember, have converted it into their home." He pointed up ahead. "It's just up there."

Julian stopped at the door of a building that had a deep veranda over the top, and rang the bell. Jade could hear it tinkling inside.

An elderly woman in a flowery dress and apron opened the door. She immediately let out a shriek of delight and flung her arms around Julian. "Ah, Julian," she said as she pushed herself away and held him at arm's length. Your hair is just as crazy. You didn't like it cut even as a child." She cocked her head sideways. "But you look well."

Julian smiled self-consciously. "Hi Bronny. It's great to see you again." He turned to Jade. "Jade, meet Bronny. She and her husband, Brant, have been family friends forever. Brant used to skipper tugs here in the Port."

Jade held out her hand. "Hi."

Bronny took her hand, pulled her close, and gave her a hug. "Any friend of Julian's is a friend of ours."

Jade just managed to stop herself recoiling in surprise. This was not Chinese behavior.

"Am I hearing that rascal, Julian?" A deep voice boomed from the depths of the house.

Julian yelled into the interior. "Put the kettle on, Brant – and make yourself presentable for someone very special."

It took a moment for Jade to realize he was referring to her. She was conscious of a flush of warmth coursing through her body.

A big bear of a man appeared behind Bronny. Braces held up his trousers, and the top button of his shirt was undone to reveal a mass of curly black hair. He looked at Jade. "A comely maiden indeed," he said and held out his hand.

Jade put her hand into his great paw and was grateful for the gentleness of his handshake.

When Bronny and Brant were in the kitchen getting tea and scones, Jade whispered to Julian, "Why am I here?"

"Because it's about as safe a place as you will find in Adelaide. Bronny and Brant will spoil you and fuss over you – and protect you with their lives. They are fiercely loyal."

Brant came into the front parlor holding a plate of scones and some side-plates. He addressed Julian. "Now, young lad. Tell me about the danger you are in. Whose head do I need to bang?"

"No one's head, Brant." He nodded toward Jade. "Some of Jade's Communist countrymen have been trying to pressure her over some of the technical work she is involved in. It's got a bit ugly, so I need her hidden for a while until I can figure out a way through it all."

Brant nodded. "Is ASIO involved?"

"I've got them standing in reserve. They know about us, but I'd rather trust you than them when it comes to hiding Jade."

Brant held out the plate of scones to Jade. "We'll look after her, boy. What I want to know is: who will look after you?"

Julian smiled. "You've done pretty well already… organizing a place for me to stay.

Brant grunted. "You'll be doing us a favor."

Bronny came in with a tray bearing a teapot and cups. Jade thought she looked ridiculously English… and loved her for it. She ventured a comment. "I understand this place used to be a pub."

Brant smiled. "Not just a pub, darling – a notorious pub. It was a place of wickedness."

Jade looked at the hand-stitched cushions on the sofa and found it hard to believe. "Why's that?"

Brant scratched his stubble. "Well, in days of yore, pubs had many functions. First, they kept the maritime population happily drunk. Second, they were unofficial recruiting agents for crew."

Jade frowned. "What do you mean?"

Brant gave a rumbling laugh. "They got sailors drunk, knocked them on the head, and had them carried out to ships that were in need of crew. The ship's captain used to pay the publican quite well."

"Wow!"

"But that's not all. The pub had cellars where the beer was kept cool. Because they were cool, they also served as the local morgue." He laughed again. "They had earth floors. So if there was a king tide, water used to seep into the cellars, and some of the coffins would float."

Jade wondered how much of the story was true. She suspected that it was rather more than she would have liked.

Julian got to his feet. "I must go."

Bronny immediately protested. "Stay for dinner, Julian. It's getting late in the day."

Julian shook his head. "Thanks, Bronny. I need some time alone to think." He looked at Jade. Instinctively she got up from her seat. It seemed the most natural thing to do to give him a kiss. But she didn't. The thought of being parted from him alarmed her. "Where are you going?"

"I'll be very close by." Don't worry. Brant and Bronny will look after you."

Brant rumbled. "We will." He turned to Julian. "I'll come with you Julian and settle you in."

Jade couldn't repress a sense of trepidation as she watched the pair of them leave.

Brant unhooked a blue boiler suit from the back of the door and threw it at Julian. "Wear this. You'll look official." Then he handed him a set of keys. "Do you know how to start the generator?"

Julian nodded.

"Then I'll leave you to your domain. You're the night watchman, and I've asked for your help because there's been some vandalism." He looked at Julian. "Got it?"

"Got it."

Julian walked across the gangplank with him to the wharf. It was twilight, and the few tourists that were around had long since left.

They stood for a moment by one of the iron bollards. Brant turned to him. "Don't fret. Jade is in safe hands." He sketched a wave and walked back into town.

Julian turned and surveyed his new abode. He was living aboard the steam tug, *Yelta*. She was moored adjacent to the lighthouse. On a few days of the week, a team of men – all retired – descended on the *Yelta* to polish, clean, oil, and paint. On very rare occasions, the engines were fired up, and the *Yelta* chugged her way up and down the Port River. Officially, the ship was part of the Maritime Museum.

Julian loved her. She was a classic tug that looked as if she had come straight from the pages of a children's storybook. The *Yelta* had, in fact, been the last working steam-powered tug in Australia. And she still looked like a working boat. Truck tires hung from her gunwales.

A paneled wooden wheelhouse sat on top of her superstructure. Behind it was a tall funnel that had the ship's 'hooter' attached to it. Curving mustard-colored vents could be seen all over the vessel. The insides of them were painted red. Their gaping maws helped the ship to breathe. Everything about the tug charmed him – the green-blue glass in the portholes, the varnished wood… and, particularly, the mighty engine.

Yelta was, in essence, a floating engine, and the engine was huge. It stood two stories high and was a showpiece of old-fashioned industrial engineering. Machined steel was married to brass, and decorated with oiling pipes that curled their way from brass oil-cups. The size of the shafts and pistons was awe-inspiring.

Around the engine there was a plethora of metal wheels that were used to open and shut valves in the arteries of the vessel.

Whilst love and care had been lavished on the engine, the same could not be said of the crew's quarters located two levels under the wheelhouse. They consisted of little more than a few bunks, and offered only the bare essentials. Julian knew he wouldn't be spending much time there. His favorite place was sitting in a chair under the canvas awning strung over the stern deck. From this vantage point, he had a commanding view of the *One and All* moored just fifty yards away – where Dillon was staying.

Chapter 19

Dillon steeled himself as he stood on the gunwales and gripped the shrouds. The ratlines soared above him to a giddying height. It was early in the morning, and the only other crew member up and about was Sven, the cook. Dillon knew that he either had to climb now, or not at all.

Taking a deep breath, he began to mount the ratlines. It was only the second time he'd done it, and this time he was on his own. There was no Julian to coax him and guide him.

He tried to remember all Julian had said. *Take your time. Look straight ahead*. Then he came to the backward-sloping shrouds that ran to the end of the crosstrees. This was the big test. Dillon didn't dare let himself pause for breath. He gripped the shrouds and worked his hands and feet up until he was ready to haul himself to the safety of the crosstrees. The tools that were hanging from his belt exaggerated the sensation of hanging backward over the ship. For a few desperate seconds, he fought the terror rising up within him. Then, with a final heave, he hauled himself around the end of the crosstrees.

Fifteen minutes later, Dillon was back on deck, and just in time to join the rest of the crew as they stumbled sleepily to the main cabin for their first mug of coffee and breakfast.

Not long afterward, they were all at work. Mick had asked Dillon to daub linseed oil on the jib boom of the bowsprit. The jib boom speared forward from the ship, as if pointing the way. Underneath it on the stem-head of the ship was the figurehead − a bare breasted woman looking steadfastly at the horizon. Mick had told him that she must never look down, for that would mean the ship would sink.

Dillon sighed with exasperation as Mick told him how to hold a paint-brush, and how to load up the brush with the right amount of paint − or in this case, linseed oil. Fortunately, he understood the wisdom of what he was being taught before he voiced any protest.

A short time later, the tin of linseed oil was hanging from a wire hook on the jib boom, and Dillon was having the surreal experience of standing on the netting hanging under the jib boom − with nothing underneath him but water.

He didn't see Julian until he appeared on the wharf beside him... and it took a moment for Dillon to recognize him. Julian was dressed in a blue boiler suit and had his hair in a tight bun under a beanie.

"How's it going, mate?" Julian asked.

Dillon wiped his brow. "Pretty good. I've nearly finished here. Mick says he's going to teach me how to 'worm, parcel, and serve' − whatever that means.

Julian smiled. "You'll find out soon enough." He paused. "I've got a pre-paid cell phone for you, so you can contact me if you want to. I've already put my number into it."

"Where are you and Jade staying?"

"Jade's with friends nearby − just a couple of hundred yards from here."

"You not staying with her?" he asked archly.

"No."

"Why?"

"Because I'm keeping an eye on you."

Dillon looked at him questioningly. "Yeah? From where?"

Julian pointed to the old tugboat moored further along the wharf. "From there."

Dillon looked at the tug with disbelief. "You're joking."

Julian did not smile. "When it comes to your safety, mate, I don't joke."

Dillon felt deeply humbled.

Jade had done her best to milk Brant and Bronny for as much information about Julian as she could. She was particularly keen to learn about Julian's past affairs of the heart.

Bronny was happy to tell her. "Julian has only had one serious relationship. In fact, they were engaged to be married."

"What happened?"

Bronny shook her head sadly. "It was tragic. She died of cancer – a brain tumor."

"Oh."

"Yes. Such a shame. They were very much in love."

"What was her name?"

"She had an unusual name: Tansing."

Jade let herself reflect on the name. With a shock, she realized that she wasn't sure she felt fondly towards Tansing. Was she jealous? Would Tansing continue to compete for Julian's heart... or could he give his heart away again?

She ventured to ask: "Was it Tansing's death that made Julian become a monk?"

"Bronny smiled. "I once asked him exactly the same question."

"What did he say?"

"I've never forgotten his words. He said it stopped him 'skating lazily over the top of life, uncritically absorbing its mantras.'"

"What do you suppose he meant by that?"

"I think it began him on his search for truth."

"Oh."

Jade wondered whether she'd been skating... but daren't let

herself think too much about it. The things Julian had already said to her were unsettling enough.

Bronny stood up and began collecting the teacups. She turned a twinkling eye to Jade. "Is there a romance between you and Julian?"

Jade dropped her head. "I'm not sure." Even as she said it, she knew it was a lie. She had felt his smoldering passion – even if it had not been allowed full expression. "And even if there was," she added quickly, "he couldn't allow it to develop. He's a monk."

"Yes, dear. I suppose you're right."

After they carried the afternoon tea things into the kitchen, Bronny led her upstairs to her bedroom. The carpeted wooden stairs creaked as they made their way up them. It was a curiously comforting sound. She ran her hands along the carved wooden handrail and felt its history.

To her delight, she discovered that her bedroom opened out to the balcony through a pair of French doors. Once she'd unpacked her belongings, she opened the doors and listened to the buzz and hum of the Port. There were hoots from ships, the occasional siren, and the vibrating thrum of big diesel engines.

She did not see Julian again until the middle of the next morning. Her heart leaped when she heard his voice downstairs. Moments later, she could hear the stairs creak as he made his way up them.

Jade stood by her bed and waited.

He knocked on the door.

She cleared her throat. "Come in."

When he opened the door, she was surprised to see him dressed in a blue boiler suit.

"How are you?" he asked.

Only his eyes gave a clue to his deeper feelings.

"Fine." Inwardly, she chided herself. *That was pathetic.*

As if seeking safe neutral ground – away from the bed, they both migrated onto the balcony and sat in the two chairs there.

"I like it here," she said. "It allows me to feel the heartbeat of the port, but from a safe place."

After a lengthy silence, Jade decided to broach the subject of him being a monk again – but in a tangential way that had reference to her own culture.

"What do you think of Buddhism?"

"I respect it."

"Then why are you not a Buddhist?"

He looked her briefly. "Buddhism negates all passion."

Jade suddenly felt flushed in the face. "Is that all?" It was a brainless riposte, but it was the best she could muster given her unsettled equilibrium.

"If I understand Buddhism correctly, it is essentially negative. The sole goal of a Buddhist is to escape this world to Nirvana. Buddha's last words were, 'always exert the mind, seeking the way out.'"

"So Buddhism has no attraction to you?"

"If passion dies, joy dies, and if that dies, you are left with a shriveled husk of a human being."

Hoping her face was not turning red, Jade countered, "If passion dies, you don't hurt yourself, or others, by wanting things."

Julian looked at her. "If passion dies, morality is simply reduced to that which is most efficient. Personally, I think that is inadequate."

"But surely it's a good thing for the Buddha to tell us that we must strive harder."

"Or it is a cruel thing… for everything then depends on your own ability."

Of course everything depends on your own ability, she thought. Aloud, she said, "In what way is Christianity different?" She could hear the petulance in her voice.

"It's not about what we can do to reach God; it's about what God has done to reach us."

Jade wasn't sure she'd achieved anything through her conversation, so she lapsed into silence.

Julian seemed to pick up on her turbulent emotions, for he made his apologies and got up to leave. His only token of affection was to lay a hand against her cheek, briefly.

She wanted to cover it with her own, but didn't.

After Julian left, she was quite unable to sit still and paced up and down the balcony. Finally, she tired of her own company so much, that she left the house in order to buy some flowers for Bronny… and a red ribbon.

Jade dived through the French windows of the balcony to her bedroom the moment she heard their voices. They were heavily accented Chinese voices.

She crept to the landing of the stairwell and listened.

Bronny had answered the door, but almost immediately called for Brant.

"What do you guys want?" Brant asked with commendable brusqueness.

"We are looking for this woman."

There was a moment of silence – presumably as Brant was shown a picture of Jade.

"No mate. People sometimes board here, but that photo doesn't bring anyone to mind."

"Are you sure? We have evidence that she is here."

"Well sonny. I'm the evidence that she is not."

"It is important that we find this woman. The Chinese consulate need to locate her – for her own well-being."

"None of that changes the fact that she's not here."

"Perhaps the woman who lives here with you, knows."

Jade heard Brant's tone change.

"Look sonny; this is my home, and I'm the master here. You don't go running behind my back to speak to my wife. Do you understand me?" Brant's voice had a dangerous edge to it. Jade could picture him standing in the doorway like an indomitable rock, with his arms folded across his chest. By any measure, Brant would be a difficult man to get past.

She again heard the Chinese voices. "No, no. We go now. Maybe we come back and ask later."

It was a notion that received little encouragement from Brant. "Don't be in a hurry to come back."

She heard the sound of the door shutting.

Jade slumped down on the top step and leaned against the banisters. It was all too much. Despite Julian's best efforts, Wang Lei and his men had found her just twenty-four hours after her arrival at Port Adelaide.

Below her in the hallway, she could hear Bronny's voice.

"'I'm the master here,' she parodied. Really!"

"Sorry darling," said Brant. "It was all I could think of in the moment."

Bronny sniffed and made for the stairs.

Moments later, she was seated next to Jade with an arm around her.

Jade started to weep.

Brant came lumbering up the stairs. He came to a stop halfway up them and addressed her.

"Well, my darling. Whoever's looking for you hasn't wasted much time in finding you."

Jade shook her head. "It's impossible. How could they?" she sobbed.

The big man shook his head. "Don't worry girl." He managed a reassuring smile. "It just calls for plan B."

Julian was seated on the bench seat beside the engine-room door when his phone rang. He answered it immediately.

Brant's distinctive rumbling voice spoke. He gave no introduction.

"Julian, my boy; we have a problem."

With growing alarm, Julian listened to Brant's account of what had happened. As he listened, he massaged his forehead and tried to think.

"They must have tracked Jade via her phone. There can be no other explanation." Even as he said it, he realized that his own phone could be equally problematic. He would need to get a prepaid phone for himself. Luckily, Dillon already had one.

Brant grunted. "I suppose you're right, boy. I don't really understand much about these things."

"Can you get rid of Jade's phone for me... send it somewhere,
preferably?"

The big man gave a low chuckle. "I'll slip over to Dry Creek and
put it on one of the railway goods wagons going to Melbourne."

If the situation hadn't been so dire, Julian would have smiled.
He settled for saying, "Yeah, that should do it."

"But what do we do then?"

"I think we have to assume the place is being watched, so we'll
have to implement plan B."

"Okay son. What time's the pick-up?"

"Two hours from now."

The phone went dead.

Chapter 20

J ade watched with bewilderment as Brant pulled back the carpet to reveal a wooden trapdoor. He lifted it up by an iron ringbolt.

"This goes to the cellar," he said. "Follow me."

Halfway down the steps, Brant reached for a switch and flicked it on.

Jade saw a large dank cellar and various items of stored junk. Only the wine rack looked as if it had been regularly visited. It was situated close to the bottom of the steps.

"Where are we going?" she asked nervously.

Brant helped her to the bottom of the steps and chuckled. "I'd like to say that you being billeted with us had everything to do with my magnetic personality and charm, but alas, that would not be the whole truth." He heaved away two tea chests stacked on top of each other to reveal a rusted steel door. Brant gestured to it. "This is the other reason."

He retrieved an old-fashioned key from his pocket, unlocked the door, and pushed it open. It creaked and groaned in protest.

The inside of the tunnel was pitch black.

Brant took his cell phone from his pocket and selected the flash-light function.

What the light revealed, didn't fill Jade with confidence. Old bricks, covered with damp and strange-looking fungi extended into the darkness.

Jade had given Brant her phone to dispose of two hours ago, so all she could do was to follow Brant, as he crouched down and entered the tunnel.

"Where does this go?" she asked, nervously.

"I told you this was a wicked house. Whenever there was a sailor who needed to be transported to the wharf without being seen… or perhaps a barrel of brandy that needed to come from the wharf; they used this tunnel."

"So this is plan B."

"Yeah."

Jade had no idea what awaited her at the end of the tunnel. All she knew, was that the bottom of it was slimy and wet. Occasionally her feet splashed through a puddle. She tried not to think of what she was treading in.

Jade estimated that they would have walked about fifty yards when their way was blocked by another steel door. It opened with the same key that had unlocked the first door. When it opened, Jade could see that she was in another cellar. But this one was full of marine-looking equipment in wooden crates. Pumps and valves were nested in wood-shavings inside plywood boxes. At the end of the cellar, she could see daylight streaming through a crack above her. The light came from the edges of a wooden trapdoor.

Brant stepped onto a box, opened the bolt, and threw open one of the leaves of the trapdoor. He beckoned Jade to stand next to him, and in the next instant, she felt herself being lifted through the opening to a pavement outside.

With a wave, Brant closed the trapdoor above him and was lost to sight.

She was on her own.

It took a moment for Jade to get her bearings. She discovered she was in a laneway, just twenty yards from the end of the wharf… and there, sitting on a bollard, as calm as you like, was Julian.

Relief flooded through her. She ran to Julian and clung to him fiercely.

He buried his face into her hair. "I've got you," he said. "You're safe."

After a few moments, Julian drew back and pointed to a steel ladder that led down to the water. "This way."

Jade looked down and saw the inflatable dinghy from the *One and All* tethered to the bottom rung.

Julian climbed into the dinghy after her and started the outboard motor.

"Cast us off," he said.

Jade understood enough to untie the rope tethering them to the ladder.

Seconds later, the outboard revved, and the boat was skimming over the water.

"Where are we going?" she shouted.

Julian was looking disturbingly grim. "Somewhere really safe… and I'm sorry to say, somewhere really remote."

Jade had no idea what to expect.

Jade had been so anxious and bewildered by everything that was happening to her that she barely noticed the harsh industrial features of the Port River. She was dimly aware of giant sheds and silos. But as the inflatable slapped and juddered its way over the water, she began to settle down and take some interest in her surroundings.

Up ahead, she could see a brutally industrial power station. Its huge buildings looked rusted and slightly run down. She was surprised to learn from Julian that it was still in use.

"We're going to branch off and head down the North Arm." Julian had to shout to make himself heard. "The power station sits on Torrens Island. It's the biggest island in the Port estuary." He pointed over to the right. "The little island that's squeezed between Torrens Island and the mainland is Garden Island. We're going under that bridge over there, and we'll slip between the two islands to the mangrove swamps."

Jade wasn't at all sure she liked the sound of that, but Julian distracted her by giving her a running commentary on the things of interest they passed. After skimming under a low bridge, Julian throttled the engine back so they could speak easily.

Jade was amazed at the bird-life around her. Julian pointed out the various birds: spoonbills, ibis, and cormorants.

"What's that?" she asked. She pointed to the rusted remains of some old iron ships. The rusted behemoths only had a few of their bones left – enough to give an indication of their former elegance – reminding her of a time when ships were beautiful.

"This area is known as the 'ship's graveyard.'"

It didn't look to Jade as if a ship had come here to die for at least a hundred years. Some had been reduced to just a few spikes of rusted metal that were draped in weeds.

Julian pointed to a marina they could see on Garden Island. "Warm water from the power station triples the rate weed and fouling grows on the bottom of those boats." He grinned. "What the owners save in mooring fees they have to spend on cleaning the weed off." He paused. "Keep your eyes open for dolphins. The whole area is a dolphin sanctuary."

Julian piloted the inflatable between the two islands and out into a wide estuary. "Yachties and powerboats use this eastern side of Torrens Island to play in. You only need to be caught in the wake of a tug from Port Adelaide in the main channel once, and you won't do it again."

Jade nodded dumbly. She couldn't think where Julian might be heading.

He steered the boat to the eastern side of the estuary where the bank was covered with mangroves.

Jade looked at Julian with puzzlement.

"I used to canoe around here with my mates. It's the best place in the world to hide." He pointed to the mangroves. "These are gray mangroves. The pencil-like aerial roots poking up from under the water enable the roots to breathe."

Julian throttled the engine back to a low burble.

This gave Jade a chance to look into the water. She could see schools of tiny fish and the occasional crab. "Wow! The water is amazingly clear."

"The mangroves are a nursery for a host of marine creatures. Ecologically, they are very important."

Julian nosed his way up a narrow river between the mangroves. "This is Swan Creek. It's an outfall for the Little Para River."

Jade had no idea what he was talking about. She could see an occasional sandy beach. Each one looked inviting. But Julian ignored them and steered the inflatable out of the river into a twisting channel. It was so narrow and overhung with mangroves that it looked as if they were going through a tunnel.

Jade's sense of disquiet was greatly heightened when Julian cut the engine. She looked round her. "We're in the middle of nowhere," she protested.

"Precisely," said Julian.

She watched with disbelief as Julian unpacked a green bundle from a waterproof sack. "This is an army hammock they use when they're in the tropics. I pinched it from the lazarette on the *One and All*. It has a built-in roof, and the sides are made of mosquito netting. Believe me, you'll be grateful for the netting."

"Me!" she stuttered.

Julian climbed out of the inflatable into the trees, and in short order had strung a hammock between two branches. Next, he hung the roof over the top. It all looked as if it was made of nylon."

"Am I having to get into that?" she asked incredulously.

"Not until I put a sleeping bag inside. You'll need it at night, and you will need it to stop the mosquitoes biting you through the nylon."

Jade couldn't believe what she was hearing.

"Hop in," he said. "You'll find it the most comfortable thing you've ever laid in."

To her surprise, she allowed herself to get into it. The green nylon sagged, but held her firm. "It is comfortable," she conceded.

"Good." Julian pulled some bottles of water from the sack, and followed this up with a box of muesli energy bars. "Pack these by your feet and legs."

"How long do I have to be here?" she asked nervously.

"Until I sort some things out, and I know it's safe to get you." He reached into his pocket and handed her a cell phone. "That's a pre-paid phone. You'll see my number, and Dillon's number, in there. Ring me if you are concerned about anything at all… or just need to chat."

She nodded dumbly. But then the full reality of her situation dawned on her. "But what shall I do? I've nothing to read."

Julian rubbed his stubble, and then pulled a small book from the breast pocket of his overalls. "This is a pocket New Testament." He shrugged apologetically. "It's all I've got. Try one of the biographies of Jesus – Matthew, Mark, Luke, or John."

"But what if I need to…" she paused, embarrassed. "You know… go to the toilet?"

"Climb out, put your feet on one bough, hang on to a higher one – and let fly." He smiled. "Use leaves and seawater to wash up. Just be careful getting back into the hammock that you don't knock your food into the water."

"Is that likely to happen?" she said, alarmed.

"No. This hammock has a low center of gravity. It's very stable. But be careful."

"I suppose it's no use me protesting?"

He shook his head. "Not when your safety is at stake." He paused. "Try and enjoy the experience. Times of peace are rare."

"I'm not a monk," she cried out… but she wasn't sure Julian heard her above the revving of the outboard.

Chapter 21

Dillon was feeling seedy and wretched. Mick, in contrast, looked hale and hearty – completely unaffected by the crew's 'run ashore' last night. The same could not be said of Dillon. He had drunk too much and was now paying a heavy price for it.

"Your behavior last night wasn't great, mate." The bosun looked at him darkly. If you want to stay part of the crew, you need to learn not to be a dick-head."

Dillon hung his head.

If you vomit for any reason other than seasickness on this ship, you'll become a pariah. Do you understand?

Dillon thought it was ironic. The very reason he'd drunk with such bravado the previous night was so that he could fit in. It had badly misfired. He held his head in his hands wishing he didn't feel so wretched... and guilty. Faintly through the fuzziness of his thinking, he was also aware that despite behaving stupidly last night, he had changed. The mere fact that he could tolerate Mick giving him a dressing down was testimony to that. Three weeks ago, he would have reacted angrily, hurled abuse, and stormed off. His time with Julian had changed him.

Mick continued on. "You're in no shape to go to the workshop today. Your job is to clean the focsle so that it's spotless and smells great. Okay?"

Dillon nodded. He hated the idea of not going to the workshop. He'd discovered that the *One and All* had a workshop in the end of the giant shed by the wharf. They'd got a timber store and all sorts of wood-working machines: planers, a band-saw, and a drill press. When Dillon had seen them, he was thrilled.

A bearded man called George, stooped with age, was in charge of the place. He was a retired industrial arts teacher, and he took meticulous care of the machines under his care. Dillon had worked with him the previous afternoon and loved every moment of it. George had even let Dillon use some off-cuts to make three seat-bases to take back to Second Valley for his stick chairs.

Mick was leaning against the Sampson post on the foredeck of the *One and All*, and Dillon was sitting on a hatch cover. The bosun shook his head. "I sometimes think that the worst thing a sailor can do when they come into port is to go ashore." He laid a hand on Dillon's shoulder. "You'll feel better after a good sleep. Make sure you drink lots of water. "

Dillon wanted to find a place to curl up and die.

"How are you?" Julian massaged one side of his temple as he asked the question. Jade had spent a full night on her own."

"I'm okay."

He was relieved to hear her voice. She sounded remarkably positive. Jade was an showing extraordinary inner strength. Few could have endured the inactivity and isolation she'd had to endure.

"Have you any idea of what a mangrove swamp sounds like at night?" she said.

"No."

"There are splashes and clicking noises – and you have no idea what's causing it."

"Are you managing?"

"Yes."

Her assurance wasn't quite convincing.

"I feel like a caterpillar trapped in a cocoon."

"Have you managed to get out of the hammock?"

"Yes. I climb out every few hours during daylight, hang onto some branches and do some exercises."

"You're amazing."

"How long do I have to be here?"

"I hope to collect you late this afternoon."

"You mean I have to wait an entire day?"

"Yes." He paused. "If I'm not with you by 6pm, ring Dillon. He'll get Mick to collect you."

"What are you going to do?" she said.

Julian wondered how much to tell her. "I'm tired of being hunted," he said evasively.

"What do you mean?"

Julian could hear the concern in her voice.

"Nothing," he said. "I'll explain more tonight."

What Julian didn't say, was that he was furious at the evil that was being visited on those he loved… and he was determined to attack it.

It was time for him to go hunting.

Julian had the description of Wang Lei's car – a black Audi. Jade had even managed to tell him the number-plate. Wang Lei, evidently, was based at the Chinese consulate. Julian was driving there now. He'd borrowed Mick's battered old Land Rover.

The difficulty he faced was being allowed to actually speak to Wang Lei. No doubt all sorts of polite obstacles would be put in his way.

He drove down Crittenden Road until he came across the consulate. It was a surprisingly modest single-storied building, surrounded by a wire security fence.

Julian drove the Land Rover into the car park and motored

down its length. There, at the end of the car park was a black Audi. He checked the number-plate.

It was the one he was looking for.

Julian reversed, and then drove forward in a wide arc, lining up the blunt nosed Land Rover with the car's passenger side door.

The steel fender on the Land Rover crashed into it.

Julian was dimly aware of metal crumpling, and a side-door air bag inflating.

The peace of the morning was abruptly shattered by the sound of the car's security alarm going off.

Julian got out of his vehicle and inspected the damage, acting for the sake of the security camera's, the role of a concerned driver.

He was not alone for very long. Six men ran out from the building shouting and gesticulating.

Julian held up his hands placatingly. "So sorry. So sorry. My foot slipped onto the accelerator. So sorry. So sorry. Who owns this car? I will make everything right."

A youngish man in skinny tan jeans, tee shirt, and jacket pushed through to the front. "This is my car, you idiot."

Julian looked at him. So this was his enemy. It was an uncanny experience to see him face to face. Here was the man who had kidnapped Jade – and very probably had a role in Caleb's murder. The man was dressed very fashionably and had a haughty tilt to his chin. His eyes gave away nothing.

Julian was instantly on guard.

He smiled at the man and said: "Sit with me in the front of the Land Rover and let's do the paperwork."

Wang Lei looked at the Land Rover, much as someone might look at some dog excrement on a pavement. His face looked grim and veins were standing out on his neck.

After a brief conversation in Chinese, the other men returned to the building.

Julian was quite sure, however, that he was being watched closely through security cameras.

Wang Lei and Julian climbed into the Land Rover. It was not a vehicle that offered much comfort. The vehicle's seats were little more than pads. Julian approved. The last thing he wanted was for Wang Lei to feel comfortable.

Wang Lei slammed the door shut. "You have caused many thousands of dollars damage. I hope you are well insured."

Julian nodded. "Wang Lei," he said softly.

The man froze, and then looked at him with a frown.

Julian continued. "ASIO are taking an interest in you." He paused. "Your name has been linked with the torture and murder of Caleb Kuznetsov. And recently, it has been linked with the attempted abduction of a Chinese student here in Adelaide, Jade."

"Who are you?" Wang Lei demanded.

"I am the one you believe has information on Dr. Kuznetsov's research."

Wang Lei's eyebrows shot up in surprise.

Julian continued. "I am also the person a group of thugs was sent to torture for information." Julian conjured an affable smile. "I'm the man you sent Jade to seduce and extract information from."

Wang Lei pointed to him. "You're...."

"Yes. My name is Julian Alston."

An uncomfortable silence hung between them.

Julian knew he had to maintain the initiative. "I'm here to tell you that if you wish to deal with me, you must do so directly. You are not to do so by attacking Jade or any of my friends." He looked at Wang Lei. "Your actions, so far unproven, are bringing disgrace on your government – who will be made aware of all the facts, if you continue your attacks on my friends. Is that clear?"

Wang Lei did not move. His face was now a blank mask. After a few moments, his lip curled. "Hah," he said dismissively. He ran his eyes over Julian's stained canvas smock top and long hair. "Look at you. You are nothing but..." words seemed to fail him.

Julian helped him finish the sentence. "I'm the one who is telling you that you will pay for the damage to your own car." He paused. "Now, get out."

It occurred to Julian as he parked the Land Rover back in the shed from where he'd collected it, that he needed to ring one or two people in Second Valley and ask them to take over the running of the Sunday service at St. James. He shook his head. It was surreal. One moment he was contending with kidnap and murder... and the next, concerning himself with who would read the prayers at his church.

He deliberately didn't let himself dwell on the other massive issue in his life – his love for Jade. Julian had learned that some things needed time. He'd showed his heart to God... and was content to leave it there.

What he could do, however, was collect Jade.

Was it safe to do so? He didn't know for sure. Julian did feel, however, that something had shifted in the dreadful game that was being played. What was in no doubt, was that Julian had painted a giant target on his own back. Wang Lei had been maneuvered into a corner with the threat of diplomatic action at a very high level. The big question was, of course: was that threat enough to keep Jade, Dillon, and Leah safe? He'd thrown down the gauntlet to Wang Lei, and ensured that the issue he had with Julian was now personal.

It was not an entirely comfortable thought.

He walked to the *One and All* and lowered himself into the inflatable that was tethered to the ship's side. Dillon was nowhere to be seen, but that was not surprising. Mick ambled over to the gunwale, unfastened the mooring lines, and tossed them into the inflatable.

Julian nodded his thanks and asked, "How's Dillon doing?"

Mick smiled. "He's a bit sorrier and wiser than he was yesterday. Currently, he's asleep."

Julian thought it wise not to ask any more questions.

He primed the outboard, set the engine to neutral, and fired it up.

It started straight away, and soon Julian was skimming across the surface, making his way down the Port River.

There was only an hour of daylight left by the time he had threaded his way through the mangroves to the lair he'd chosen for Jade.

Jade signaled his arrival by lifting up the side mosquito netting. She lay there in her cocoon with a small smile on her face. "Nice of you to turn up."

"Oh, I was just passing… and I wondered if there were any damsels in distress that need rescuing."

"Well, you can rescue this one," she said handing him the first of a number of empty bottles and the cardboard remains of her box of muesli bars. Then, with fluid ease, she climbed out of the hammock and began helping Julian pack up the sleeping bag and the hammock.

The pleasure of sharing this simple task with her brought Julian huge joy.

Only when they both climbed into the inflatable did they kiss. They knelt on the bottom of the inflatable and hugged each other. Julian kissed and caressed her hair. It took a moment for him to notice that she was crying.

"It's okay," he said.

"I know… 'I've got you,'" she quoted, managing to paste a smile on her tear-stained face.

He nodded. "I have indeed."

Julian piloted the inflatable through the mangrove channels back to the eastern estuary of the Port River. He was just turning into the North Arm when Jade pointed.

"Look! Dolphins."

Julian glanced to where she was pointing. He was rewarded by the sight of two adult dolphins and a calf. Their shining gray backs arched through the water as they swam close by the mangroves looking for fish.

Julian couldn't help but wonder who would now be looking for him.

Chapter 22

Julian walked with Jade from the *One and All* to Brant and Bronny's house, making no attempt to remain unseen. He was acutely aware that he was playing a dangerous game. Julian had to behave as if he was confident that ASIO had extended its protective arm around them. He'd intimated as much to Wang Lei with the hope that by so doing, Wang Lei would tread carefully, knowing he was on the edge of an international scandal. If it blew up, the Chinese Government would, of course, deny everything and make counter-accusations… but they would nonetheless be displeased at the public exposure. The CCP were not known for being very forgiving. Wang Lei would need to be careful.

Julian and Jade dawdled along the shops of St. Vincent Street until they came to Brant and Bronny's house.

Julian murmured to Jade, "I have little doubt that we are being watched. So let's enact a little pantomime." He glanced around. "If we were being watched, where's the most likely place they would be watching from?

Jade answered straight away. "From one of the cars parked on the other side of the road – probably about one-hundred yards away."

Julian nodded. "I agree." He then pointed to the row of cars and whispered in Jade's ear. "Rhubarb, rhubarb, rhubarb."

She looked at him with puzzlement. "What?"

Julian pointed again to the row of cars, and then made an ostentatious show of getting out his cell phone.

A minute later, he was rewarded by the sight of a blue Nissan peeling away from the curbside, doing a three-point turn, and driving off in the opposite direction.

Julian watched it leave, unsure if he was pleased by the sight or not.

When they turned to knock on the door, he noticed that one of the lower floor windows was boarded up.

Bronny answered the door. Julian pointed to the window and raised a questioning eyebrow.

Bronny sighed. "A half-brick through the window." She waved a hand. "Easily fixed."

Julian was appalled. "Bronny, I'm so sorry. I'll organize the repair."

"Brant's already got it organized, dear. Don't worry." She looked at them both. "Can you both stay for dinner?"

Jade looked at Julian and nodded. "We'd love to," she said. "Just promise me it won't be muesli bars."

Julian couldn't help but think that there was a touch of the 'last supper' about their meal together. Jade had said she wouldn't be returning to Second Valley and would finish writing up her thesis in Adelaide.

Julian heard the words with a rising sense of despair. Could everything end so tamely? Could what they had both experienced simply be allowed to fizzle out like an untended fire – because there certainly had been fire.

He cast a covert glance at Jade.

She was looking very poised and in control. Only her hands

gave her away. She was systematically destroying a bread roll with them.

Jade interrupted his mournful thinking. "Julian, can you tell us why we are now making no attempt to hide from Wang Lei?" She shrugged. "I don't understand."

The question brought him up with a start. "Um, because I had a chat with him."

"What!" She looked at him incredulously.

"Yes. I got his attention, and had a chat."

"How on earth did you get his attention?"

"I drove into his car at the Chinese consulate with Mick's Land Rover." Julian shrugged, almost apologetically. "I destroyed his front door."

Jade looked at him in disbelief, and put her head in her hands.

Julian continued. "I let him know that ASIO was keeping their eyes on him over Caleb's death and your abduction."

Jade shook her head. "But it's not true…" she paused. "Is it?"

Julian pursed his lips. "I may have gilded the lily somewhat." He glanced at Jade. "You know Wang Lei better than I do; what do you think he'll do?" He paused. "I, er, didn't volunteer to pay for the repairs to his car."

Jade groaned. "He loves that car. I can't believe you did that."

Julian was unrepentant and said again, "What do you think he'll do?"

"Wang Lei is naturally vindictive, and he'll want to have the last word." She sighed. "You'll have to expect more bricks through the window and perhaps some graffiti. It could go on for a long time. Just look at what they did to that Australian swimmer who refused to share a podium with the Chinese champion – the alleged drug cheat." She shrugged. "They intimidate."

Julian twisted round and took out his pre-paid cell phone. "Jade, can you give me Wang Lei's number?"

She looked at him in disbelief. "You can't seriously tell me…"

"Please," he insisted.

Jade reeled off the number. Julian noted that she did so from memory.

The phone was answered almost immediately with some abrupt words in Chinese.

Julian spoke clearly and slowly. "Wang Lei, this is Julian Alston. Your petulant behavior in throwing a brick through my friend's window has been noted, and ASIO have been informed. Your national ambassador will be called to explain your behavior if you fail to put two-hundred dollars in an envelope, and place it my friend's letter-box by this time tomorrow. Do I make myself clear?"

Julian rang off and pocketed the phone. He knew he was engaged in an appalling game of brinkmanship. Julian forced a smile. "There; I hope that's fixed it."

Jade shook her head.

Half an hour later, Jade led Julian out onto the veranda from her bedroom in Brant and Bronny's house. She could see from the carriage of Julian's shoulders that a deep sadness had settled upon him.

It was one she shared.

They sat themselves in the two chairs and listened to the gathering quiet, as evening fell over the port.

Julian made to say something, but Jade had a premonition about what he was about to say, and she wasn't ready to hear it. She put a finger to her lips, and held out a hand for him to hold.

"Let's just enjoy the quiet together for a while."

Julian took her hand, and nothing was said for a long time.

Jade knew, however, that there were issues that must eventually be broached. She squared her shoulders, removed her hand from Julian's, and said, "Okay. What do we need to talk about?"

Julian glanced at her. She could see the pain in his eyes. His voice told her one thing, his eyes another.

"Will Wang Lei use you to get to me?"

She nodded. "You have to expect so." She lowered her head. "The best thing is for me to stay away." She paused. "And you are a monk."

Julian nodded slowly. "Ours is a meeting of hearts, but it is not yet a meeting of souls."

"What do you mean?"

"If we end this now, there will only…" his voice wavered… "be a broken heart. But at least there will not be a deadened soul."

Jade wasn't at all sure she understood. But she knew enough to know she didn't like what he was saying.

"What are you suggesting?" she demanded.

Julian shrugged. "Everything is against us: culture; circumstances and controlling beliefs…"

"What do you mean, 'controlling beliefs?'"

"Different belief systems."

She nodded. "You being a monk."

"Yes. Me being a Christian monk."

Jade knew herself to be in a state of turmoil, unable to define what her controlling belief was. All she knew was that it wasn't what it used to be. Old certainties were no longer certain, and concepts, once scorned, were now commending themselves.

"Some things are destined not to be," she said, weakly – not believing her words for a moment.

Julian said nothing. His eyes were closed, and he had a fist pressed against his forehead.

The very idea of being without Julian was disorientating – a thought too terrible to contemplate. She felt sick with the anguish that was piercing her heart.

Even the night was quiet, as if it too was holding its breath. There was only the occasional whoosh of a car. The unique sounds of the port had stilled.

Julian broke the silence. "What will you do?"

Jade sniffed, and held her head upright. "I won't go back to Second Valley. I'll drive to my flat in the city tomorrow morning. Her eyes started to fill with tears. She dropped her head again. "I share a flat with two other Chinese students."

It was an inane thing to say, but it was all she could manage.

Julian parked Mick's Land Rover on the roadside opposite St. John's church. It stood at the end of Halifax Street in an area that was a peaceful backwater of the city. The street was lined with old blue-stone cottages, and gave way to Victoria Park at its end. Julian loved the area.

He walked behind the church, past the modern resource center, to the undercover walkway that led to an old stone house. It had a bull-nosed veranda, so typical of the old buildings of Adelaide. A small garden was all that separated it from the church. The two buildings had traveled through time together... and were at peace with each other.

Julian was not at peace.

He pushed through the heavy front door into the hallway, and tapped on the door to the right.

"Come in."

Julian recognized the voice of the prior, Andrew Prescott.

The prior's study was a reflection of the house. It was quiet and dignified... and harked back to a time when things were more certain, and life moved at a slower pace.

The prior appeared unsurprised to see Julian. He let his eye run over Julian's appearance, and waved him to one of the armchairs in the room. Then he came out from behind his desk and sat in the other.

"How are you going?" he asked.

Julian dropped his head in his hands. "Pretty wretched, actually. That's why I wanted to see you."

The prior nodded. "I'm at your disposal... all morning if you need it."

For a long while, all that could be heard was the ticking of the clock on the mantelpiece... *tick, tick, tick*, in slow measured beats.

Julian leaned back and closed his eyes. "I'm having trouble with my vows."

The prior waited for him to say more.

Julian continued. "Despite my best efforts to be poor, God has not allowed me to be so. I own two cottages and gain income from renting the second."

The prior nodded. "The church was unable to finance you... and you found a way to support yourself using your own hands. You bought and renovated a cottage, I understand." He paused. "Very sensible."

"But right now, I'm struggling with the chastity thing."

The prior frowned. "Have you honored your vow?"

"Yes. But it's been a close-run thing."

"You have a duty to stand guard over your heart." The prior paused. "You have more control than you think. If you didn't, all of us would be brute beasts, led by the nose by our feelings."

"Yes. I have been careless." Julian went on to give a highly edited account of his meeting with Jade, and of Jade being kidnapped in an attempt to force Julian to hand over classified technical information belonging to Caleb.

To his great credit, the prior showed no surprise. He simply asked if the police and ASIO were aware of the facts.

"ASIO is aware, and it is reasonable to expect they have involved the police as much as they wish them to be involved."

"And are you, and the young lady, Jade, safe? I wouldn't want the same thing to befall you as happened to your friend, Dr. Kuznetsov."

"I think Jade is safe... and I'm fairly sure I can manage my own safety."

The prior shook his head. "I think it would be safer for you if you moved back here into community."

"It may be safer, but I don't think it would help the issue to be resolved."

The prior grunted. "Well, just remember: that option is always open to you." He drew in a deep breath. "Which leaves the question of your heart." He paused. "The vows you took are sacred and binding. It is no small thing to consider breaking them."

Julian nodded. "I am determined to remain under your authority."

The prior sighed. "You place a heavy responsibility on me. In reality, you come under the authority of the order... of which I happen to be the head."

Inside the house, a bell rang to signal one of the offices of the day. Then the silence was again taken over by the clock: *tick, tick, tick.*

"Do you wish to be free of your vows?"

"I don't know." Julian massaged his forehead. "I've loved being a brother… and appreciate the extraordinary privilege of it… the privilege of time, the time to be still, to be close."

The prior put his fingertips together, tilted his head slightly, and looked at Julian. "I think you are destined never to fit in wherever you go in life, Julian; whether it is with us, or as a priest, or as a scientist."

Julian looked up at him in surprise.

"I thought I fitted in, or at least tried to fit in."

The prior shook his head. "We were the wrong order for you to join. We have been heavily influenced by the Oxford Movement. We love ritual, theater, and tradition. You, on the other hand, love simplicity, reality, and existential truth. "If you were Catholic, you would have found a home with the Cistercians. They love asceticism."

Tick, tick, tick.

The prior broke the silence with another surprise. "The bishop of Adelaide has let me know that he has had a number of complaints about your role as acting priest at Delamere. Evidently, some are saying that you are not traditional enough. You don't stick to the words in the Book of Common Prayer. Is that true?"

"Yes. I tend to use the prescribed liturgy as a template rather than a rule book."

"It is arrogant to think you can come up with better words than the Anglican Church's finest theologians."

"The issue is not what words we prefer… but which words are real and true to God's ears."

The prior smiled. "And there we have our conundrum. The inflexibility and safety of tradition, or the existential reality and danger of home-spun spirituality." He tapped his fingers together. "Tell me how you do your services."

"The congregation is very small. In many ways, my expected role there is one of palliative care – presiding over the inevitable death of a church community. They have very little energy, very little hope, and not enough people to fill key positions. They've had to struggle without an organist for months."

"So what have you done?"

"I use the Internet and a data-projector. They now sing to the best music in the world. And on the rare occasions I am away, they can listen to the best preachers in the world. More of the parishioners are now involved in running the service, and I want to start a couple of mid-week Bible-study groups – one of them for youth."

The prior nodded.

Another silence ensued.

Julian wondered what was going in the mind of his superior – a man he greatly respected.

Eventually, the prior broke the silence. He waved a hand. "The complaints are nothing. They are simply the symptoms of life returning to a church. But be careful not to run too far ahead of your people."

Julian nodded.

"As for you losing your heart; you have, to date, honored your vow. I would ask you to continue to do so. Meanwhile, I will think about your situation." He got up from his chair. "In many ways, Julian: you have been more of a monk than any of us. I wouldn't want the special gift you bring to the world to be lost." He smiled. "Now, go join your brothers in the church."

Chapter 23

There was only one bus a day that took people from Adelaide to Second Valley. Julian had never taken it before, and it was a luxury to allow someone else to navigate the winding road down the Fleurieu, whilst he sat in relative comfort next to Dillon.

Dillon's luggage had now grown to four shopping bags. This was impossible for him to manage because he was also transporting the three wooden seat-bases he'd made in the *One and All's* workshop. Julian had therefore slung his duffle bag onto his shoulders and carried the seat bases for him. It was no surprise that Dillon valued them so much. The seat bases were the hardest things to construct, ordinarily. He'd taken full advantage of the machines in the workshop and done a good job.

The bus came to a stop outside the old stone mill with a hiss of brakes. Julian and Dillon got out, collected their luggage from the bus luggage compartment, and, after a brief walk, were at the back door of the cottage. It was, as usual, unlocked.

Julian looked for signs of someone having entered the cottage, but found none.

He laid the fire and started it burning, whilst Dillon took his prized seat bases over to the workshop.

It was a surreal experience being back. The peace he usually felt when he was alone in the cottage eluded him. Julian paced about, feeling unsettled and on edge. It wasn't hard for him to discern the reason. Jade. She was not with him… and may never be with him again. Julian squeezed his eyes shut and massaged his temples.

Instinctively he put his hand in his pocket for his New Testament, only to remember that Jade had it. She hadn't given it back. He pulled his larger Bible off the shelf and opened it to the Psalms. He loved the raw emotion and honesty of its words.

But even then, his thoughts began to wander. The real problem was that the issues surrounding Caleb's death, and the attempts by Wang Lei to obtain his intellectual property, had not been resolved. Until it was, everyone remained at risk. The thought of those close to him continuing to be in danger appalled him.

If anything was going to be done to bring things to a head, it had to happen quickly. Julian wondered if simply telling Wang Lei that ASIO were now in possession of Caleb's intellectual property could solve the problem. The trouble was, ASIO were not in possession of it, and Julian had little confidence that he could pretend they did.

He needed Caleb's hard drive and micro computer. Without them, he had no bargaining chips to play with. He could only pretend… and pretending was dangerous.

There had to be an ending, an ending that he could control. The trouble was; any ending almost inevitably would involve violence, and violence was something he abhorred.

Perhaps he should have shared more of these thoughts with the prior and asked for his wisdom.

As he massaged his forehead, the kettle began to boil.

Julian opened the back door, and gave a shrill whistle. He could hear Dillon banging away at something in the workshop. "Tea's ready," he yelled.

Dillon came to the door, removed his boots, and sat at the table.

Julian handed him his mug of tea.

Dillon nodded his thanks and looked at Julian quizzically. "What's up with you, mate? You look grim."

Julian gave a wan smile. "Sorry Dillon. Somehow I've got to bring the whole business of Caleb's murder, his intellectual property, and the threat to Jade and yourself, to a close."

"Isn't that the job of the police... or the secret service, or whatever?"

"Yes. But they can't nursemaid all of us for ever."

Dillon frowned. "How would you go about ending it – if you could?"

Julian leaned back and sighed. "I'd need to lure them into the open, so that their link with Caleb's murder can be positively established. Then I'd somehow need to corral them, together with the evidence... and call in reinforcements."

Dillon snorted. "That doesn't sound very likely."

"I know." He paused. "There are places where I might be able to corral them. The problem is, I've nothing to lure them there with." He shrugged. "I've got no chips to play with."

Dillon nodded slowly. "A gambler with no chips. That's not good. What would you need?"

"I need Caleb's hard-drive and micro-computer. Without them, I can't bargain. And, believe me, I would give them to anyone in a heart-beat, if it meant keeping you all safe."

Dillon stared into his cup with a frown, and then seemed to come to some sort of decision. "Julian, what if I could get you Caleb's stuff?"

Julian looked at him with bewilderment. "What?"

"Seriously. Would that change anything?"

Julian sat bolt upright. "Are you telling me you know where Caleb's stuff is?"

Dillon nodded. "Yeah."

Julian didn't know whether to be furious, or to hug him. In the end, he did neither and settled for saying, "You'd better tell me the full story."

Dillon looked at him apologetically. "I only took it because I thought it would help." He hurried on. "I didn't want to cause you any trouble, just protect you from yourself."

"What do you mean?"

"Well… I was at the back door taking off my boots when I heard Jade make you promise not to be bullied into giving this Wang bloke Caleb's stuff, because Wang would never hurt her. Well, I laughed to myself because blind Freddy could see that you were always going to be a soft touch – particularly when it came to Jade."

Julian was mortified that he was so transparent. "But how did you do it?"

"We were at Leah's when you got the phone call about Jade being held captive." He shrugged. "I knew what you would do, so I said to Leah that I'd steal the hard-drive."

Julian shook his head. "But how did you know where it was?"

"Oh, that was easy. You'd spoken some rubbish about stones and stuff… and of course I thought about the stone you call your prayer rock. It was pretty easy to find."

"But what about the micro-computer?"

Dillon waved a dismissive hand. "Leah always knew where you'd put that. She said something like: 'Silly boy. Did he think that I wouldn't feel an extra bump on the martyr's stone?'" Dillon did a fair job of imitating Leah's husky voice.

Julian was tempted to smile, but didn't.

The boy continued. "Anyway: she dropped me off down the road, and then drove on to the church." Dillon shrugged. "And that's pretty much how it happened."

Julian was both appalled and amazed. Leah and Dillon had been a step ahead of him all the way – but in being so, they had imperiled Jade's life. For a while, he couldn't bring himself to say anything.

Finally, he managed to ask: "Where's the hard-drive and the micro-computer now? Do you have them?"

"Yeah! Leah handed me the microcomputer as she gave me that handshake when she left us. She'd put it into a tiny capsule that once held the leads of propelling pencils."

Julian raised his eyebrows. "And where is that now."

"Safe."

"Where?"

Dillon rocked the base of his tea mug round on the table top. "I bored a half-inch hole into the topmast of the *One and All*, stuck it inside, and used silicon to seal it up."

"You what?"

"I climbed the ratlines and hid the capsule in the mast." He shrugged. "It's still there." He smiled. "I was pretty pleased with myself, actually."

Julian shook his head in disbelief. "What about the hard-drive?"

Dillon got up from the table and made for the back door. "Come and see."

After slipping on his boots, he tromped over to the workshop. Once he was there, he selected one of his new seat bases. Julian noticed the timber planks used to construct it were significantly thicker than the others.

A suspicion started to form in his mind.

Dillon looked at him with a grin. "I've used dowels to join the planks for the seat – except for this one joint." He placed the seat base on the workbench so that it hung over the edge. Then he laid a piece of scrap wood over the edge of the seat, and thumped it with a mallet.

The glued joint instantly gave way to reveal a cavity that Dillon had bored into the edge of one of the planks.

The boy hooked out the hard-drive and handed it to Julian. All the wrapping that had previously protected it had been removed.

"Here you are," he said. "Will this make a difference to your plans?"

Julian knew he had to bring things to a head one way or another, and there was only one place he could think of where it could be done which gave him a chance of surviving. One thing he was very certain of, was that he needed to do this alone. Everything was just too chancy. He was glad that Jade was safely back in Adelaide, even though he missed her terribly.

Julian tried to think what it was about her that was so captivating. She was beautiful, certainly – outrageously so. But Julian had never accorded much significance to outward appearances. In fact, he was slightly bewildered by current society that was so obsessed with outward appearance, and so careless of inward character. No: the easy grace Jade displayed when she moved, matched an inward grace. There was an inherent goodness about her, a depth… even a spirituality that was currently a sleeping dragon, waiting to be aroused. She was also passionate. He could feel it smoldering just under the surface, controlled for now, but no doubt wonderfully dangerous and expressive when released. Julian had never seen it released. He'd only seen evidence of its darker side – the fury she'd unleashed protecting him from those who had come to hurt him.

He shook his head. That whole episode now felt like a dream, something impossible to believe. Only the pain and ache in his heart told him it was real… and that this remarkable woman had changed him forever.

Julian had left Dillon, who was happily engaged with his projects in the workshop, and driven back to Adelaide. His first priority was to recover the microcomputer from the *One and All*. He had to concede, that when it came to hiding places, the one Dillon had chosen was hard to beat. Accordingly, he had furnished himself with a short length of half-inch dowel and some epoxy.

An hour and forty minutes later, his pick-up squeaked to a halt on the wharf in front of the *One and All*. He didn't want to involve Mick or any of the crew in what he was doing, so he simply gave Mick a wave, retrieved some tools from the lazarette, and put them in a tool belt. Then he climbed the rigging until he was standing on the capping of the foremast. The topmast was bolted onto it with huge iron brackets.

It wasn't hard to see the small lump of silicon left by Dillon. Julian prized it out of the hole with a screwdriver and hooked out the tiny capsule with a piece of wire. Moments later he'd lathered a section of dowel with epoxy and driven it into place with a hammer.

Mick accosted him when got back down on the deck. "Anything I should worry about up there?" he asked.

"No, very minor. I remembered seeing a small hole that I never got round to fixing. All good now, but I'll need to come back later this afternoon to sand the plug smooth and put a coating over it."

Mick nodded his thanks and returned to his task of overhauling the forward lifting plate.

Julian walked back to his pick-up and drove to Rundle Street in the city to visit a camping shop there. He bought some rope, lights, pitons, carabinas, and two camping mattresses. After snatching lunch at one of the many pavement cafés, he returned to Port Adelaide to finish his repair on the *One and All*.

When all was done, he drove back to Second Valley late in the afternoon – having first stopped off at Normanville to buy some lengths of timber. By the time he got home, Julian was bone tired.

None of the weariness was due to physical exhaustion. It came from the emotions that haunted him regarding what he proposed to do.

Dillon never felt happier than when he was in the workshop. Julian was there so rarely these days that he'd come to look on the workshop as his own domain. He just wished that it wasn't so primitive, and that he had access to some of the machinery he had been taught to use in Port Adelaide. His abiding ambition was to build a Windsor chair with a two-tiered back. The chair was impossible to build in the traditional style, because it required the steam-bending of green wood. However, Dillon felt he could construct a curve using composite bits of wood joined together.

He was mulling over the problem when his phone rang. It gave him quite a shock as he had almost forgotten that he had it in his pocket. The phone was the pre-paid one that Julian had given him in Port Adelaide.

"Hello," he said cautiously.

"Hi Dillon. It's Jade. How are you going?"

Dillon smiled with pleasure. "Hi Jade. What's up?" He paused.

"We're doing okay… although Julian's not been around much. He's busy with some project of his own, which he's not letting me be part of."

There was a pause at the other end of the phone. Then Jade asked. "Any idea what he might be up to?"

Dillon wrestled with his conscience about how much he should tell.

Jade interrupted the silence. "Dillon, please tell me everything. Julian is up against something very big and may need some help." She paused. "You and I can't give it unless we both know what's going on."

Dillon rubbed the back of his neck, desperately trying to come to a decision.

"Dillon. If you have any regard for me… and for Julian, tell me, I beg you."

Her words persuaded him. "We've recovered Caleb's stuff."

"What?"

"Yeah. And now Julian's away a lot, doing things he won't tell me about. He's been really secretive."

"What do you suspect he's doing?"

"Dunno. But if I had to guess, I reckon he's organizing some sort of 'guts and glory' thing."

"Guts and glory? I don't understand."

"He's going to make things happen, you know… end things."

"Oh. Who with?"

"It's got to be with that Wang fellah that nabbed you. He's probably planning to do some deal with him to keep us all safe."

"Oh no!"

Dillon could hear the despair in her voice.

"What's the matter?" he asked.

"Dillon. This could go badly wrong. I know Wang Lei. He's not a person you play games with." She paused. "Look, can you and I make an agreement? Let's keep each other informed of everything, so we can protect Julian? Is that a deal?"

The idea of being important – particularly when it came to

looking after Julian, appealed to Dillon. "Yeah," he said. "I'll do that."

Only after the phone call ended did he wonder whether he'd done the right thing.

Chapter 24

There was only one place Julian could meet with Wang Lei that would allow him any chance of success, or indeed, survival... and that place was Talisker Mine. It was one of the most dangerous places on earth, and Julian had taken his life in his hands as a teenager exploring it. He shuddered when thinking back to the headstrong things he'd done. The fact that he was still alive was little short of a miracle.

The upside of his foolhardiness was that he knew the mine well and understood some of its secrets. He suspected that little would have changed in the intervening years – just a few more rock falls, and more dry rot in the timber frames holding up those sections of roof that were loose and friable. If the roof wasn't dangerous enough, the numerous shafts that went down to Hades itself made navigation of the tunnels a perilous undertaking.

Julian loaded his pick-up with all the things he needed and then drove south to Delamere. When he got to St. James', he parked under the yew trees and unlocked the church door.

The morning sun was shining through the eastern windows, casting rainbow colors over the pews and flagstones. Rainbows, he knew, represented God's covenant – God's promise of blessing.

Julian felt in desperate need of it now so, careless of the chill, he knelt on the flagstones and lost himself in that deep place – the place of prayer.

He wasn't sure how long he was there. It didn't matter. It was enough to know that he now had the energy and confidence to do what needed to be done.

Julian nodded his respect to St. James in the lead-light window, and to the martyr's stone… and made his way to the front of the church. There, he picked up the data-projector and a battery pack – and returned to his pick-up.

He sat for a moment, unmoving in the front seat, thinking about the martyr's stone.

If there has to be a martyr, he thought grimly, please let it be me and no one else.

───

Jade sat at the desk in her bedroom resting her chin on her hands. Her room, which had felt perfectly adequate in the years she had lived in the unit with friends, seemed small. It was as if her eyes had seen bigger horizons that now left her restless, ready for more.

The problem, of course, was Julian. It had been three days since she'd seen him, and it seemed like an eternity. She shook her head in irritation. The last thing she wanted to be was a neurotic woman morbidly dependent on a man for her identity. But even as she thought it, she knew it wasn't true. She was very much her own woman – except with Wang Lei. Wang Lei owned her, and she knew it. He held her future, and her parent's well being, in his hands.

No, she was not being neurotic. She was in love. It was as simple as that. Jade had known it for a while, of course, but only now, in the grief of parting, had she allowed herself to reflect on it. The strength of her passion had caught her by surprise. It was simultaneously both thrilling and alarming… and now, deeply tragic.

The irony, of course, was huge. She'd been sent by Wang Lei to 'get close' to Julian. A more brutal term would be 'seduce,' but that had sexual overtones. She was very sure she would not have let it get that far. But now her fantasies took her down that path.

It was impossible. He was out of reach. All she could do was to watch over him from a distance through Dillon, but even that was not an arrangement that could last.

Julian was in every sense, different. He was counter-cultural in his dress, but appeared to be completely unaware of it. The very way he presented himself seemed to highlight a way of living that showed up the crassness of commercialism. His hair was long and wild, but he didn't wear it to be noticed. The paradox was, of course, that it was noticed – certainly by the girls.

But it was his character that was particularly arresting. He had a gentleness and a depth of understanding that was exceedingly rare.

Calling him to mind caused her to smile sadly. Julian was a man of truth. Truth was important to him. Jade loved him for that. Just knowing that men like Julian existed gave her hope. He was also a man completely unwedded to the clock… and silence was his friend. She felt that some of her most eloquent times with Julian had been the silences.

Jade reached out and picked up Julian's New Testament. The small book showed evidence of much use. She held it against her heart briefly then flicked through its pages. How many times had he done the same thing?

She'd read it every day since he'd given it to her. At first, she'd expected to find wise and moralistic words, like those of Confucius. However, what she'd encountered was a story in which Jesus made claims about himself that were deeply disturbing. When she searched for evidence of megalomania or madness, all she came across were words of grace and profundity. Whatever else was true, the Galilean was certainly not mad.

She'd checked the accounts of his life in all of the biographies of Jesus, and although they differed slightly, as one would expect from different witnesses, they were broadly similar.

Jade was in shock.

And she was faced with a choice.

The ballroom did not look like a ballroom. It looked like a huge underground cavern with a craggy, steeply sloping roof – which is exactly what it was. Julian had no idea who had given the cavern its name, and didn't much care. The cavern had been carved out by Cornish miners as a result of them coming across a particularly large pod of ore. Once it was all mined out, they'd used it as their 'crib,' the place they met to have their lunch.

The rest of Talisker mine was a maze of vertical shafts, the deepest being 430 feet. The shafts were connected at different 'levels' by 'drives' tunneled between them.

For the last two days, Julian had worked alone in the mine, perfecting his plan. This had necessitated him swinging from ropes, cutting wood, and hinging balks of timber to each other. The operation had been perilous, because he'd done it completely on his own. Two flashlights had given him the light he'd needed, but even so, the exercise had been physically testing and emotionally exhausting.

Every moment down the mine had been a time of moral torment. He knew that there was a good chance that people might die as a result of what he was doing. The very idea that he might cause anyone's death was abhorrent to him. He had a good deal of sympathy with the Quakers and their pacifism. Julian had reflected on the moral quandary of Christian villagers in Latin American countries who had to take up arms to fight off marauding government troops. Their struggles had led them to develop their 'Liberation Theology.'

Julian also reflected on the life and death of Dietrich Bonhoeffer, the German theologian who had joined with some fellow Germans in a plot to kill Hitler. Raw evil that thought nothing of torture with a blowtorch and killing, had to be challenged. He would, of course, give the option of surrender, but he would not back down in visiting terrible consequences on those who murdered. The lives of Jade and the others he loved depended on it. But even so, it was a distasteful thought; one that troubled him greatly.

Catching a group of murderers, all of whom would doubtless be armed, was not something Julian had any experience in, and he was acutely aware of it. The challenge of how he was going to do it had occupied his mind for three days. In the end, he had sought inspiration from his scientific research; specifically, from that strange 'other world' of quantum physics.

In the quantum world, sub-atomic particles could appear and disappear.

He too needed to be able to disappear.

The quantum world also displayed the extraordinary phenomenon of 'entanglement'. Once two sub-atomic particles had become 'entangled,' i.e. had interacted with each other… and subsequently separated; everything that happened to one particle was instantly mirrored in the other – regardless of where it was. If one spun to the right, the other instantly spun to the left. It was a phenomenon that completely bamboozled Einstein who referred to it, somewhat disparagingly, as "spooky action at a distance."

He hoped it would live up to its name.

It was too early to call anyone. That fact didn't bother Julian at all. He rang Wang Lei.

His first call went through to the message bank. So did his second. Wang Lei answered the third, but with obvious ill grace. There was an angry torrent of Chinese.

Julian waited for him to finish and then said, without introducing himself. "Wang Lei. I have good news for you. I have located Caleb Kuznetsov's hard-drive."

There was a moment's silence, and then Wang Lei spoke. "Julian Alston…" He seemed unable to say anything more.

Julian gave him no time to recover his wits. "The price for me giving you Caleb's hard drive is the assurance that you will leave me and my friends alone. You will have the hard-drive, so there will be no benefit in pursuing any of us. Is that clear."

"How do I know you have not copied the information on the hard-drive."

"You don't. All I can do is give you my assurance that it hasn't been copied."

For a moment, nothing was said.

Wang Lei eventually spoke. "Then I too will give a promise to you. If I find any evidence of Caleb Kuznetsov's intellectual property being in any hands other than mine, I will exact my revenge on you and on anyone associated with you. Is that clear."

Julian swallowed. "Perfectly." Not caring to hear any more of Wang Lei's threats, he continued. "Meet me at the main mine shaft of Talisker mine on the Fleurieu Peninsula, south of Adelaide. I will give instructions once I see you are there. Come prepared to go underground… and understand that your cell phone will not work once you are in the mine. You are to be there at 10 this morning."

Julian rang off before he could hear any objections. For a moment, he sat there staring at his phone. It shook slightly in his hands. Inside, his mind was a storm of emotions. Not daring to give himself any more time to think, he punched a familiar code into his phone and sent it off as a message.

His phone rang three minutes later.

Edwina Stanthorpe spoke with her typical economy of words. "What's occurred?"

Julian drew a deep breath. "I've located Caleb Kuznetsov's harddrive."

"Who had it, and why was it hidden?"

"Doesn't matter." He paused.

Edwina came back at him immediately. "Are you able to keep it safe for the next two hours?"

"Why?"

"Because I'm sending people down there to collect it right now."

Julian drew a deep breath. "Actually no."

"Why?" she demanded.

"Because I'm going to use it as bait to trap Caleb's killers."

There was the briefest of pauses. "No, you're not," she said. "You are involved with something that is way over your head. This is an issue that touches on national, even international security. If you compromise Australia's interest in any way, there will be dire consequences. I'm talking about lengthy prison terms. Am I making myself clear?"

"Perfectly. But I have no confidence that you will be able to wrap things up in a way that will keep those I care about safe. I think I can, but I need your team to be in place at Talisker mine on the Fleurieu Peninsula, south of Adelaide – at midday today."

Edwina's angry voice interrupted him. "Julian, you are not to do anything other than sit tight."

"Edwina…"

"Don't call me Edwina. Only my friends call me…"

Julian ended the call.

Dillon didn't intend to eavesdrop. He was simply awake and alert to the sounds of the morning. It was not yet fully light, and he could hear Julian speaking quietly into his phone. That he should be on his phone so early in the morning was a surprise. Julian was usually outside on his rock at this time of day.

Dillon only managed to catch some of the conversation, but what he heard caused the hairs on the back of his neck to rise. Julian had called Wang Lei and organized to meet with him at Talisker mine.

Then he'd rung someone else, and from the sound of it, the person on the other end of the phone wasn't too happy about it.

He lay still in his hammock until Julian had finished the call. It didn't take long. Moments later, he heard Julian leave the cottage by the back door.

Dillon was out of his hammock in a trice, and fumbling for the phone in the pocket of his jeans. He punched in a quick-dial button and waited impatiently for the phone to be answered.

He breathed a sigh of relief when it was. "Hi Jade. I think things are going to happen today with Julian."

All semblance of sleepiness instantly left Jade's voice. "What things? Tell me everything?"

"I don't know much, Jade. But I overheard Julian tell someone

199

that he's going to ask this Wang fellah to meet him at Talisker mine. I think he wants to give him Caleb's stuff, so we'll all be safe."

Dillon could hear Jade groan in anguish.

"Jade, I don't know what to do," he continued.

Jade's reply did nothing to encourage him. "Julian is being headstrong. Wang Lei can't afford to let Julian live, even if he gets Caleb's hard-drive." Dillon heard her groan again. She sounded like a woman in labor – someone in pain.

After a few moments of hesitation, Jade continued. "I'll come down. In the meantime, don't let Julian out of your sight... and keep in contact with me."

Dillon was relieved that Jade would join him and share in the responsibility of looking after Julian. To say he was alarmed was an understatement. Jade's comments had forced him to understand the appalling danger Julian now faced. He rubbed the back of his neck. Everything was spiraling out of control.

Chapter 25

Dillon had no idea how uncomfortable it would be lying under a tarpaulin in the back of Julian's pick-up truck. He bounced up and down like a cocktail in a cocktail shaker. It was a bruising business. Things got even worse when Julian left the bitumen and drove on the dirt track leading to Talisker mine. He was heartily glad when the vehicle finally pulled up with its characteristic squeak.

Dillon listened as Julian got out of the pick-up and walked away. When he judged Julian to be well away, he risked a peek over the edge of the tray.

He saw Julian bending down heaving aside a large metal plate from what Dillon presumed must be a mineshaft. The shaft was about seventy yards away from the main mine site. With some alarm, Dillon watched Julian disappear down the hole.

Everything was quiet… or as quiet as it ever gets in the bush. Parrots screeched and somewhere in the distance came the distinctive sound of a kookaburra.

Dillon pulled out his phone and rang Jade.

She answered almost immediately.

"What's happened?"

"I'm at the mine in the back of Julian's pick-up. He doesn't know I'm here."

"And where's Julian?" she asked.

"He's gone down some sort of mine shaft."

"Okay." There was a pause. "Can you make your way to the top of the dirt track but keep yourself hidden?"

"Sure. What do you want to do?"

"I'll pick you up from there. I'm about twenty minutes away. Then we'll figure out what to do."

"Right."

"Oh, and Dillon: make sure you stay hidden. If I know anything about Wang Lei, he will be unpredictable. He could turn up at any time."

Dillon caught sight of the large black saloon well before it passed him. He had plenty of time to duck down behind the mass of thin, spiky leaves of a yucca bush. The bush looked as if it was wearing a Hawaiian grass skirt – except it was upside down.

The car went past with a gentle purr. Dillon could see three men sitting in the back seat and two in the front.

Dillon had positioned himself near the point where the dirt road began. After a moment's indecision, he decided to stay where he was.

Waiting, he decided, was one of the hardest things to do. The inaction nearly drove him mad.

In the event, he didn't have to wait too long. Jade's pale-colored Corolla came barreling down the bitumen, and then turned off onto the dirt track.

Dillon ran from his hiding spot and waved his arms.

She came to a halt, and Dillon climbed into the front seat. "Wang's lot are already here," he said. "They are only a few minutes ahead of you. He's brought a small army. There are five of them."

Jade groaned and rested her head on the steering wheel. "Five's too many. Somehow we've got to lower the odds, otherwise, Julian won't stand a chance."

For a moment, nothing was said.

Jade eventually leaned back and turned to Dillon. "Can you drive my car? It's got an automatic gearbox."

"If you show me how?"

A few minutes later, Dillon was getting a crash-course on how to drive Jade's car. After some experimentation, he got the hang of it. He grinned. "Nothing to it. Much easier than a manual."

Jade got out of the car and shooed him away. "Go," she said.

Jade left Dillon and jogged up the side of a small scrub-covered hill. When she got to the top, she could see the mine site laid out before her. Julian's pick-up was parked to one side… and more disturbingly; five men were gathered round what she knew to be the remains of the main shaft entrance. Even from where she stood, she recognized Wang Lei.

She shouted out to them. "Hey!" then scuffed her way down the hill and walked across the mine site toward them.

"Didn't you see me wave to you?" she said. "You drove right past me."

Wang Lei looked at her darkly. "What are you doing here?"

"I'm giving you your instructions," Jade then took a gamble. "You didn't turn up at the time we expected, so I've had to chase after you."

Wang Lei lifted his head so his chin stuck out arrogantly. "And what are these instructions?"

"They are instructions on where to find the hard-drive."

"And where's that?"

"If you take Julian's pick-up and turn down the first track on the left, it will take you through a farm gate and alongside a hill with views over Kangaroo Island. Stop just before you get to the ruins of some old stone stables. On the uphill side of the road, you should see an old stone rainwater tank."

"What of it?" Wang Lei demanded.

"There are two car tires in the south-western corner of the tank. They're easily seen. The hard-drive is inside the bottom rim of the bottom tire."

"And how do we get it?"

You will need the rope ladder. There's one in Julian's pick-up. The keys are in the ignition. There's a metal stake next to the sediment trap that you can hook the ladder to."

Wang Lei reached forward and flicked her painfully under the chin. It wasn't the first time he'd done it to her, so she was half expecting it.

She didn't react.

"You had better be telling me the truth *Too Bee-eh.*"

Wang Lei turned to one of his men, and nodded to him.

Without a word, the man made for Julian's pick-up.

Julian watched the pantomime going on at the center of the mine site with a sense of disbelief. He'd wedged himself into the top of the mineshaft seventy yards away, where he could watch them unobserved. The bile in his gut churned at the sight of Jade in the company of Wang Lei and his men. He massaged his forehead. Somehow, he had to modify his plans, so that she could get away from them. He had no idea how. One thing he was very sure of was the need to keep the initiative. And at this stage, that meant staying with his original plan for as long as he could.

Julian reached for the phone and rang Wang Lei.

It was answered straight away. Wang Lei's voice came through to him. "Enough of your games, Alston. We've got Jade and we've sent someone off to get the hard-drive. Come out from whatever hole you are hiding in."

Hearing that someone had gone to get the hard-drive completely bewildered him. Julian's knuckles turned white as he gripped the top rung of the steel ladder, and he wondered what it could mean. His plans were already beginning to unravel. Earlier, he'd unscrewed the bolts holding the steel plate over the shaft entrance and had pushed it to one side. It was now lying alongside a pile of rocks.

The rocks were not there by accident.

Julian thought furiously about how he should reply. Trusting his instinct, he said, "You are early, Wang Lei. Clearly, you are not someone to be trusted. But it doesn't matter." He paused. "I do require you, however, to let Jade go."

Wang Lei laughed unpleasantly. "That's not going to happen, Alston. Why should I? You've got nothing to bargain with."

"Oh, but I have. In my pocket I have a plastic capsule. Inside it is Caleb Kuznetsov's micro-computer. If you want the complete package – and you'll need it, by the way – then you'll do as I say."

"I don't think so, Alston. Come out and talk to us, or Jade will suffer." With that, Wang Lei gave Jade a vicious back handed slap across the face.

She staggered sideways.

Julian was conscious of a slow boiling anger rising up within him. He said between gritted teeth. "I'd prefer it if you come to me, Wang Lei. There's a mineshaft about seventy meters up the hill from you. It leads down to a cavern. I'll leave a light on to guide you."

Wang Lei tried to interrupt him, but Julian spoke over the top of him. "I'll speak to you there from one of the tunnels. This is the last you'll hear from me on this phone. Cell phones will not work underground."

Dillon had parked Jade's car in the ruins of the old stone stable. Before he left it, he had the presence of mind to throw some handfuls of dust and sand over it, and scuff over the tire tracks. He then climbed the fence and made his way up to the water tank. What he was looking for was a place where he could hide. The ruined hearth of the old cottage offered no protection at all, and the overgrown pile of disused rocks ten yards from the tank was too obvious.

In the end, he chose to hide in a hollow behind a tussock of grass. He suspected that sheep had discovered the dip and used it to shelter from the wind.

Dillon flattened himself in the hollow and waited.

He wasn't a moment too soon. He could hear the rasping growl of Julian's pick-up grinding its way along the rutted track toward him.

The engine stopped. Dillon peered through the grass but could see nothing.

An eternity later, a burly Chinese man came into view. He was carrying Julian's rope ladder. The man dropped the ladder by the gully trap and walked around the water tank. He then inspected the overgrown pile of stones, checking he was alone. Finally, the man looked around the rest of the site. Dillon did not believe for a moment he was admiring the view.

Seemingly satisfied, the man returned to the water tank, hooked up the rope ladder, and threw its free end into the tank. In quick order, he eased himself over the edge and started to climb down.

Dillon was instantly on his feet. He ran to the gabled end of the stone tank and risked glancing over the top.

The man was now at the bottom. His legs had sunk up to his calves in oozing mud and filth. Dillon heard him cursing under his breath as he began to splosh his way to the corner of the tank toward two old tires.

Dillon ran to the rope ladder and began heaving it up the wall.

There was a shout and a yell of indignation.

Dillon was too terrified to look over the edge. He gathered the rope ladder in his arms and stumbled down the hill to the track.

He threw the ladder over the fence, climbed after it, and carried it to Julian's pick-up. Once he'd stowed it away in the back, he jumped into the cab.

What should he do now?

He had no idea.

Chapter 26

J ulian had prepared his field of battle with meticulous care, but
the arrival of Jade had thrown his plans into disarray.

He stepped off the final rung of the ladder onto the floor
of the cavern. Julian had left a camping light at the bottom of the
shaft. It only cast a feeble light – and he had chosen it for that very
reason.

The cavern, or 'ballroom', may have been a place where miners
gathered to eat lunch, but it was a treacherous place. Two tunnels,
diametrically opposite, led away into the darkness. Between them,
on the cavern floor, lay the gaping maw of a shaft. Julian had never
seen the bottom of it. Piles of rock and dirt littered the cavern floor.
Julian crouched down behind some rocks near one of the entrances
of the tunnel,

…and he waited.

It didn't take long for him to hear the scraping of boots on the
rungs of the ladder. Occasionally there was a small fall of dirt and
stones caused by people brushing the side of the shaft.

Julian watched them arrive through a space between two rocks.
He saw three men and Jade. That meant that one man would be

standing guard at the top of the shaft. He presented a problem that Julian would have to deal with later.

Three men and Jade: three killers… and the woman he loved.

Until he'd seen Jade, his plan had been relatively simple. He had just two objectives. The first was to get conclusive evidence of Wang Lei's involvement in Caleb's murder. The second was to trap Wang Lei underground, until the police could collect him and his men. Julian's primary objective now, however, was to ensure Jade's safety – and he had no idea how to go about it. There was no time to strategize. Julian allowed himself just a few seconds to bring his emotions under control, then he lifted his head and shouted out to the ceiling of the cavern.

"Wang Lei, there's a good chance that only one of us will leave this place alive. If you have any ambition that it be you, you will do exactly what I say."

Julian's voice echoed in the chamber, bouncing off a million rock surfaces. It was a disorientating sound.

Wang Lei shone his flashlight this way and that seeking the source of the voice. It steadied briefly on the shaft at the other end of the cavern.

"Come out, Alston, or things will get seriously unpleasant for Jade. I'll give you ten seconds."

Wang Lei jabbed a foot in the back of Jade's legs, forcing her to kneel on the ground. Julian caught sight of a flash of red in her hair. Jade was dressed for battle. He didn't dare let himself think what that might mean.

Julian called out again. "I've got nothing to lose. Caleb Kuznetsov's micro-computer will be tossed down a mine shaft if you don't let Jade go. You can't afford for that to happen."

Wang Lei's answer was to slap Jade on the side of her face.

This time, she yelped in pain.

Wang Lei drew a pistol out from behind his jacket and called out. "The next sound you will hear, Alston, will be me shooting Jade in the leg."

Julian winced… and gritted his teeth in anger and frustration. It was time to take things to the next level – and bring some quantum entanglement into play.

Crouching low to keep behind the piles of rocks, he made his way into the tunnel entrance and slipped into the darkness. He was fortunate that he made his move when he did, because moments later, Wang Lei directed the two men with him to stand by the entrance of each tunnel.

The man standing at the entrance of the far tunnel had a muscular build and must have stood over six feet tall. He was pointing at Julian's footprints in the dirt and jabbering away in Chinese. Julian's view of what was going on was partly obscured by the silhouette of the other man standing guard at the end of his own tunnel. He willed the man to move to one side with every fiber of his being. *Move, move, you blighter. Get out of the way.*

A few seconds later, the man moved.

Julian lifted his arm and pressed a button on the remote control for the data projector. He had placed the projector on the floor of the opposite tunnel.

The projector instantly came to life, and for a few seconds, an image of Julian was projected on the white limestone rock at the end of the far tunnel.

Almost as quickly, Julian switched the image off.

The sight of Julian's image sent the man at the entrance of the tunnel off on a crouching run, his flashlight flickering over the tunnel walls. Julian noticed that he was holding a pistol.

Entanglement. He had to be in two places at once.

Julian called out to the man standing guard at the mouth of his tunnel. As he did, he shone a flashlight on himself.

"Do you want a piece of me, mate?"

Julian switched off the flashlight and then ducked behind a boulder, squeezing himself into a low cavity in the tunnel wall.

The man at the end of his tunnel began running toward him, his flashlight roving this way and that.

Two things happened simultaneously. Julian couldn't see either of them, but he could hear them. There was a yelp of surprise… and a scream. The man in the far tunnel had run over the top of the wooden cover that had been placed over a shaft entrance. Julian was familiar with it. He hadn't trusted it for a moment when he'd put the data projector in place. In fact he'd taken pains to climb along the tunnel wall around it, much like a rock climber. The big Chinese man had not done the same. His scream seemed to hang in the air like a tortured spirit.

Julian closed his eyes in anguish. The man would have fallen down at least to the next level, forty feet down, and would not have survived. Julian had no time to dwell on it further, as the guard at the end of his own tunnel was now blundering past him.

Julian waited until he judged the man was beyond the section of tunnel that had been shored up by pit props, then he pulled the rope that lay at his feet. The rope led deeper into the tunnel. It would have been invisible to anyone, as Julian had covered it with dirt. He'd looped the far end of it round one of a pair of pit props that held up a roof beam. The beam was braced across a friable section of the tunnel roof. None of the pit props in that section of tunnel were in great shape. All of them had been eaten away by dry rot. The one Julian had looped the rope around was particularly rotten.

He gave the rope a savage jerk.

There was a cracking sound of breaking timber, and Julian was able to pull the rope freely toward him. The loop at the end must have passed through the timber. But nothing happened.

Julian gathered the rope to himself, sick at heart that his plan to trap one of Wang's men on the other side of a roof fall had not worked.

Then all hell broke loose.

There was another cracking sound of breaking wood… and then a trickle of dust fell from the roof.

The man who had blundered past Julian must have heard it, because he turned and began to run back to the entrance of the tunnel.

There was another crack, and then a terrible crashing sound of thudding rocks. The earth shook as the roof of the tunnel smashed down in a blinding cloud of acrid dust.

Julian had anticipated the rock fall and had looped a handkerchief around his neck. He pulled it over his mouth and nose as the earth shuddered and rumbled around him... and Hades coughed out its filth.

A deathly hush followed. All Julian could hear was a ringing in his ears. He had positioned himself in the section of the tunnel that had solid rock above him, but he was only yards away from the friable section where the roof had collapsed. Hundreds of tons of rock must have fallen. Julian dared not think of what had happened to the man who had been trying to flee to safety. His body was probably unrecoverable.

But there was no time to think, no time to grieve.

The dust was still thick in the air as he stood up from behind his boulder and stepped back into the tunnel. He shone his flashlight in front of him but the dust was so thick, it was only of limited use. Julian staggered forward, feeling his way, until he came into the main cavern.

Here, the dust had more space to disperse and visibility was better. Wang Lei had thrown an arm over his face and was cowering away from the tunnel entrance.

Jade was still on her knees. She had her head turned away, so he couldn't see her face.

Wang Lei straightened up as Julian stepped through the dust. He could have been stepping through the smoke of a battlefield. Julian halted midway between Wang Lei and the gaping shaft at the edge of the cavern.

Wang Lei looked around him apparently disorientated. He did not, however, remain bewildered for long. He took in the dreadful significance of what had happened all too quickly and turned on Julian.

"You bastard."

Julian had not intended to kill, but he dared not argue the point. He wanted to retch, but he forced himself to remain under control.

"I warned you, Wang Lei. Let Jade go... and who knows, you may yet live."

Wang Lei snarled. "If you think I will let you live, any more than

I let Kuznetsov live, you are mistaken." He lifted the pistol and pointed it at Julian.

It took a moment before the full import of Wang Lei's words registered. Julian blinked. Wang Lei had been present at Caleb's death. Julian had the proof he needed.

Wang Lei then turned the pistol so that it was pointing at Jade. "I am going to shoot Jade first in the legs and then the arms… and continue shooting, unless you give me the micro-computer.

He pointed to a rock that lay half way between them. "Leave it on that rock and then step…"

Wang Lei got no further. The instant the gun no longer pointed at her, Jade unwound herself like a spring. She lashed out with a foot, kicking Wang Lei behind the knees.

Before he buckled to the ground, Jade was on her feet. Her next kick sent Wang Lei's pistol spinning from his hand.

To Wang Lei's credit, he regained his feet and crouched into a fighting pose.

Julian looked on with amazement at the flurry of kicks, parries, and punches that were being exchanged. It quickly became evident that Wang Lei was no match for Jade. She was systematically destroying him. Jade landed blow after blow, until a final kick left Wang Lei on all fours, barely conscious.

She looked down at him with obvious disgust, then turned and picked up the pistol.

To Julian's great bewilderment, she began to step backward toward the tunnel where the big Chinese man had fallen down the shaft.

She looked at Julian with pleading in her eyes. "This shaft is deadly, yes?"

Julian made to reach out to her but she waved him back.

"Jade," he cried. "What are you doing?"

As he spoke, he was half aware of Wang Lei getting back onto his feet, staggering as he tried to keep his balance.

Julian took another step toward her.

Jade raised the pistol. "Don't come closer," she ordered.

Julian couldn't believe what she was saying.

"Jade; what…?"

She looked at him imploringly. "Don't you see, Julian?"

"No!" he shouted.

Jade shook her head. "It's impossible, Julian. It always was. I could never compete with your true affection… nor should I."

"Jade," he shouted. "There is a way. There has to be. This is ridiculous." His was on the edge of hysteria.

"Oh no. It's not ridiculous. Wang Lei, or someone else from the CCP, will always be able to use me. I can't escape. This is the only way." She started to step backward.

Julian started to think furiously. "No, no, Jade. Don't jump into that shaft. It only goes down to the next level. You may not die, but you'll be terribly hurt." He paused. "If you must jump…" Julian pointed to the shaft entrance in the main cavern. "Then use this one. Although I strongly urge you to…"

She waved him to silence and edged round to the other shaft. All the while, she kept the pistol aimed at him. "You don't see, do you?"

"See what?" he yelled. "Jade don't…"

She interrupted him. "Julian, listen to me." She paused, and then said very deliberately, "Wang Lei is my brother."

Julian's mouth dropped open. "Your brother?"

"So, you see it's impossible for me, Julian. She looked at him and smiled. "I love you so much… so much, that it hurts."

Jade dropped the pistol at her feet, paused for a second, and jumped.

Chapter 27

Julian leaped toward the edge of the shaft; scooped up the pistol, and aimed it at Wang Lei. For the briefest of seconds, he wanted to pull the trigger, but something made him stop.

Dust was still swirling around the chamber. The camping lamp turned the cavern into a hellish scene from Dante's Inferno. He saw Wang Lei staggering back onto his feet. The man held his head with both hands and eventually steadied his gaze on Julian.

"You don't care that my sister is dead?" He laughed unpleasantly. "Maybe I misjudge you. You are more mercenary than I thought." He waved a hand dismissively. "Pah. My sister's affections were wasted on you."

Julian was only half listening. He was mentally calculating what Jade would have experienced... and desperately hoping she was safe. Jade had inadvertently used the escape ploy he had designed for himself. She would have fallen eight feet down onto a broom handle that held open a miniature drawbridge. The drawbridge was sloped at a forty-five degree angle and padded with two layers of camping mattresses.

Once the broom handle had been knocked away, the drawbridge would have been pulled shut by the weight of two stones.

These had been tied to ropes that passed through metal rings and fastened to the corner of the drawbridge. The drawbridge would have scooped Jade up as it closed, and she would have tumbled into the side tunnel. The gate would have snapped shut over the tunnel's entrance much like a giant's mouth.

Jade would be sore, certainly. But she would be alive.

Julian affected a savagery that he did not feel, and asked a question that he'd been longing to ask.

"Are you really Jade's brother? Her name is Jade Zhou. She has a different surname from Wang."

Wang Lei was now standing fully upright. His eyes didn't leave Julian for a second. "My parents were poor. So I was raised by a rich uncle and adopted his surname. He was a moderately important person in the Communist Party." He paused. "I have since overtaken him in seniority."

For a moment, nothing was said.

Wang Lei pointed at Julian. "I didn't think a monk would kill a person. But now I see you more clearly. You are a brutal man… and you don't care about my sister's death." He paused. "I think perhaps you might shoot me."

Julian nodded. "Make one false move, and you'll find out." Internally, he was thinking furiously: *I don't even know if I've switched the safety catch off.*

Wang Lei lifted his chin. "What happens now?"

"I think you can kiss goodbye to your senior post in the Communist Party. You will be put on trial here in Australia, and it will be a show trial – very much in the public eye. The media will have a field day. Your government will, of course, say that the charges against you are fabricated. If they run true to form, they will arbitrarily arrest an Australian citizen on some trumped up charge and fill their news channels with concocted outrage. But they will nonetheless be embarrassed." Julian forced a smile. "And then you will be imprisoned for life. Any memory of you will be memories of shame… and you will never be able to expunge it."

Julian started to walk toward the steel ladder of the entrance shaft. As he did, he rapped out his orders.

"I will climb first. You will stay two yards below me on the ladder. This gun will be pointed down at you at all times. If that distance should vary by as much as a foot, I will shoot you. Is that clear?" Julian waved him toward the ladder. "Alternatively, you can stay down here. But I can tell you; there's no way out other than by this shaft."

To Julian's great consternation, Wang Lei circled round him until he stood on the edge of the shaft down which Jade had so recently jumped.

Julian had a dreadful premonition of what was to come.

Wang Lei pasted a parody of a smile on his face. "What is life?" he said.

Julian kept the pistol aimed at him, knowing very well that he could never fire it.

"What's worth sacrificing everything for, Lei? What's worth living for? Did you find it? Did you even come close?"

"Damn you Alston."

Wang Lei jumped backward into the void.

This time, there was no salvation. The padded drawbridge had closed. The jaws of life had shut.

Julian heard a nasty sounding bang as Wang Lei's body hit something on the way down… and then a distant thud.

Julian knelt down in the dirt and put his head in his hands. He was overwhelmed by a sickening guilt. This was not how it was meant to happen. Everything that had occurred was the stuff of nightmares. There was, however, one positive outcome; Jade should be alive and well. And yet, he couldn't let himself savor that reality. His soul screamed in torment at the violence and death that had occurred. He wanted to weep. His plan had been to lure Wang Lei and his men underground, and then jump into the shaft. That would have deposited him into a tunnel that led out to the side of the hill – not far from the main shaft to the cavern. He was then going to slide the metal plate over the entrance of the shaft, pile rocks on the top of it... and call for help.

But as it was, three people were dead. It was an appalling ending.

And he wasn't even sure things had ended. What had happened to Jade? Was she all right? He had to get back to the surface, find the entrance to the tunnel, and then crawl down it in order to find her.

Julian walked over to the steel ladder. It would be a long climb to the surface.

Aware that one of Wang Lei's men was standing guard at the surface, he tucked the pistol in his waistband and began to climb.

Jade was bleeding. She could feel its sticky wetness. But that wasn't her main problem. Every bone in her body felt as if it had been dislocated.

She struggled to make sense of what had happened. But one fact was incontrovertible – she was still alive.

How could that be?

She was lying on a stony floor in pitch-blackness... and she ached – everywhere.

With a groan, she reached into her pocket for her cell phone and switched on the flashlight function.

The entrance of the tunnel was blocked with some sort of wooden gate that had been padded by some mattresses.

Slowly, it occurred to her that Julian must have been responsible for it. The thought gave her a sense of relief, for in the instant before she'd jumped, she'd wondered at Julian's calmness. She'd felt a pang of hurt. And then she'd jumped.

But Julian knew she would be all right. Somehow, he'd rigged up an extraordinary contraption that had scooped her to safety. He'd probably rigged it to engineer his own escape – but it had saved her life instead.

The very knowledge that Julian cared, rekindled a hunger for life. She shone the flashlight down the tunnel. There was nothing beyond the edge of the light beam but darkness.

Jade began to make her way along it. Progress wasn't easy. She had to walk whilst doubled over, and navigate her way over and around rocks and rubble.

Jade continued to press forward, now motivated by a new instinct to survive. She couldn't help but think that life was perverse. Moments earlier, she'd been prepared to die.

Her head hurt abominably, but she used the pain to keep herself focused.

Two factors now motivated her. The first was her concern for Julian. He was with Wang Lei, and she knew her brother was a killer. The second factor was the thought of her parents. It would be too much to expect them to cope with the shame and grief of having a daughter who was dead, and a son who would doubtless end up in prison.

No, she decided. She owed it to them to stay alive.

Her thoughts returned to Julian. She'd left the gun at her feet knowing that Julian was very much closer to it and would get to the gun first, but she also knew that he would never use it. He was therefore vulnerable.

The thought of him caused her to quicken her pace. As she did, she had to concede that her heart was inseparably connected to Julian – and always would be. It was a realization that brought her both joy and pain.

After what seemed like an eternity, she could see a pinprick of light up ahead. The pinprick eventually resolved itself as the tunnel's entrance. She was conscious now of tree roots dangling down in front of her, and cobwebs.

Jade shuddered and brushed through them.

Something near her feet slithered to the side. She shone the flashlight down just in time to see the retreating tail of a snake.

It was with considerable relief that she pushed through the scrubby vegetation at the entrance, until she was able to stand up in the sunshine. The spring sun bathed her in its optimism. Jade breathed in the eucalypt-scented air with relief – feeling as if she'd escaped from the pit of hell.

But every joint in her body continued to scream in protest. She felt for the cut on her head. The blood had ceased to flow and was beginning to cake over.

That was good.

But where was she?

Jade looked around, and realized that she was near the bottom of the small hill that had the entrance to the original access shaft at its summit. She started walking up the slope. It wasn't long before she could see the man Wang Lei had left to guard the entrance. He was sitting on a fallen log not far from the entrance.

The man represented a danger to Julian – and that was not to be countenanced.

Taking a deep breath, she called out. "Hi! Has Wang Lei come out yet?"

The man's hand went inside his jacket, and he looked at her with a frown of incomprehension.

Jade gave him no time to work anything out. She twirled and lashed out with a foot, kicking him in the neck. The man spun round, staggering to keep his balance.

Jade chopped down hard on the back of his neck.

He fell to the ground instantly and did not move.

She stepped over him and pulled his arms behind him. Using her belt, she tied his hands together.

When she finished, she stood up, alerted by a new sound.

She looked down the hill.

Dillon was making his way up to where she stood.

When he arrived, he looked at the comatose man on the ground and nodded his approval. "Wow. That was pretty cool."

Two things then happened at once.

The first brought tears of delight.

Julian emerged from the mineshaft.

She ran to him.

He held out his arms and enfolded her within them. For a long while, he simply held her, saying only, "Don't worry. I've got you." He said it over and over again.

After a while, Julian leaned back and explored the gash on her head. However, before he could attend to the wound, a sinister-looking black Land Rover roared into the mine site. The vehicle had been equipped with a bull-bar, spotlights, aerials, and green bullet-proof glass. Four men jumped from the vehicle, wearing black helmets and bulletproof jackets. All were carrying assault rifles.

The men fanned out and ran up the hill toward them shouting, "On your knees. Hands on your head."

Dillon's eyes were as round as saucers. "Woah!"

Jade thought it propitious to say, "Better do what they say."

The three of them knelt down and put their hands on their heads.

A few moments later, they were all handcuffed, and the pistol in Julian's waistband had been confiscated.

"Are there any more people?" one of the men asked.

Jade nodded toward the man she had knocked out. "Make sure he's secure. He's a killer."

Julian interrupted. "Are you STAR Force?"

"Yes, matey, so do as we say."

Despite having his hands cuffed behind his back, Julian was heartily glad to see the STAR Force officers. They were efficient and left nothing to chance.

"Who else is there?" one of them asked.

"Three dead." Julian nodded toward the unconscious man. "And there's him."

Dillon interrupted. "And there's another guy trapped in a rain-water tank…" he trailed off and turned at Julian. "…At your great, great, whatever's place."

Julian looked at him with incredulity, but the next comment from Jade forestalled any more questions.

"So my brother is dead."

Julian nodded. "I'm sorry, Jade. He jumped to his death rather than lose face by being arrested."

She lowered her head. "It is perhaps for the best."

One of the officers pointed to the gun that was now inside a plastic bag. "Is that gun yours?"

Julian shook his head. "No. It belonged to Wang Lei of the Chinese consulate. You'll find his prints and mine on it."

"There's no clear and present danger then?"

"No." Julian then gave a brief account of all that had taken place in the mine.

The officer listened grimly. When he had finished, the officer reached for the padlock keys and unlocked Julian's handcuffs. "Right. We'd better have a look at the carnage that's evidently taken place down there. You're coming with us."

Julian climbed back down the ladder. Two STAR Force officers climbed below him and one above. They were taking no chances.

It was a full hour before they all returned to the surface.

When Julian finally clambered out into the sunshine again, he was pleased to see that both Jade and Dillon also had their handcuffs removed. A STAR Force officer hovered in the background.

The foreground was dominated by the diminutive figure of Edwina Stanthorpe, and a stranger he did not recognize.

The STAR Force officers also emerged from the shaft and began talking into phones, making arrangement for the recovery of two bodies from the mineshaft. The officer had agreed with Julian that there was little hope of recovering the third.

Edwina wasted no time on pleasantries. She pursed her lips and said, "Where's the hard-drive and micro-computer?"

Julian was still catching his breath after his long climb back up the shaft. He spoke whilst bent over.

"There're in the glove compartment of my pick-up."

"What?" said Edwina with disbelief. "You casually throw something of national importance into the glove compartment of your truck?"

Julian waved an apologetic hand. "It seemed a safe place to put

221

it. I've taped the capsule with the micro-computer onto the side of the hard-drive."

Edwina shook her head and marched down the hill toward Julian's pick-up. Except for on STAR Force officer, everyone else followed her. The remaining officer continued to guard the entrance to the shaft.

When Edwina got to the pick-up, she held out her hand. and demanded the key.

"It's not locked," said Julian.

Edwina shook her head… and a few seconds later she was holding Caleb's hard-drive in her hand.

Julian was heartily glad to be rid of the thing.

The man who was with Edwina hovered around her – almost hopping from foot to foot with impatience.

Edwina handed him the hard-drive, and introduced the stranger. "This is Dr. Adrian Potter. He's from Michigan University, and he was a colleague of Dr. Kuznetsov."

One of the STAR Force officers interrupted them. He clapped Dillon on the shoulder. "Right ho, lad. Let's go and get this other bloke you've got penned in the tank."

Dillon pointed to the black Land Rover. "Do I get to ride in that?"

"You do. Get in."

Dillon grinned. "Brill!"

The vehicle drove off, leaving behind one STAR Force officer.

Julian looked at the American scientist dourly. "What's the big deal with this thing? Does it just make small computers that help kill people?"

The scientist's head jerked round with obvious affront. "Oh no. This technology is vital for many reasons. As powerful as they are, modern laptops are slow compared to modern supercomputers. The new Titan supercomputer being built for the U.S. Department of Energy is set to become the world's fastest computer. It will be able to perform 20,000 trillion calculations per second." He pointed to the hard-drive. "The technology in here will enable us to build the next generation on from that."

Julian pretended he understood and nodded – already weary with the whole affair. He turned his attention to Jade.

She had her arms crossed and her head bowed, no doubt trying to process all that had happened.

He stepped over to her and held out his hands.

Jade glanced up and then, hesitantly, put her hands in his.

Julian closed his eyes, savoring her presence. Then he drew her to himself and wrapped his arms around her. "I'm so sorry for your loss," he said – his voice muffled by her hair. "And I'm so grateful you are still alive." Then he pulled back from her and said with a touch of sternness, "Don't ever try and destroy something so sacred again!"

"You mean me?"

Julian nodded. "I mean you."

His comment was met with a smile, and she stepped forward back into his arms.

Chapter 28

The tires screeched as the giant aircraft landed at Beijing International Airport. Jade had been in the air for over thirteen hours and was bone weary. The aircraft taxied into the newest terminal: Terminal 3. It was the equal of almost any International airport in the world, but Jade barely noticed it.

She caught the train into Beijing West; and then the high-speed train to Taijuan. There, she had a long and wearisome wait, as the train from Taijuan to Lüliang only ran once a day.

Eventually, she was on her way again.

Finally, the train began to approach her last destination. Agricultural scenes of orchards growing jujube, so prized by the Chinese for their medicinal qualities, gave way to Lüliang's ugly suburbs. Despite being on the Sanchuan River, Lüliang was not a pretty place. It was a city that had hoped to succeed, but had fallen short of its ambitions. The main industry that supported the city was mining – coal being particularly important.

Jade watched as the industrial squalor gave way to tall apartment blocks. Many of them were unoccupied because of the slowing economy. It didn't help that the city mayor had been imprisoned for corruption. The city may not be beautiful, but it was her home, and she felt the nostalgia of returning to it acutely.

Moments later, the train pulled into the station.

Jade felt grimy, sweaty, and weary beyond belief.

However, she cheered up hugely when she caught sight of her father. He was looking thin and stooped, but appeared as cheerful as ever.

They embraced… and wept.

Not many words were spoken.

Her father led her to where he'd parked his car. It was a tired old Dongfeng that had been made in Wuhan ten years earlier. He drove her to Fengshan Residential District, where they parked and took the stairs to her parent's third floor apartment.

When they reached the apartment, Jade saw that a white banner had been hung over the front door. It was a sign that the family was in mourning. She shook her head. So much had happened in the two weeks since Wang Lei's death – mostly concerned with inquests and legal matters. Jade was glad to be finally free of it all.

Her parents would have wept at the death of their son, but done so privately.

The CCP had brought his ashes back in a diplomatic bag. Lei had been cremated on the 7th day after his death, as was the Chinese custom. Jade's mother and father would have held a wake that lasted all day. But they would not have cried – at least in public. In Chinese custom, an elder was not allowed to show respect for someone younger – even in death. In fact, as Wang Lei was a young bachelor, his ashes could not even be brought home. They had to remain in the funeral parlor. And strictly speaking, her parents were not even allowed to offer prayers for their son.

Both life and death could be cruel.

As she entered the apartment, her mother struggled to get out of the armchair. Jade saw her wince as she pushed down on the sides of her chair.

Jade ran to her and eased her back into it. Then she knelt down, and embraced her.

They both sobbed.

Later that night, she listened to the sounds of the city that were both so familiar and yet so strange. Then she fell into a deep sleep.

Jade woke twelve hours later, put her feet into her slippers, and slopped her way into the family room. Her face was puffy with sleep, and her hair was a mess.

Her mother was in the kitchen leaning against the bench-top. She'd been preparing Jade's breakfast – soy milk and *youtiao*. The aroma was wonderful.

"Where's father?" she asked.

"He's teaching."

Jade nodded. "Is he still on a basic salary?"

Her mother nodded. "The same as ever."

Jade grunted in disgust. "It's so unfair. He's one of the best teachers in the school and works harder than anyone."

"But he's not a member of the Communist Party."

Jade nodded her understanding.

A little while later, they were both settled in armchairs drinking jasmine tea.

She could see that her mother was itching to ask her questions, but daren't. Jade watched her jiffle and fiddle until she could bear it no longer. "Mum; what is it that you are bursting to ask?"

Her mother lowered her head, embarrassed.

"What?" insisted Jade.

"It's your brother, dear. We've not been told anything. The CCP simply said he died honorably whilst doing his duty. They made him out to be a hero, but I doubt whether that was the case."

Jade raised her eyebrow. "You doubt your son?"

Her mother lifted her head. "I know my son."

For a moment, only the distant hum of traffic could be heard.

Jade was thinking furiously, trying to gauge how much she should divulge. Eventually, she cleared her throat.

"Lei was very patriotic… which is a good thing, isn't it?"

Her mother nodded, but without much conviction.

"Lei was trying to steal some intellectual property from an Australian scientist, so he could give it to China."

"…and make a big name for himself," finished her mother.

Jade nodded. "But he was caught and chose to commit suicide rather than shame China."

For a while, her mother searched Jade's face, looking for the words that were not said. In the end, she nodded. "Thank you, dear. I will tell your father."

"Mum, I'm so sorry. I wish it could have been me instead."

Her mother's neck stiffened. "Don't say that, Jade. You have always been a good girl." She wiped away a tear. "Your father and I are proud of you... of the sort of woman you have become."

Jade looked at her in shock. This was the first time she had heard such words.

For a while, the only sound was the hum of the morning traffic.

Jade was far from sure that she would continue to enjoy her mother's favor. She drew a deep breath and said, "Mum, I've met a man."

Her mother's face suddenly came alive. "Have you dear. Is he nice? Tell me everything."

Jade held up her hands. "Mum, we're just..." she swallowed, "good friends at the moment. It's just that I'm not sure what to do?"

"Why's that, dear?"

"He is an Australian."

"Yes?"

"...and a monk."

Her mother frowned. "A monk! You mean a Buddhist monk?"

Jade lowered her head. "No mum. He's a Christian monk."

The expected reaction of dismay and outrage never came. Jade was puzzled, and she looked at her mother closely.

She seemed to be smiling.

"Can monks marry, dear?" asked her mother, demurely.

"I don't know Mum. Everything's very uncertain at the moment."

"Oh, I see."

Another silence descended on them, until Jade could bear it no more.

"Mum, what are you not telling me. Come on. Spit it out."

Her mother looked at her for a long while and then nodded,

perhaps to herself.

"I'm going to tell you something that would be in your best interests to keep confidential."

Jade frowned. "What?"

"Your father and I are Christians." She shrugged. "We have been for about six years."

Jade spluttered, "But you never told me."

"Oh no, dear. We attended a house church – all very illegal. But six months ago they arrested our pastor, and he's been sent to prison for five years. We have to go to the official 'Three Self' church in the city, now."

"But you can't keep your faith a secret if you go there."

Her mother nodded. "So far, it's quite legal for us to worship there. But the church has been forced to take down the cross outside, and they've insisted that a poster of the Chairman be hung next to the cross inside."

Jade shook her head. Having experienced the freedom of Australia, the very concept of what she was hearing was discordant.

Her mother sighed. "But that's not the worst of it. The CCP have installed facial recognition in the church. We're all being watched."

Jade whistled. "Wow. No wonder Dad hasn't had a promotion."

Her mother leaned forward and laid a hand on Jade's knee. "I hope you are not too scandalized, dear."

Jade shook her head. Then an idea came to her. "Do you have a Bible?"

"Oh no dear. They burned them."

"Well, we'll have to fix that." Jade got up and went to her bedroom and picked up Julian's pocket New Testament.

When she got back to the family room, she handed it to her mother. "Here's a New Testament. It's in English, which I know you and dad read well. It belonged to my… special friend." She rushed on. "I'm sure he wouldn't mind you having it."

Jade's mother took the New Testament in both hands and looked at it with disbelief.

Then tears of joy rolled down her face.

Chapter 29

Julian accepted the mug of tea gratefully and held it between his hands, warming himself. It had been an unusually cold spring morning. The chill reminding him that winter was not yet ready to surrender to summer.

He had walked down the path from his cottage to the village by the beach in order to visit Leah. She'd been eating her breakfast when he called, and the smell of toast still lingered in the air. Leah welcomed him in and hugged him against her ample bosom.

It was the first time Julian had seen her since he'd dropped her off in Adelaide, and he was anxious to see how she was going. He also wanted to share all the recent developments – and assure her that no more threats were forthcoming.

"I gather I wasn't very successful in hiding the micro-computer from you," he said.

Leah smiled. "No you weren't. As soon as I felt the martyr's stone, I knew what you'd done."

"It gave me quite a fright to see it missing from the window."

She chuckled. "Do you want me to fill in the hole? Almost nobody will notice, but it should probably be done."

Julian nodded his thanks and then proceeded to tell Leah all that had happened since they were last together.

Leah was in shock. "Wow! People died."

"Yes."

"And Jade was kidnapped."

"Yes."

For a while, both of them were lost, deep in thought.

Leah interrupted his ruminations by saying, "What are you going to do with Jade? You're a monk, and even if you stop being a monk, you will always be monkish."

Julian smiled. "What's monkish?"

"Oh, you know: not earthed in reality, over-educated, spending huge times in quiet… living as frugally as a church mouse."

"You make it sound irresistible."

"Seriously, Julian. If you harbor any ambition of a future with Jade, you will have to make some changes." Leah shook her head. "I just don't want the real Julian to be repressed in the process, though. Much as it pains me to say it, the world needs people like you."

Julian recognized her sincerity. "Thanks, Leah."

She grunted. "Thanking me is not going to solve the problem. What are you going to do?"

Julian smiled. "I'm going to trust… and I'm going to plan."

"Plan what?"

"I've drawn up plans to extend my cottage. It's never been renovated, except for the bathroom."

Leah leaned back in her chair. "Hallelujah. About time. What will you build?"

"A family room with a kitchen and two bedrooms."

"What will you build it with? It's a heritage area down there, isn't it?"

"Yes, so I'll be building with local stone and corrugated iron."

Leah nodded her approval.

"Are you pleased to be back?" Julian asked.

"Very much so. The people I stayed with are dear friends, and I love their children hugely. The kids were sad to see me go, but I suspect the parents were less so." She smiled. "There are only so many butterfly stickers you can fit on the garden chairs and gnomes in their garden."

Julian was not given much time to enjoy the peace of Second Valley. In fact, he and was having the fortnight from hell. He'd needed to spend most of his time at St. John's priory, as he was required to keep himself on hand for inquests and interviews. These were proving to be wearing and disturbing affairs. The main reason they were disturbing was that they kept raising the issue of Julian being responsible for the deaths of two people.

He didn't need reminding. The reality of what he had done plagued him with a thousand accusations. It was difficult to dodge the facts: He had engineered a rock fall that was designed to entrap, but it had killed.

Julian had spent hours with the prior, pouring out his heart. It didn't matter what absolution the prior gave him – he still felt wretched.

The wounds in his soul had left blood in the water… and Detective Inspector Edmonds, the officer investigating the case, had smelled it. He chased Julian down every few days, requiring him to re-tell the story over and over again. Edmonds was relentless. The dingy interview room, with its recording apparatus, had become Julian's second home, and he hated it.

Julian was there again today and feeling particularly vulnerable. Jade had left for China and wouldn't be back for another week. Julian felt that a piece of him was missing.

The detective inspector drove a finger into the desktop.

"You deliberately set out to entrap and kill. That's not even manslaughter. It was premeditated."

"No. The rock-fall was designed to entrap, not kill. And the death of the other man was entirely unforeseen."

The detective scoffed.

"Might I also point out," said Julian, "that both men were armed, and that Jade's life was under threat."

"But was that really the case?"

Julian rubbed his forehead wearily. "We've been through this already, many times. They were planning to shoot Jade Zhou in the legs and the arms."

"Can that be corroborated?"

"Jade can... and I suspect, has; as you very well know."

The Inspector scoffed. "She is hardly an independent witness. Isn't it true that she is romantically involved with you?"

"She has become a very dear friend, but Jade is not my partner... and I have not had sex with her."

The policeman rolled his eyes, making it clear that he didn't believe a word he said.

Edmonds was gearing himself up for his next assault on Julian, when the door of the interview room banged open.

Julian sat back with a start and stared in amazement as Edwina Stanthorpe swept into the room.

As usual, she wasted no time on small talk.

"My name is Edwina Stanthorpe, and I am Julian Alston's legal representative." She paused. "I am also a busy woman. I have a senior role in ASIO, and I'm booked for an on-line meeting with the Federal Minister for Home Affairs in thirty minutes."

Edmonds looked at the diminutive tornado with evident disbelief. Eventually, the Detective Inspector regained enough of his wits to say, "I was just interviewing your..."

Edwina interrupted him. "It didn't sound like it. It sounded to me like harassment."

"We were just going over some questions."

"Are these the same questions you asked two days ago... and two days before that... and after a whole day last week going over his statement." Edwina looked at him contemptuously before turning to Julian. "Are you being asked the same questions over and over again?"

"Yes."

Edmonds felt obliged to protest. "Of course the questions are the same. We get more information by asking the same questions in different ways."

Edwina looked down her nose at him – shriveling him into silence. It was no small achievement given Edwina's diminutive stature.

"No," she said. You don't get more information. What you get is a tired, harried witness, whose testimony, in consequence, becomes increasingly unreliable." She leaned forward on the table. "So let me spell this out for you: You may not ask the same questions again. You may only ask something if you have a new line of inquiry." She stood up. "Do you have a new line of inquiry?"

The Detective Inspector didn't answer.

Edwina continued to sally forth on her white charger.

"Nothing to say? Well, perhaps I might help you. The salient question is: Did Mr. Alston have good reason to seek recourse to lethal force?" She paused. "What do you think the answer is, Inspector?"

The Inspector sat in stunned silence.

Edwina Stanthorpe ticked off the relevant points on her fingers.

"First, his friend Dr. Caleb Kuznetsov is brutally tortured and murdered.

"Second, people came for him at night with a gun and a blowtorch." She glared at the Inspector. "Do you think that might have given you cause for thought, Inspector?"

She didn't wait for an answer. "Third, his friend, Jade Zhou, was abducted by Wang Lei and used to make a ransom demand.

"Fourthly, Wang Lei threatened to shoot Jade Zhou in the legs and arms if Mr. Alston did not hand over highly classified information that is vital to Australian and American interests." She paused. "In other words, he was simply trying to save the lives of his friends and be a patriot." She drew in a deep breath. "I therefore submit that there is no case for Mr. Alston to answer… and you haven't come within a bull's roar of establishing the remotest suspicion of one."

"He could have done it for money," said Edmonds. "One of the Chinese men we're holding has suggested that Alston was trying to sell information to the Chinese."

When Julian heard the accusation, his mouth dropped open. He was appalled.

Edwina laughed. "Have you seen where Mr. Alston lives… and how he lives? He freely chooses to live as a hermit." She waved a hand. "You stupid man. He has no time for money. You have simply allowed a desperate killer to make a baseless slur against him… and I, for one, would like to explore your motives for doing so." She paused. "How many times have you visited China in the last five years, Inspector? Who's whispering in your ears?" She looked at him grimly. "What will I find if I do a background check on you?"

"I'm only doing my job," the Inspector protested.

"Bullying, intimidation, and being a crass idiot are not in your job description."

The Inspector sighed and closed the file in front of him. "We will be in contact with your client again," he said.

"No, you won't. If you want to have any dealings with Mr. Alston, you will do so through me. You've run the poor man ragged, calling him in for questioning time after time." She slapped her hand on the desk. "This ends now." Edwina stood herself back upright. "Is there any legal reason why Mr. Alston is not free to go now?"

"No."

"Good, then it is finished. If you wish to pursue things further, you must contact me." She waved a finger at him. "And let me tell you, I do not take kindly to bullies or fools who take up my time needlessly."

Edwina took out her phone and glanced at it. "I must rush." She beckoned to Julian. "Come with me."

As they walked down the corridor toward the front door, Julian whispered: "Are you really a lawyer?"

Edwina Stanthorpe smiled. "A true poker player never reveals their hand."

They descended the front steps and stood on the sidewalk. Julian had the feeling of being reborn – of being free.

Edwina turned to him. "I have read the reports of this sorry affair, and I want to thank you on behalf of the Australian Government." She smiled. "I'm afraid I can't give you an Order of Australia or anything, but I'm pretty handy at cutting through red tape if ever you have a need."

"Thank you, Ms. Stanthorpe."

She waved a hand. "Call me Edwina."

So saying, she held out a hand and flagged down a passing taxi.

Julian and the prior were sitting in white cane chairs under the bull-nosed veranda of the priory. It was one of Julian's favorite places to sit, because it was beside the garden. He appreciated its peace. It was a peace that managed to transcend the hum of the city traffic caused by the last of the office workers returning home.

His future was very much up in the air, and it was disturbing. And always... there was the deep ache in his heart for Jade. His world had been turned upside down and could never be the same again.

When he'd shared with her his grief at causing three people to die, Jade reminded him that it was a grief that she shared. She was by no means sure that any of the three men she had attacked outside of Julian's cottage had survived. It was difficult to think that they could have. Jade had talked about the grief of this with Julian a number of times in the last few weeks. She'd done so, she said, because she desperately needed some of Julian's peace.

Julian shook his head. The irony was huge.

He was now talking with the prior about his own sense of guilt – pouring out his heart, desperately hoping for some form of absolution.

The prior listened, and for a long while, said nothing. Eventually, he cleared his throat. "Mercifully, I've never known this sort of grief. But I have had occasion to talk with army veterans who have." The prior paused. "We ask young men to brutalize their sensibilities on the battlefield... and reward them on their return with neglect, or even worse, with derision." He shook his head. "Killing is not kind to the soul. A bit of you has to die for you to be okay with it."

The prior pointed to Julian. "You are not okay with it, and I am glad. You are, however, wounded; and this means you are well placed to help others with similar wounds." The prior put his fingers together. "It is a hard burden to bear, but it will deepen you... not that you were ever shallow."

For a long while, the only sound came from the city traffic.

Julian's old mentor then changed the subject. "Let's talk about your future."

This comment caused Julian to blink and sit himself upright. He wasn't sure he was yet ready to think about the future. He was even less sure when the prior added fuel to his discomfort by suggesting, with brutal candor, that Julian made a terrible monk – in the conventional sense. He was too earthy, too simple, and too rigorous. The prior tapped his fingers together. "Your very presence here in the priory seems to throw out a challenge to the other brothers?"

Julian was amazed. "Really? I had no idea."

The prior smiled. "Of course you didn't. That's part of your appeal. You are an innocent." He paused. "It's therefore ironic and somewhat unkind that you, of all people, should be here wringing your heart over the fact that you have been responsible for the deaths of three people. That is not a burden any of the other brothers have ever had to carry."

Another wave of anguish washed over Julian, and he put his head in his hands.

The prior laid a hand on his shoulder… and allowed the silence to continue.

Julian eventually sat himself back upright. "I just don't know what to do"

"Well, I'm sure God does." The prior smiled. "And it's our job, as his imperfect emissaries, to co-operate with God's purposes." He paused. "Speaking of which: You and I are booked in to see the bishop at ten o'clock tomorrow morning. He and I have come up with some possible scenarios regarding your future."

Julian blanched. "Wow! That's not much notice." He had planned to be driving back to Second Valley at that time.

The prior smiled. "Sometimes time is not a friend. And I think this may be such a time."

―――――――

With some difficulty, the prior managed to find a car park and walked with Julian down King William Street to St. Barnabas House. The old stone building was located on the other side of the road to St. Peter's Cathedral. The cathedral's soaring bulk rose into the sky in defiance of the growing secularism of the city.

They walked up the stone steps and passed through a sliding glass door into the atrium. A receptionist rang through, and soon the Bishop's PA came in to lead them through to the Bishop's office.

Julian hadn't met the Bishop before, but the Right Reverend seemed affable enough. The bishop came out from behind his desk and invited them to sit down in the chairs that had been set around a coffee table. After organizing tea and coffee, the cleric sat back and closed his eyes.

Peace, of a sort, descended on the room.

After a minute, the bishop opened his eyes. "So you are Julian. The prior has spoken much about you. Tell me: all this dreadful business over the death of your friend, the scientist – has it been resolved?"

Julian nodded. "I think so. But it will take time for me to come to terms with all that's happened."

"Hm… with three people dead, I can understand it.

The story had been reported in the newspapers, but in a muted and edited form. Julian suspected that Edwina Stanthorpe was behind that. The papers had simply reported that some Chinese nationals had died, one through suicide, and two by misadventure. The deaths had occurred when police were closing in on them to question them in relation to the murder of Dr. Kuznetsov.

The Chinese consulate had issued an angry denial and was making counter-claims.

The Bishop stretched his neck. Julian wondered whether it was an involuntary action he'd developed when he'd first worn a dog collar. "So what is to become of you, Julian?"

Julian thought it propitious to say nothing. It was an odd feeling having his future decided on by a man he'd never met before.

The Bishop continued. "The prior tells me that your love of God is as firm as ever. Is that right?"

"Yes, Bishop." It was the simple truth.

"You live a radical lifestyle; you have great gifts in working with teenagers; and you fit badly in the high church style of Anglicanism we practice here in Adelaide." The Bishop sucked in his cheeks. "Have I missed anything?"

"And I am in love with a Chinese national, and am struggling with the idea of chastity."

"Ah, yes. I was coming to that."

Another silence hung in the room.

The bishop sighed. "Is this person with whom you seek a liaison, in any way compatible with your life-style and faith?"

The Bishop's question hit Julian hard. It was the very question he'd been wrestling with for weeks.

"With your permission, Bishop; I would like to bring her here so you might ask that question of her yourself."

The Bishop inclined his head. "Interesting idea. Yes, I'd be open to that. But tell me: what is your gut feeling?"

"I believe Jade is on a journey. Her old certainties have been thrown into the air, and she is discovering truth." Julian paused. "She's been reading the gospels for the last few weeks."

The Bishop nodded. "I wish the students here at St. Barnabas College would be as diligent. That's good to hear. Very good, in fact." He paused. "Which brings us to your life-style…"

Julian waited for the ax to fall.

The Bishop continued. "You wish to be released from your vows. Personally, I think that is a very good idea. You've not fitted in well with the brothers of the Society of the Sacred Mission. You're too radical."

Julian lowered his head and waited for the Bishop to say more.

"But you have been theologically trained, and you've acted as locum at Delamere for two years. In other words, you have both the training and the experience to be a priest."

Julian's eyes opened wide.

"A priest?"

"Yes." The Bishop put his hands together. "So this is my proposal. I will license you to be a priest – and as a priest, you will be able to conduct chapel services… and be free to marry." He held up a finger. "However, this is conditional on you agreeing to be a tutor living in residence here at St. Mark's college." He smiled. "As you know, St. Marks is the Anglican college for the University… and it is full of people in need of your guiding hand. You have a research degree, and a degree in theology. This makes you eminently qualified."

Julian rubbed his forehead. "Wow!"

The Bishop stretched his neck again. "May I suggest that 'wow' is an inadequate response?"

Julian struggled to find words to fit the storm of emotions going on within him. "I currently have a home at Second Valley," he said, lamely.

The Bishop nodded. "You will only be required to be in residence here at St. Marks during term time. For the rest of the time, you can live at Second Valley." He paused. "What do you think?"

Julian suddenly felt the loose pieces of the puzzle fitting into place. It gave him a surge of delight… and hope.

"Yes," he said.

"Yes, as in you accept?" asked the Bishop.

"Yes, sir. And thank you for your wisdom. I'm more grateful than I can say."

The Bishop smiled and put his hands together. "I very much suspect that St. Mark's has no idea what's coming their way."

Chapter 30

Dillon looked up at the mountain of a man standing before him and was too terrified to say anything.

The big man spoke. "My name is Brant, and there are three things I hate. The first is stupidity; the second is laziness, and the third is selfishness." He sniffed. "So, you tell me. Are we going to get along?"

Julian, who was standing behind Dillon, laid a hand on Dillon's shoulder. "Relax, mate. His bark is worse than his bite."

Bronny came to the front door and pushed Brant aside. "Don't frighten the boy, Brant. Come on in, you two. I've made a fresh batch of Anzac biscuits."

Dillon edged his way down the hallway to the kitchen. He'd never been in a house like it before. Everything was old… as in *really* old. And the floorboards squeaked. But it was the man who dominated everything. He was formidable.

Julian spoke from behind him. "Dillon, these are two of my best friends. Brant is a master mariner. There are not too many types of ship he hasn't sailed in. For the last ten years or so, he captained the tugs here in the Port. Fortunately for the worthy denizens of the area, he's got Bronny to keep him civilized. She used to be a school teacher."

Dillon was only dimly aware of what he was saying. He was looking everywhere. Everything looked old and intriguing. It was like stepping into Hogwarts – except it was homely.

At Bronny's prompting, he sat down at the well-scrubbed kitchen table.

The big man sat down on a protesting chair and stuck his thumbs behind his braces. "So, you'll be working at the *One and All* workshop with George, learning the ropes, before you apply for a cabinet-making apprenticeship." He nodded approvingly "George is a good man."

Dillon hung his head. The goal he'd set himself seemed a million miles away – impossible to attain. He'd left school in year ten, and was very much below standard with his writing, reading and math. He'd expressed his misgivings to Julian earlier – hating the fact that he was 'dumb.'

When he used the word 'dumb' to describe himself, he had been surprised at Julian's response. It was the nearest to angry that Dillon had ever seen him. Julian had said to him sternly, "I don't want to hear you ever say that about yourself again. I've watched you problem-solve in the workshop, and you are far from dumb. You've simply not been inspired, or given the opportunity to excel at school."

Dillon had looked at him, willing himself to believe it was true. He still had massive doubts.

Julian accepted a cup of tea from Bronny and blew over the top of it to cool it. Then he turned to Dillon. "I've been talking to Brant and Bronny, and we've decided on how things will be whilst you are here… if you want to stay here. It's up to you."

"What things?" he asked guardedly.

"You get up at seven – because that's what you'll need to do in the real world. Make your bed, and then come down for breakfast. After breakfast, clean and tidy your room. Tidiness needs to be an obsession if you're going to learn a trade." Julian looked at him for a moment. "And this is the bit I haven't told you."

"What?"

"Bronny has agreed to teach you reading, writing, and math each morning until lunch time." He paused. "It is an amazingly generous gesture. But I don't want you to waste her time. Are you up for it?"

Dillon found himself nodding before he'd even thought about it. Something deep and primal within him was reaching out for hope.

Julian grunted his approval. "George will expect you in the workshop at 1pm each week day."

That was the bit that really appealed to Dillon, and he was looking forward to it hugely.

After a while, Julian got up from the table. "I'll head back to the priory now." He clapped Dillon on the shoulder. "I'm proud of you, mate." And then he left.

Dillon thought they were probably the best words he had ever heard.

George handed the plank of wood over to Dillon.

Dillon obediently took hold of it.

"Now look at the edge of the plank, son, and tell me if the grain is running up to the surface, or down. What's it doing?"

Dillon looked at the edge of the plank, and for a while couldn't make out the grain pattern at all because it was overlaid with the striations from the saw blade. But as he looked closer, he thought he could detect the movement of the grain.

"Up," he said.

George looked at the plank. "You're right. And that's what you do before you do anything with a plank of wood. You must see where the grain is going."

"Why?"

"Because you need to put a plank on the planer so the blades don't lift the grain and leave tiny pock-marks on the timber."

Dillon had hoped to begin his time in the workshop making his

Windsor chair, but George had him selecting pieces of timber and planing right angles on them – hour after hour.

"A perfect right-angle is one of the hardest and most crucial things to learn." George gave him piece after piece to plane smooth. Dillon had to learn what to do when the timber was cupped or bowed. It was a whole new world, and he despaired of ever understanding it. If Dillon wasn't learning to plane wood smooth, he was being given a lecture on safety.

"Always safety. Safety first, second, and third." George grinned. "And if you abide by that rule, you will reach my venerable age with all your fingers intact, and with your two eyes still in your head."

Dillon applied himself as best he could. He loved the new world he'd discovered. The smell of the wood, its warmth, and the potential of what it might become when used, was amazing.

Dillon felt a sense of importance walking between Julian, who looked cool with his hair, and Brant who looked terrifying. It was a good feeling.

They walked to an old pub that had a wide veranda. Evidently, it had a reputation for good food.

They made their way inside, ordered some beers, and sat down at a table.

Brant placed both of his beefy hands on the table. "Well Dillon, this is an important celebration." He picked up his glass and raised it. "Here's to you, kid. You've made eighteen."

The simple ritual of a glass being raised in his honor brought a curious feeling to Dillon – one he couldn't describe. He just knew it was nice.

"Now lad," he went on. "It's the job of us old codgers to teach you a thing or two."

"Oh yeah. What?"

"We have to teach you to control your brain, your balls, and your belly – because you won't be a true man unless you can."

"What do you mean?"

Brant shook his head in a show of despair. "Oh boy. This lad's got a lot to learn."

Julian grinned. "That's why I've put him in your tender care, Brant."

The big man drew in a deep breath. "Righto, son. Lesson one: How much beer will I drink tonight?"

Dillon frowned. "I dunno."

Brant glowered at him. "Well a man should know. How else will he stay in control when his mates want him to drink more?" Brant paused. "So, how much beer will I drink tonight, boy?"

Dillon shrugged. "One?"

"Blast, boy. This is your birthday – your eighteenth birthday. One beer is never going to cut it. On special occasions like this, I drink two." He waved a finger. "But on all other occasions, just one."

The big man leaned back and scratched his chest hairs. "And what happens if I'm dumb enough to let others persuade me to drink more?"

Dillon knew the answer to this. "You become a dickhead."

"Yeah. You become a dickhead."

Brant nodded slowly. "You've just had your first lesson on how to be a man."

Dillon had the impression this would not be the last piece of wisdom Brant would be sharing.

The three of them worked their way through a steak-and-Guinness pie, with mushy peas and chips. When they'd finished, Brant burped loudly and thumped his chest.

"You've done well this last week Dillon, and if you want it, I've got a reward for you."

Dillon pulled himself up from a slouch. Tiredness was beginning to creep over him. "Oh yeah. What?"

"A trip on *Tusker*."

Dillon frowned. "What's *Tusker*?"

"She's a bloody great tug boy; a bloody great tug." He'd barely got the words out when the big man leaned back and said, "Well I'll be jiggered. Look who's here."

Dillon spun around… hoping… and was rewarded by the sight of Jade standing in the aisle between the tables. She was looking sensational as usual, and just a little self-conscious.

"Is this party for men only?" she said with a smile.

Julian was on his feet in an instant. "When did you get back?" he stammered.

"This afternoon.'

Dillon grinned. "I rang her."

Chapter 31

Jade waited for Julian on the sidewalk outside her block of flats in the city. She kept craning her neck, looking down the street, willing him to arrive. Jade was desperate to feel his arms around her again, to see him smiling at her – to be lost in his love.

She glanced at her phone. It told her that she was five minutes early. Her hands had clenched into fists with impatience…

…And then, there he was. He was also early. His battered pick-up, with its rasping engine, came toward her in a line of traffic.

She found herself waving before she realized it.

Julian pulled into the curb, and careless of the 'no parking' restrictions, jumped out of the cab, ran round to her and scooped her up in a hug.

Jade let her head fall back as he pressed her to himself, and she laughed with delight. She wanted to laugh and laugh. And then they kissed – a soul satisfying, hunger satiating, kiss.

Some indignant tooting of car horns reminded them that time was at a premium, so they untangled themselves and dived into the cab of the pick-up. Somewhat self-consciously, they nosed their way back into the Adelaide traffic.

Jade's visit to her parents in Lüliang had lightened her heart more than she could say. Having their blessing was liberating – a precious thing to be cherished. It had set her free to follow a dream, as impossible as it was, and that meant everything to her.

It occurred to her that she didn't know where Julian was taking her; somewhere quiet and beautiful, she hoped – somewhere where they could be alone. She had so much to tell him.

Julian glanced at her. A smile was hovering on his lips.

"I've got some plans... and an idea I want to share with you," he said.

It was an enigmatic comment, but she could hear the hope in his words.

"And what's that?" she said. Jade was leaning against his shoulder as he drove, hugging an arm, reveling in his nearness.

"Before I tell you, I want to introduce you to someone who would like to speak with you."

"Oh. And who's that?"

"Um. The Archbishop of Adelaide, actually."

Jade pulled back "What? Did you say the Archbishop of Adelaide?"

Julian looked at her and nodded. "Yes."

She shook her head. "No."

"Why?"

"I, I'm not... dressed..."

Julian lifted his head and laughed. "My darling Jade. Look at me. Do you think I'm dressed to visit an Archbishop?"

Jade started to smile and ran her eyes over his woolen shepherd's shirt. "Well... I guess not. And I doubt you ever will be." She reached over and brushed his hair aside. Then laid a hand on his cheek. "If you did dress up, you wouldn't be you... the man I love."

Julian explained the difficulty there was in parking near St. Barnabas House, and that he had therefore allowed plenty of time.

But of course, they found a park straight away, so they killed time having a coffee at the Good Samaritan Café on Kermode Street.

Jade held Julian's hand over the table, her fingers roving over his restlessly. "My parents send you their greetings," she said. Her comment sounded stiffly formal when said in English. Jade wished she could convey the real significance of what it meant. Perhaps she would explain, later.

All too soon they left and walked down the road to St. Barnabas House. The place felt old and reeked of history, even though modernity had shouldered its utilitarian way into its story, as evidenced by the atrium and modern extension on the back.

With a sense of unreality, Jade followed Julian as they were escorted through the old section of St. Barnabas to the Bishop's office.

Julian made the introductions.

"Jade, may I introduce you to the Right Reverend Tony Clements, the Archbishop of Adelaide."

The Bishop held out his hands. "Please call me Tony." He looked at Jade. "You've just come back from visiting your parents, I understand. Are they well?"

"Fairly well. My mother has trouble with arthritis, but still copes." Jade managed a smile. "At least she can cook, and that is everything to a Chinese."

The Bishop chuckled, and turned to Julian.

"Julian, why don't you wait for us in the atrium. I'll organize for you to have some tea. Or would you like coffee?"

"I'm fine sir. I've just had a coffee."

When Julian had gone, the Bishop waved her to a seat.

"A remarkable man, Julian," he said.

"He certainly is," said Jade, with more feeling than she'd intended.

The Bishop tapped a finger against his mouth. "I hear you are reading the gospels."

She shook her head. "Not anymore."

"Oh. Why?"

"I gave my New Testament to my parents. They're Christians. Evidently they have been for six years. I never knew. Their Bible had been confiscated, so I gave them Julian's New Testament." She shrugged. "It was the least I could do."

The Bishop nodded. "Well, having a New Testament is pretty good." He paused. "So you currently have no Bible?"

"No."

"Well that will never do." He got up from his seat and went to the bookshelf that lined one of the walls. The Bishop pulled out a book, pondered it, and put it back. Then pulled out another. It was a beautiful leather-bound Bible with gold edging.

"Here," he said handing it to her. "It's a modern translation. Quite good."

Jade's mouth dropped open. "It's beautiful."

The Bishop smiled. "Yes. It is."

"Are you sure?"

"Never surer."

She took it in her hands and opened its pages. "I'm, er, not very sure how I should go about reading this." She looked at the Bishop apologetically. "I've never been taught."

"I'll give you a little pamphlet that will help you, but I imagine Julian will give you all the help you need."

"Yes," she smiled. "He would."

The Bishop sat himself back down again.

"Would you describe yourself as a Christian, Jade? I ask this not to pressure you in any way, but simply to establish what our starting point is."

Jade had been asking herself the same question for the last few weeks. She chose her words carefully. "I found that the truth I thought I knew, lacked integrity; and the truth I didn't know, had it."

"Hm. Do you wish to marry Julian?"

Jade's hand instinctively went to her throat. "Yes. With all my heart: yes."

The Bishop nodded.

"And would you like to remain resident here in Adelaide?"

"Wherever Julian is… but I like Adelaide. It is a lovely, gentle city. So, yes, I would like to live here."

"But you would be happy going anywhere?"

"Anywhere, as long as I was with Julian."

The Bishop smiled. "Well, I won't be sending him to Tasmania, but I needed to be sure that you were not romantically attached to him simply so you could get permanent residency here."

The very notion that she should be doing so, bewildered Jade. She struggled to get her words of protestation out.

The Bishop held up his hands. "Please relax. I am quite convinced of the sincerity of your love." He paused. "I have a plan that would enable you to live right here in North Adelaide – only a couple of hundred yards away, actually."

Jade's mouth dropped open.

The Bishop continued to outline the proposal that he said he'd put to Julian on his previous visit. "It is an arrangement that would enable you to continue with your social contacts and university studies here in Adelaide, yet enable you to retreat to Second Valley during the term breaks." He leaned back. "How does that sound?"

It took a moment before Jade could speak. "It… it sounds perfect."

"Then that's what we'll do."

The Bishop got up from his chair and pushed an intercom button. "Please send Mr. Alston up to join us."

When Julian entered the Bishop's office, both Jade and the Bishop were on their feet.

Without any preamble, the Bishop said to him, "As I am about to free you from your earlier vows, I'm going to ask you, Julian, to make three new ones. You'll recognize echoes of your last vows in each of them." He pointed to the cross hanging on the wall. "Can I ask you to kneel before that cross?"

Julian immediately fell to his knees.

"And perhaps you too, Jade."

With just the slightest hesitation, Jade knelt down beside Julian.

"I'm going to invite you to make three vows. But I want you to make them only if you agree with them. Is that clear?"

Both Jade and Julian nodded.

"The first is simply this: Will you vow to remain faithful to your spouse for as long as you live?"

It took a moment for Julian to understand the full import of what the Bishop was saying.

"Yes," he said huskily. To Julian's ears, what he was hearing sounded very much like a wedding service. Perhaps it was.

"Yes," said Jade.

"Secondly," said the bishop. "Will you vow to live with simplicity, eschewing the excesses of commercialism, and embracing the way of Christ?"

"Yes," they said together.

"And finally: Will you vow to abide by the consistent principles you find in Scripture?"

"Yes," they said again in unison.

The Bishop helped Jade get up from the floor. For a brief moment he held both Jade and Julian by the hand. Then he smiled. "You both give me hope." He turned round. "Now away with you both, and leave me to my dull administration."

In something of a daze, Julian walked hand in hand with Jade back out to King William Street. He was too wired to think of returning to his pick-up, so he walked Jade past the Cathedral along Pennington Terrace until they were in front of St. Mark's College. Julian pointed through the ornate iron gates to the old stone buildings beyond. "That's our new home."

Jade's eyes widened. "It looks very grand."

They continued on until they came to the statue of Colonel Light looking over the city he would build. Julian and Jade settled themselves on one of the park benches and looked across Adelaide oval and the River Torrens to the city. It was a spectacular view.

Jade rested her head on his shoulder.

For a long while nothing was said.

Then Julian rummaged in his pocket and pulled out a pendant. He disentangled himself from Jade so he could hang it round her neck.

She fingered the stone, turning it over so she could inspect it. The stone was dark green with splashes of bright red.

Julian explained. "Believe it or not, this stone came from a stained glass window in a church. Leah gave it to me when she replaced it with a piece of red glass." He smiled. "I'd like to give it to you."

"Thank you," she said. "It's a remarkable looking pendant. What sort of stone is it?"

"Technically, it's called a blood stone, but I call it 'the martyr's stone.'" He paused. "Its story brought us together. I'll tell you about it some time."

They settled back in the seat together.

"Will it be difficult for me to get permanent residency in Australia?" she asked.

Julian was nuzzling her hair. "I have a friend who is good at cutting through red tape."

"Hmm."

Jade then surprised him by saying, "I like my name, 'Jade'. I think I will keep it."

He looked at her questioningly.

Jade continued. "But I also like my Chinese name."

"Ah," he said. "I asked you what that was once. And you wouldn't tell me."

She took hold of his chin and turned it toward her. "Would you like to know what it is?"

"Yes."

"My Chinese name is Yenay."

"Yenay. That's nice. What does it mean?"

She smiled. "It means 'she who loves.'"

Note from the author

Thank you for reading *The Martyr's Stone*. I hope you enjoyed it. If you did, please consider leaving a review on Amazon to encourage other readers.

I'm pleased to be able to report that the "Stone Collection" has grown to include:

The Atlantis Stone
The Peacock Stone
The Fire Stone
The Dragon Stone
The Celtic Stone
The Syrian Stone
The Viking Stone
The Pharaoh's Stone

To find out more, sign up to my mailing list at www.author-nick.com. New subscribers will receive an exclusive bonus novelette, *The Mystic Stone*, a complete story, six chapters (15,500 words) in length. It is an adventure that takes place on Caldey Island off the rugged Pembrokeshire coast.

About the Author

Nick Hawkes has lived in several countries of the world, and collected many an adventure. Along the way, he has earned degrees in both science and theology—and has written books on both. Since then, he has turned his hand to novels, writing romantic thrillers that feed the heart, mind, and soul.

His nine novels are known as, 'The Stone Collection.'

His first novel, *The Celtic Stone*, won the Australian Caleb Award in 2014.

The inspiration for this novel, *The Martyr's Stone*, came from his experience of living in the delightful hamlet of Second Valley on the rugged coast of South Australia. Some of the adventures he encountered whilst sailing on the *One and All* around the coast of South Australia also make their way into the novel.

Also by Nick Hawkes

The Syrian Stone

Chelsea is part of an international team of archaeologists who are making the most of a tenuous cease-fire in the Syrian civil war to excavate and conserve the historic remains of the ancient kingdom of Ebla. A dramatic discovery of a new library of clay tablets inscribed with cuneiform writing brings to the surface international tensions between Syria and Israel. Chelsea must call on the help of a small boy who has looted his own artefacts. She must also recruit the help of a shadowy character, Tony. He has military training, but is now seeking a new life, one that will allow him to deal with his own demons.

Chelsea and her friend, Beanie (an IT genius) must manage the greatest archaeological discovery of the century—one that has international consequences, whilst keeping those she loves alive.

More details at www.author-nick.com

(See next page for more)

Also by Nick Hawkes

The Viking Stone

Adam Hollingworth is unsure whether he wants to live or die following the death of his fiancé. In deep grief, he journeys from Australia to England, and finds his way to the tide-ways and byways of the Thames estuary, an area renowned for its secrets, and its smuggling. Amidst the marshes, Adam is mentored by an old man, and his niece—a talented artist. They introduce him to a love for the sea and the world of ancient wooden boats.

Adam secures a job teaching in one of England's oldest boarding schools. It is an alien environment in which he must find a reason to live. The violent world of smuggling soon makes its presence felt, and Adam must fight to keep himself, and the people he loves from being murdered. Whether they survive, and counter the evil pervading one of the mightiest waterways of the world, will depend on their ability to use a secret of ancient Norse navigation—the Viking Stone.

More details at www.author-nick.com